Lurking in the shadows...

a darkness threatens their joy.

Heaven's Song

Heaven's Song

MARILYN KOK

BETHANY HOUSE PUBLISHERS
MINNEAPOLIS, MINNESOTA 55438

Published by Bethany House Publishers
A Ministry of Bethany Fellowship, Inc.
11300 Hampshire Avenue South
Minneapolis, Minnesota 55438

Printed in the United States of America.

Library of Congress Cataloging-in-Publication Data

Kok, Marilyn, 1955–
    Heaven's song / by Marilyn Kok.
        p.   cm. — (Portraits)
      ISBN 1-55661-990-1
      I. Title. II. Series: Portraits (Minneapolis, Minn.)
PS3561.O378H43 1997
813'.54—dc21   97–33833
                                              CIP

For Randy,

who knows something of both God and chemistry,

and my sister JoAnne,

who knows about faith and darkness and holding on.

I love you.

Portraits

The Balcony

Blind Faith

Endangered

Entangled

Framed

Gentle Touch

Heaven's Song

Impasse

Masquerade

Montclair

Morningsong

Shroud of Silence

Stillpoint

Walker's Point

MARILYN KOK is a daughter of missionary parents who served in both India and Taiwan. Schooled overseas, she is also a graduate of Texas A&M University and Wheaton College. Marilyn has recently retired from her teaching position at Millikin University to concentrate on writing. The parents of six children, she and her husband make their home in Illinois.

"I have seen the burden God has laid on men. He has made everything beautiful in its time. He has also set eternity in the hearts of men; yet they cannot fathom what God has done from beginning to end."

ECCLESIASTES 3:10–11 (NIV)

One

Cassie McCormick slipped her gaze away from the boarding area and toward the airport windows. It was late March, a time when the sun should be shining and temperatures in St. Louis warming, but all Cassie saw outside was snow—a thick, blanketing, opaque mass of whirling whiteness, obscuring everything beyond the glass enclosure.

The snow had started soon after Cassie's commuter flight arrived from Springfield, Illinois. By eleven, the wind had picked up. Now at noon, when her flight was scheduled to depart, the wind had escalated to a blizzard, and all planes were grounded.

A sign that she shouldn't go? She squashed the notion and went to find a phone.

"Stay overnight in St. Louis if necessary," Cassie's contact at Texas A&M University said. "Or in Houston if you get there after the last limousine leaves for College Station. Either way, don't worry. We'll make sure you see enough to make a decision about attending A&M."

Cassie returned to the waiting area and took her seat. Many of the business passengers had vanished, presumably to find a quiet place to work. A few others, perhaps from the St. Louis area, had also left the airport. But a few passengers were still arriving.

Including the man against the far wall.

He was in his late twenties and tall, with a strong face, intelligent eyes, and a determined jaw. His three-piece suit said boardroom, but his dark hair was wrong somehow, the cut off-beat. And he was wearing cowboy boots.

So not a businessman. What, then?

He was standing at the window, gazing out at the increasingly dense snow. With one hand he tapped a folded newspaper against his leg; with the other he rubbed the back of his neck. He was clearly troubled about something.

Tall, handsome, *and* brooding?

How intriguing.

When he did turn away from the window, he spared one sustained glance around their end of the passenger lounge. He passed quickly over Cassie and paused, blinked, and swung back to meet her gaze. Caught, she smiled briefly and looked away, but not before she saw a flicker of interest in his cool blue eyes.

She made a show of opening her book but couldn't resist glancing up one more time. This time he was waiting. A slow grin spread across his face, and his hand lifted in a brief salute. His eyebrows communicated the question: So what's your pleasure, little lady?

Cassie's lashes fluttered down. This was crazy. She had dressed for the trip with her customary carelessness: jeans and a sweater, dark brown hair pulled back in a utilitarian clasp, no makeup. In two seconds she could pick out three or four women much more likely to attract the interest of a man like this one. Why her?

Polished leather boots appeared on the carpet before her. "Heading to Houston?"

She blinked her eyes up and nodded. His voice was like his eyes, deep and mellow, with a hint of Texas twang.

Definitely a cowboy, she decided, from the High Lonesome, used to facing the elements and not easily intimidated—in spite of his earlier melancholy.

He lowered himself into the seat beside her. "You going to wait here till this is over?"

She nodded, then lifted her book for him to see. "Sorry. Things to do."

"As in 'places to go, promises to keep'? Your name wouldn't be Robert Frost, would it?"

She smiled briefly and determinedly opened her book.

He leaned forward to see the title. "Ah, a Trekkie. Live long and prosper."

But he didn't seem anxious to pursue the conversation. He sat in that lazy, relaxed way confident men have, looking not the least bit clumsy or awkward. Every now and then she heard him hum an odd snatch or two of music. Probably the latest country hit. She wasn't up on the country music scene, but he looked the part. What was he doing in St. Louis anyway, dressed in a suit, when he clearly belonged on a Texas spread in his jeans and boots?

She sneaked another look. His hands were smooth and strong, with trimmed nails and not a bit of dirt under them. So. He was a desk jockey somewhere, not so rough and hardy.

He still didn't say anything, but the fingers on one hand lifted slightly from his knee and gave a little wave. A laugh bubbled irresistibly inside her.

"Ah, she smiles."

Her glance slid up to his again.

"Hey," he said, coaxing her smile to stay. "I'm Nick. But don't tell me your name if you don't want to. I'll guess it. Hazel, right? No, no—Nettie."

She drew back to get a better look at him. Where had the brooding cowboy gone?

"No," he said with a boyish grin. "Something much more glamorous. How about Diana or Penelope?"

She rolled her eyes.

"Come on . . . Diana? Penelope? Help me out here."

She hesitated—but really, why resist? It was going to be a long day.

"Okay, think Greek myths. If you stick to those, you'll get there eventually."

"Great! Ariadne? Andromeda?" His grin became sly. "Not Aphrodite. . . ?"

"Please."

"Then, give me another hint."

She paused, searching for the right information. "All right. You're not going to believe it, but this blizzard will last for days."

"That's a hint?"

"And the Greeks will attack the Trojans . . . on a horse, no less."

"Ah-ha. You're Cassandra, daughter of King Priam and Queen Hecuba, cursed by Apollo never to be believed. No one believed you about the horse, and the Greeks won the war."

Expensive suit and messed-up hair, a touch of down-home Texas drawl, all coupled with Robert Frost and an intricate knowledge of Greek mythology?

"I'm impressed. You should go on *Jeopardy*. But *Cassie*, please." She let her eyes wander over him. "You don't look well-read."

He laughed and waved away her comment. "I know. It's the hair. Someone told me I should change the style, but hey, give me advice, and I'll probably ignore it."

"What were you doing in St. Louis anyway?"

"Chasing dreams, I think."

She waited, but he didn't add anything more.

"Dreams?"

He was staring at the floor with such concentration that Cassie thought he hadn't heard her.

"Nick? Did you catch any?"

He gave her a blank look.

"Dreams, I mean."

He pushed his fingers through his hair. "Not this time, I think . . . a wasted trip." He lifted his gaze slowly to her face, his eyes laughing. "Or maybe not."

She drew back, embarrassed. "Now, wait a minute—"

"Oh, don't sound so worried." He tipped his neck and rolled his shoulders. "I'm just ready for some fun. How about we get something to eat, check out the cheesy souvenirs, do a little people watching? What do you say?"

She glanced at her novel.

"Hey," he said. "I got my rabies shots just last week. I did. I really did."

She smiled, glad to see his humor back again. "Okay. Sure."

"And we'll make a pact—no questions about our life beyond this airport, no personal details. For however long this storm lasts, we'll stay loose. And all the disappointments and frustrations out there beyond the blizzard—we'll let the rest of the world go hang. What do you say?"

He must have some story up his sleeve. Too bad she wasn't going to hear it.

"Sure. That sounds good."

She bit her lip. Maybe . . .

"Are you married?" she blurted out.

"No." He grunted. "Not that kind of trouble—not this time."

What did he mean, 'not *this* time'? She gave him a puzzled frown.

He sighed. "I just keep confusing you worse, don't I?"

"No, it's okay." She stuffed her book away. "Where to first?"

Giving her a big grin, he grabbed her backpack and pulled her up. To the attendant he said, "If the plane can take off, you'll announce the boarding over the loudspeaker, right? Great. Then we're off."

He took her first to a bank of lockers, stowed her hand luggage, then headed toward the main terminal. "Just to see what they've got here. Then we'll eat lunch and explore some more. Looks like we've got plenty of time."

For lunch, he ordered a Chicago-style hot dog loaded with tomatoes and peppers and so many other toppings it looked more like a vegetable garden than a hot dog.

"Wimpy," he declared after polishing it off. "Not hot enough by a long shot. Texas chili, four-alarm style—now, that's real food."

"So you're from Texas?"

"On the contrary. I"—he tapped his chest—"am a man of the world."

"Nick."

"Cassie." He mimicked her frustrated tone exactly. Then he laughed again. "I told you, no questions about the world out there behind the snow."

He kept her at the hot dog stand long enough to teach her his spoon tricks and then took her to the souvenir shop, where he managed to get all the perpetual motion statuettes moving at once. He insisted on buying her a hat with a corncob stuck through it and bought himself a puzzle with a huge ball trapped behind bars that could supposedly be set free. "I know someone who'll appreciate this. Might even teach her a lesson."

Her? "Someone you work with?"

"Uh-uh-uh," he objected. "Who needs to work? For today at least, I'm independently wealthy. And you're a famous heiress—how about that?"

"Rich *and* famous?"

"No, I'm rich, you're famous. You've been cruelly hoaxed out of your millions. All you have left is this paperweight to remind you of what you've lost." He held up a heavily laminated ten-thousand-dollar bill.

"Too bad it has Alfred E. Neumann's picture on it. Hmm." She lifted it up next to his face, and he obliged by pushing out his ears and spreading his lips into a smirk.

"Yes," she said. "A definite resemblance."

"It's yours then, to remember me by."

"You want me to remember you?"

"Sure do."

"Then, come on. I know our next stop."

She pulled him to a photo booth, where they sat side by side for silly grins and monster faces.

At the bookstore, they stood back to back, he in front of the horror books, and she in front of the romances. He read snatches from the gory scenes to her, and she shared bits from her books, the juxtaposition of the two styles sending them into hastily stifled spurts of laughter.

Nick finally thrust the book back into the rack. "Boy, this stuff makes a hornet look cuddly." He turned toward Cassie's side of the aisle. "Your books, however, could bear some further research. . . ."

"Time to go." She put her book back and covered it to keep him from taking it.

"You're blushing," he said. "You are."

Cassie poked a finger into his chest and shoved him away. "Don't get any ideas, cowboy. They must be having trouble with the heating system in here."

"If you say so. But I think this calls for another souvenir, don't you?"

He surveyed the book rack and chose a cover with a dark-haired cowboy and a pensive beauty, paid the cashier, and scribbled an inscription on the first page: "To Cassie, with memories of laughter in the St. Louis airport. From Nick."

He stood waiting as she read the inscription. When she looked up into blue eyes warm with infectious humor, she really did feel her heart swell. It had been a long time, too long, since she'd allowed herself to laugh so freely with a man. Not since before Richard.

Outside the bookstore, he held up his hand. "Romance is good. Let's do it right, with candlelight, soft music, cloth napkins. There must be an airport hotel around here. We'll check out the restaurant."

"Sure. You in your suit and me in my jeans."

He stepped back to look her over. "The sweater's great. Let's go buy a skirt to match it."

"Yeah, right."

Nick's expression didn't change.

"You're serious."

"Absolutely. You get the skirt, and I'll spring for dinner. Look, you're even wearing nice shoes, not tennis shoes. It was fated. Let's do it, Cassie. A thick, juicy steak. Baked potato. Hot rolls smothered with real butter. And I'm buying. How can you pass it up?"

He grabbed her hand and started down the concourse toward the gift and clothing shops.

"Okay, okay," she said. "I'm coming."

The shops offered little selection, but Cassie managed to find a slim-fitting black skirt, useful and unassuming.

"Black? What's with this black? Black won't work at all with that gorgeous sweater. Don't tell me—the sweater was a present, right? You probably would have chosen something brown or gray. Well, not tonight. I've got just what you need right here."

The skirt he held up was pale blue, cut on a bias. Once on, it hugged her hips and swirled smoothly around her legs as she moved.

"Perfect," Nick said, and Cassie had to agree.

The best the St. Louis airport offered was a restaurant specializing in ribs. Nick glanced around the crowded entrance with dismay. "Looks like everyone had the same idea."

He gave his name to the harried woman at the entrance, then led Cassie to seats in the large second-floor area. Banks of windows, placed close to the lofty ceiling, circled the space, but the only light came from within the airport. Snow continued to swirl around in the gathering darkness outside.

"What a small world this has become," Cassie said.

Nick put a hand over his heart. "But what a pleasure to share it with you."

Cassie laughed. "It has been fun. Thank you."

They sat in companionable silence until their table was called. Once seated, Nick surveyed the restaurant. "I'm sorry about the skirt. We should have checked things out before you bought it."

"We'll just imagine the candlelight and linen napkins," Cassie said. "And besides, I like the skirt." Her eyes twinkled. "To be honest, I've never gone shopping with a man—not even my father."

"My pleasure."

They had agreed to stay off personal subjects, so when Nick said the ribs didn't compare to what she'd taste in Texas, she carefully avoided asking him how long he had lived there. He did ask her where she wanted to be ten years from now—"ten years being far enough away not to break into our blizzard world, I think.''

Cassie had no idea how to respond. She had never believed she had the capacity to make a dream happen.

She'd made it into college. Great.

Didn't completely disgrace herself doing research at an environmental services lab. What a relief.

Then graduate school as a way to escape a one-sided crush on her boss? Why not?

But no long-term plans, especially related to graduate school. She knew her inadequacies even if the schools that accepted her didn't. She wasn't even sure she'd make it past the first year.

"Cassie?"

"Um . . . ten years from now? Let's see . . . finished with school, I suppose. A good job. Husband. Children. Same as everyone. Happy, I hope."

"Someplace in particular?"

"No. I think I could be happy anywhere."

"I do believe you could be, Cassie."

"What about you?"

He was no longer looking at her but at his glass of water. He had tipped it slightly; it offered a skewed vision through the ice and liquid.

"Nick?"

"What do I want?" His voice was low and passionate. "I want to live in a town where seasons change but people don't, at least not too fast. To know my neighbors and call a place home. Years and years in the same house. To plant a tree and see it grow and have my grandchildren climb in it. Pretty old-fashioned, isn't it?"

"You've thought a lot about this."

"Yes." He tipped his glass so far the water almost spilled out. "I can see it all in my mind. A big dining room with bookshelves and windows and flowers on the sill. There's a table in the middle with lots of chairs and kids on every one of them. There's hot food, one of those pot roasts with gravy and potatoes and carrots that have cooked with the meat. You know what I mean? A big family and we're all laughing and talking, and it takes a long time for the meal to end because there's nowhere we'd rather be than together."

"Nick . . ."

He saw her reaction and smiled ruefully. "Yeah, well." He took a long drink of the ice water. "Enough of that."

"Your family wasn't like that, I suppose."

"No family at all, Cassie, not after I was ten. That's when my parents died. No brothers or sisters. I went to live with a half-drunk uncle who died when I was in high school. Who knows where the idea of that supper table came from? Maybe I saw it in a movie somewhere."

"It could still happen."

"Maybe. But there's no sense in wishing for what you can't have."

"So what should we wish for?"

"The standard answer? To accept our lot, enjoy what we have, be happy in our work—that's not so bad. I could settle for that, I think, if things would just simmer down."

Cassie propped her chin up and gazed at him thoughtfully. Who was this guy, really? Was the world out there so difficult for him?

"Oh no," Nick said. "Incoming reality. Shields up! Red alert!"

Cassie smiled, but they headed back to the waiting area soon after, her taste for dessert gone. Nick told her how to speak Texas-style—"Y'all come back now" and "North" meaning Dallas and "Coke" meaning any soft drink—but for Cassie the imminent end of their special world was already pressing in too close.

At eight o'clock, when the few remaining people were beginning to wonder if they should go ahead and get hotel rooms for the night, the wind died down and the snow ceased, and the silent, shrouded world outside began to come to life.

On the plane, Nick coaxed Cassie's spirits up again, inventing wildly improbable backgrounds for the airline personnel until their laughter drew a sour look from the passenger in front of them. After this he pulled an *Atlantic Monthly* from the seat pocket in front of them and they began to work the puzzle at the back. Incredibly, by the time they touched down in Houston, they had the answer—something she'd never managed on her own.

Nick walked Cassie to the baggage carousel and waited silently beside her until her suitcase came. She longed to know more about him, or to at least give him her last name and where she lived so that she had some hope of hearing from him again. Maybe he lived in Houston. If she decided to attend A&M, he'd be close.

Nick didn't bend anyway. Before leaving he held out his hand to her. "Thanks for taking pity on me in St. Louis. The wait really would have been boring without you."

"You don't have any luggage?"

"Just the garment bag. It was a short trip for me. But one I'll remember for a long time, thanks to you."

He didn't even know her full name. Is this what he did—pick up strange women and do everything he could to keep them strange?

She took his offered hand. The grip was firm, the strength generous and real. At least she would have that to remember.

"Good-bye, Cassie."

And he was gone.

Two

"Chemistry? Graduate school?" The woman sitting next to Cassie craned her neck to look around the crowded sanctuary. "If you're at A&M, you should meet Luke Shepard. C'mon, we'll go find him."

The woman set off through the crowd at Faith Bible Church, Cassie following after her. Outside the church, in the early October sunshine, they approached a young man, about five ten with dusty blond hair. He was fending off the playful punches of three young boys.

"Cut it out, guys," he said. "Looks like Mrs. Stallings wants to talk to me."

The boys threw a last wayward punch and scrambled away, leaving Luke smiling.

After introducing Luke and his wife, Katy, Mrs. Stallings dismissed herself, intent on her next order of business.

Katy Shepard had short brown hair, rosy cheeks, and a warm smile. "Are you in graduate school?" she asked Cassie.

"Yes."

"I thought I might have seen you over there," Luke said. "How's it going?"

Cassie shook her head, unsure how much they wanted to hear. Living alone had been the hardest adjustment. She had gone to a different church for the last six Sundays, and this was the first time someone had said more than a cursory hello. "I'm doing okay."

"Have you come straight from college?" Luke said.

"No."

"You've been working?"

"Yes." Katy and Luke still looked interested, so Cassie continued. "For a company that does environmental testing. In Illinois that mostly means analyzing the effects of herbicides and pesticides."

"So you're probably looking for an analytical group to work for here at A&M."

"Actually—"

Katy held up her hand. "Wait a minute, you two. We have a hungry little girl to pick up. Why don't you come eat lunch with us, Cassie, and you and Luke can discuss advisers at leisure."

Cassie hesitated.

"We'd love to have you," Luke said.

Katy touched his arm. "Though it won't be anything fancy—soup probably."

They stood waiting until Cassie nodded.

"Good," Katy said. "I'll go get Alice."

"How old is your little girl?" Cassie asked Luke.

"Oh, she's not ours." He frowned and shook his head. "No. We're just baby-sitting. Now, where are you parked? You can follow us home."

Luke and Katy lived on campus in an old apartment building with white wooden siding. It looked a little like an army barracks.

"This way," Luke said and led Cassie up a narrow, dimly lit flight of stairs to their apartment door off a small second-floor landing. In the tiny living room, cluttered and yet comfortable looking, books and magazines covered the end tables, a Sunday paper lay over the couch, and what looked like student papers sat in piles on the coffee table. Luke went to these first.

"Katy's a high school English teacher. I'd better put these papers where they'll be safe." He smiled and tipped his head toward the little girl in the kitchen with Katy.

The little girl, perhaps three or four years old, didn't look much of a threat to the papers. From her position of safety behind Katy, she cast a blue-eyed gaze on Cassie. With one hand she was twirling her long blond hair. Under the other arm she clutched a stuffed orange kitty, bedraggled and threadbare.

Katy planted a kiss on her forehead. "This is Alice Meyers, Cassie. Her father's finishing up his dissertation this winter. He goes to church with Alice on Saturday night so he'll have all Sunday to work."

Luke swung the little girl into his arms and carried her to the living room. "Want to look at that new Waldo book, Alice, while Katy finishes lunch?"

Alice shook her head and leaned against Luke's shoulder, her face solemn. With a smile or a little warmth in her eyes, she might have been cute, but curls and dimples couldn't compensate for the wary look in her eyes. Cassie wondered where her mother was.

At lunch, encouraged by Katy and Luke, Cassie told about growing up in Illinois, her family, her work at Sanford Environmental Labs, her hopes of teaching in a small college after getting her doctorate.

After putting Alice down for a nap, Katy brought the conversation back to what kind of group Cassie wanted to work with. "Have you thought about an adviser?" Katy asked.

Cassie shrugged. "I've been putting that off."

"Don't worry," Luke said. "It's only five weeks into the semester. But you do know—everything in graduate school hinges on who you work for."

"It's positively feudal," Katy said. "They control everything about your graduate career—your research, your schedule, your holidays, your deadlines. Even when you finish."

Luke rubbed his chin thoughtfully. "With that work you did on your previous job, you might want to talk to Dr. Wrede."

Katy set her coffee mug down so abruptly that the coffee sloshed onto the table. "Oh, Luke, not Duncan Wrede! You've seen the way he treats—" Katy's eyes slid toward the bedroom, and she scowled. "Anyway, he doesn't seem quite . . . I don't know . . . quite safe."

"He is strange," Luke admitted, "but his work's right in line with what you were doing in Illinois, Cassie, and thanks to that big new grant, you wouldn't have to teach labs this year. It speeds up your progress if you can do research instead."

Katy wasn't impressed. "Ha. Money."

Cassie shook her head. "I think I might be ready for something different."

"How about Erin, then?" Katy said. "She goes to Faith, so she has that in her favor."

"Erin?"

"Dr. Moran's my own adviser," Luke said. "She does computational chemistry—pretty theoretical, and unfortunately she couldn't pay you until next year."

Katy began stacking the ice cream dishes. "Even so—better to teach labs than suffer under Duncan Wrede. Anything's better than that."

Remembering Katy's grading and her own homework, Cassie thanked the Shepards for their hospitality and made her way toward the door. Luke and Katy came out onto the landing to say good-bye to Cassie. As she drove away, she let out a long, slow breath. She'd been at graduate school for almost two months. Here finally were two people who might become her friends.

❧ ❧ ❧ ❧

Later that week, sitting in the chemistry seminar room, Sarah Morgan leaned toward Cassie and turned her head to see the back of the room. "Are the professors up there watching to see who goes to sleep, do you think, or hoping to catch a nap themselves?"

"How about the ones in the front?"

"They're here to make poor Dermot sweat, which'll be the main entertainment until the questioning period. That's when the real bloodletting starts, thanks to Duncan Wrede. He's the shorter one to the right. There's nothing he likes better than to pick a student apart. Please be suitably impressed by his carefully orchestrated attire—tweed blazer, knit vest, woolen slacks—all chosen to effect just the right touch of professorial splendor. But with those short legs and round belly, isn't it actually Tweedle-dee that comes to mind?"

"Oh, Sarah." The name did fit.

A harried younger professor introduced the day's speaker, someone lowered the blinds to darken the room for slides, and Dermot took his place. Cassie had only come to about six seminars so far—one per week—but she already knew enough to realize that Dermot had memorized his speech, a sure sign he didn't have a grasp on his research. If Duncan Wrede was as unforgiving as Sarah said, Dermot was in trouble.

No wonder Sarah, no longer required to attend seminars, had shown up for this one.

Sarah Morgan lived in Cassie's apartment building on the east side of College Station. She was in her late twenties, maybe early thirties, somewhat overweight but pretty, with long, curly black hair and big eyes. The two women had seen each other in passing outside their apartments. One afternoon earlier in the semester, Sarah had sat next to Cassie at a seminar like this one, in which a student was presenting her ongoing research. Cassie found herself laughing at Sarah's comments about the other students—several of whom were clearly sleeping. Cassie ended up eating pizza that night in the apartment Sarah shared with her boyfriend, Eliot Ross. Since that evening, whenever Sarah showed up for a seminar, she looked for Cassie.

Dermot struggled through his presentation and asked for questions, sounding like a man on a firing line giving permission to shoot. Duncan Wrede broke in immediately. From where she sat Cassie could see him clearly—pleasant looking, with a rounded face and even features. His Caesar haircut was attractive enough. But something was wrong somehow. He asked his question, waited as Dermot stumbled through an answer, and asked another. It was then Cassie realized his flaw. Duncan Wrede never actually made eye contact with Dermot. His eyes shifted from one side of Dermot to the other, making a brief connection but never staying.

Students around Cassie tittered nervously at something

Dermot said, but not Sarah. She was watching Cassie. "You see it, don't you? Get Luke Shepard or the Iceman Meyers up there—or any other student who knows his stuff, for that matter—and Wrede's nowhere to be found. He only goes after the weak ones. Makes you want to spit, doesn't it?"

After class, Cassie walked with Sarah to the mailroom. "But you work for Wrede, don't you?" she said.

"I'm not weak. He's easy enough to manage if you keep an upper hand. Why?"

"I did some analytical work in Illinois. Wrede's analytical, isn't he?"

"Yes, but I don't know if you should work for him, Cassie. It takes a certain breed to survive him. Still, if you're really interested, I'll show you around."

She led Cassie through the older portion of the chemistry building into one of the new wings. The fourth floor was quiet when they stepped out of the stairwell. In the office, desks lined the walls, with bookshelves forming a barrier down the middle. But no one was there.

"Where is everyone?" Cassie asked.

"Classes, labs, working on the instruments. We're all in our assigned places—Wrede makes sure of that. He comes through before his morning class at nine, and if everyone's not here, showing their merry little faces, they'd better have a good reason. And he often pulls a patrol in the evening to see who's still here." Sarah dropped her backpack on her desk. "So. The guys on chromatography have desks in their lab, the rest of us in here. There's space for you against this back wall, if you want."

She led Cassie down the hall at a brisk walk. The next door she opened revealed a man at a computer console. Most of the space in the room was taken up by an instrument that did nuclear magnetic resonance.

"This is Bob Douglas," Sarah said.

Bob was in his mid-twenties, his body almost as round as his already balding head. He stood up and brushed his hands off on his jeans. "Changing the probe again," he said to Sarah. "Who's this?"

"Cassie McCormick. She's thinking about joining the group."

He gave her an assessing look. "You could do worse, I guess. Wrede has some money now—did they tell you that? And his students publish pretty regularly."

"If they're willing to kill themselves," Sarah said.

Bob shrugged. "More likely they'll kill the instruments—like me right now if I can't get this thing back up."

Sarah grinned. "All right, all right, we're out of here."

In the hall, Cassie asked, "What's this grant for, the one everybody keeps talking about?"

Sarah gave a mocking smile. "Why don't we let Wrede explain—he'll enjoy gloating."

She knocked and pushed the door open without waiting for a response. Caught off guard by Sarah's entry, Wrede paused, then rose. Here in his own office he had no problems looking her in the eye. The effect was quite daunting.

The entire office, in fact, was impressive. The room had the standard furniture—a desk and bookshelves—but they were all made from wood and obviously expensive. An Oriental rug covered the floor, and behind the desk, in a far corner, a locked glass cabinet held a collection of Japanese netsuke on one shelf and porcelain bud vases on another.

A sanctum, Cassie thought.

Dr. Wrede didn't look too pleased at their intrusion, but after Sarah's introduction, he held out a fleshy palm to Cassie. "Where are you from?"

"Illinois."

Sarah pulled up a chair and sprawled her body across it. Just for a moment, Cassie saw Wrede's unguarded reaction to Sarah's rudeness. Instantly, the suave host resurfaced. "Hmm, well, perhaps we should sit as well." He indicated a chair for Cassie. "Have you done analytical work before?"

"A little, though I think I might be ready for something different."

"Well, we'll have to change your mind about that." His gaze shifted to Sarah. "You haven't been filling her with horror stories, have you, Sarah? You have at least told her about the new grant?"

"Yes, just now."

For the next fifteen minutes, Wrede described the projects he had going, in particular the two or three that would be available to Cassie. Then he said he was late for lunch and ushered them into the hall.

Sarah watched him walk away. "He's very impressive, isn't he? Always on his way somewhere, busy, busy—such an inspiration to us all." She wrinkled her nose. "Who else are you thinking about?"

"Maybe Erin Moran. She sounds fair."

"The beauteous Erin—A&M's PC pinup." Sarah's lip curled. "Would you believe she's only two years older than I am? You wouldn't think so. Erin's so scrupulous about maintaining the professorial distance, but she knows it, for all her airs. If it weren't for my ex-husband, I'd be where she is now."

The bitterness in Sarah's voice made Cassie want to step back and away from her. Fortunately, Sarah didn't seem to expect a response. She spun on her heel and headed farther down the hall.

"There's just one more room left, with the gas chromatograph. Two guys share it, though I can bet Izzy O'Donnell's not there. Why Wrede doesn't kick him out, I don't know." With her hand on the door, she paused and then grinned. "Maybe his parents are sending Wrede kickbacks—now, there's a thought. Wouldn't that be classic?"

Again she seemed to be talking to herself. She glanced at Cassie, laughed, and then pulled the door open and went in. From behind her, Cassie saw a bench, the counter on which chemists work, with the standard sinks and gas hookups and water spigots. Along the back wall was another counter, on which she saw two instruments, a gas chromatograph and a mass spectrophotometer. The man working the instruments stood at this counter, his back to the door.

Suspecting nothing, Cassie stepped forward into the room.

Three

*T*he man at the counter turned.

Cassie froze.

He was tall, with strong shoulders and a lean, lithe body. And his hair . . . still too short to be a businessman's. He was in jeans this time and a green-and-black flannel shirt. Just as handsome, with the same intelligent eyes and determined jaw, but watchful now and not smiling. He leaned back against the counter and crossed his arms.

"Cassie," he said. "Here you are."

"Nick?"

He didn't act surprised.

"You knew I was at A&M?" Cassie said.

"I've seen you once or twice since the semester began."

Months had passed since that March blizzard in St. Louis, but memories of Nick had surfaced so frequently in Cassie's mind that it might have been mere days since they parted. Now those memories were splintering, breaking apart, and reforming in a bizarre manner.

That man had been friendly, relaxed, quick to laugh. He had shown her spoon tricks and picked out what had become Cassie's favorite skirt. She felt the unbidden memory of that man's hand clasp, its warmth and strength.

This man seemed hesitant, his eyes guarded and careful, as if he wasn't sure he wanted to see her . . . as if this time she'd be adding to his burden of trouble.

Like a children's pop-up book—pull a tab and here comes the less-than-friendly twin.

Sarah was enthralled. "You guys know each other. Where'd you two meet?"

Cassie clamped her mouth shut. What would Nick say?

Nothing. He gazed intently at the floor, tracing the pattern of tiles with his foot. Scuffed-up tennis shoes today, not cowboy boots.

"Nick? Cassie? Where'd you two meet?"

Cassie finally spoke. "Last spring, in the St. Louis airport."

"Well, how interesting," Sarah cooed.

"It was just briefly." Cassie paused, giving him another chance. He was still so handsome, with muscled shoulders and a strong face, the same intense gaze. His eyes revealed nothing now of what he was thinking, except caution and an unmistakable restraint. She bit her lip. He wasn't going to say anything. "Apparently one of those inconsequential ships-in-the-night things," she said. "We've seen what we need here, haven't we, Sarah?"

Sarah looked again from Cassie to Nick. "I don't think so." A grin spread across her mouth. "Stay and talk to Nick for a minute. I have a phone call to make. I'll be right back." And she stepped through the door.

Cassie turned to follow.

"Wait," Nick said. "Please."

She glanced cautiously back.

"Please. But shut the door, will you?"

She didn't move. The hum of the air conditioner seemed louder in the silence.

His eyebrows lifted. "She's probably listening. You want her to hear this?"

Cassie looked from Nick to the door and back again. What was he talking about?

He came across the room, reached past her, and shut the door. He was close, less than a foot from her. His blue eyes looked into hers; she saw a measure of chagrin in them. For a sensitive moment he stayed beside her, holding her gaze. Then he blinked, the restraint returned, and he went back to the counter against the far wall.

"You want to sit down?" He indicated a nearby stool.

"When did you realize I was attending A&M?"

"That's the problem, isn't it?"

"You weren't surprised to see me."

He nodded and rubbed his neck, the motion so familiar to Cassie. If anything, his distress seemed even greater than in St. Louis. "Nick?"

"If I'd known you were coming to A&M, I would have handled that day differently. It was great, a day to remember. But back here things are different." He shook his head. "I'm sorry."

"So you ignored me?"

He shook his head wearily. "It's hard to explain."

"You *are* married."

He made a derisive sound. "I said I wasn't."

Cassie stood by the door, confused and frustrated. First Richard—falling so obviously in love with him, everyone knowing it, and then his marrying someone else. Now this man.

"I enjoyed St. Louis," she said.

"I did, too, but can't you see . . . it's not the same here." He grunted in frustration. "Things are crazy right now . . . you can't imagine how bad. It wouldn't be fair . . . I don't see how . . ." He stopped, set his jaw, and turned away, but instead of returning to his work, he kept his hands clasped against the front of the counter. His knuckles were white with tension, his arms stiff and tight.

"Okay," she said. "I guess I'll go."

This time he let her.

In the hall, she leaned back against the smooth coolness of the wall.

How strange everything seemed, like a beautiful dream turned into a nightmare. Since that day in March, she had indulged herself with so many fantasies, so many imagined encounters. A detective searching out her identity—that was her favorite scenario, and then the romantic declaration of undying love. What was she going to think about now as she waited for sleep?

Back in the office, Sarah looked up with interest. "Encounter in St. Louis. Sounds like a movie title for a spy thriller. I'd give anything to know what happened up there." Her gaze searched Cassie for some hint of information. "But you're not going to tell me, are you? Somehow, a little slip of a thing like you manages to crack the exterior of the Iceman Nick Meyers, and you're not going to tell me the story. It figures."

Nick Meyers. Cassie came to take a seat at the desk beside Sarah's. "You could tell me about him."

"For starters, look at that group photo."

Scattered computer readouts littered Sarah's desk, along with a few old journals and the remnants of a fast-food meal. Cassie lifted the framed photograph from behind a tissue box, found Nick, and froze.

Meyers. His last name was Meyers.

And he was holding a child in his arms, the little girl from Katy and Luke's, the one with the wary eyes and suspicious face.

What was it Katy said? Her father was finishing up his dissertation. He went to church Saturday night and worked on Sunday.

So Nick was a Christian?

"Her name's Alice," Sarah said.

"Yes, I know." Cassie raised her eyes, not caring that the other woman saw her curiosity.

"Do you know about Sydney, too?" Sarah asked.

"Sydney?"

"His wife."

Seeing Cassie's quick frown, Sarah laughed. "Sydney's dead. But the story's good. He married her his first year here. Rich, spoiled, and most definitely pregnant at the wedding. Knowing Sydney, the baby could have been anyone's, but judging from how much Alice looks like Nick, she must have told the truth for once. Anyway, Sydney left right after the baby was born. Six months later she fell off a horse and hit her head against a rock. She stayed in a coma for five weeks . . . *finally* died. Nick was with her the whole time. It really set him back on his graduate work. And taking care of Alice hasn't been easy for him either."

Cassie shook her head helplessly. "How awful."

"He made his bed, didn't he? Now all he does is work. Day in, day out, he's here all the time."

"And Alice?"

"That poor kid doesn't know whether she's coming or going. He has some sitter that keeps her into the evening. He goes by in time to get her ready for bed. A lot of evenings he parks her at Luke Shepard's for the night. They go to the same church, I think, and their apartments are back to back. But, you know, I kind of like the kid—she knows what she wants anyway."

Cassie remembered what he had said—lots of kids around that dinner table of his. How hard it must be for him to raise his child alone, and no wonder he wanted to pretend in St. Louis that the world out there didn't exist.

Now she was part of that out-there world, too.

So much for fantasies.

After Cassie left his lab, Nick stretched his tired muscles and settled wearily onto his stool.

So. They met again.

He had seen her almost the first day of the semester. He'd been standing at his desk, wondering how Alice was doing at her new sitter's, and there she was outside the window, walking down the sidewalk. She was talking to another student—a male. Nick had leaned closer to get a better view, unable to believe it was Cassie.

She smiled up at her companion, her expression as brilliant as ever, like sunshine from within. Nick had rocked back onto his feet and fumbled for his chair.

Definitely Cassie. That smile had haunted his thoughts since spring.

She hadn't smiled just now. Instead, on seeing him, she had looked puzzled, wary, and then hurt.

Nick grimaced. He couldn't—as much as he wanted to—he couldn't risk pulling her into this mess.

It all came pressing down on him again, the questions, the worries.

Could it really be true, what he suspected?

And if so, should he speak out?

If only he could have continued his work in blind ignorance—run the few remaining GC-mass spec that he needed, make his last revisions to the dissertation, defend his work before his committee, and clear out on schedule by Christmas. So simple.

Instead he was putting everything he had worked for during the past five years in danger, all that he had sacrificed of his own life and Alice's.

Alice . . . there was another problem.

A vision of her sitting across the table from him that morning came to mind. She was wearing the new dress Sydney's mother, Elizabeth, had sent, and he had clipped a ribbon in her blond hair. Somehow his efforts made her look even more pathetic, the listless curve of her hand more obvious as she lifted a bite of cereal to her mouth.

He wasn't stupid. He had seen the difference in Alice during the past weeks, the stillness in her eyes, the apprehension. And he knew why. Her familiar sitter, a woman who lived across the courtyard from Nick in married student housing, had moved away in August.

Obviously the new sitter, Regina Poole, wasn't working out.

He would have to find someone else, someone who would be willing to keep Alice late on Monday and Wednesday when he had his research group seminars and on Saturdays when he had to work. He had called nearby day-care centers as a stopgap, but the only ones good enough to consider were full.

Maybe Zoe would have a suggestion.

Whatever happened, he couldn't slow his pace, not now, not when he was so close to finishing. He'd do anything to get Alice away from this place, with its relentless demands on his time and attention.

And now this other problem, threatening to unravel all his plans.

Nick rubbed his temples wearily. Maybe Luke would know what to do.

ॐ ॐ ॐ ॐ

SATURDAY AFTERNOON, HIS OFFICE.

His beautiful, clean office. Clean desk, spotless, dust free.

And her on the other side.

If only he could clean her away as easily . . . scrape, crumple like paper, toss into the trash can, mash underfoot, and wrap in plastic, the cord on the bag pulled tight, trapping, holding, and then the garbage truck pushing her back, way back, among the other garbage, and then gone to the dump and buried deep, so small and dark—

She cleared her throat. "Did you hear me?"

That cloying, noxious perfume. Last time the odor had lingered . . . nauseating, repulsive . . . until hours later he'd found the wad of perfume-soaked tissue, there, where she had placed it, in his trash can—another torment.

"Tomorrow, don't forget. I want it tomorrow."

His anger spilled out, words piling on words, pure invective, the worst he could disgorge.

"My, my—aren't we testy today. But I still want it tomorrow."

"I can't."

"Fine. You know what I'll do."

"It's too soon. Give me till Monday."

She sat a moment longer, watching him, and shrugged. "All right." She rose, went to the office door, reminded him—"Monday"—then gave an insolent salute and left.

Anger coursed through his body, heat spreading down his arms to his hands, his fists clenched so tightly his fingernails drew blood.

A man could stand only so much. She should know that, the wretched creature, inhuman, ungrateful, sapping a man of all dignity and strength. Stupid, never knowing what she was forcing—yes, forcing him to do.

He slid his hands over the smooth surface of his desk. Everything in his life well ordered, just as he'd planned. No one thought it would happen, but all there now, everything, all he wanted . . . his . . . earned.

Lousy cards he'd been dealt from the beginning, the worst, and yet against all odds he'd won the hand. He had everything he wanted.

Now her.

So. A gun? Or fire—yes, fire. He smiled, the image of her trapped in a burning building, screaming . . .

Who would know?

Pleasure stimulated his lungs, spread in tremors down arms and legs until he could hardly bear to hold the shout in.

No, stay calm. Someone might hear. And wonder. And no one must know.

Four

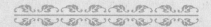

On Sunday Cassie slipped into the fellowship hall. The fragrance of brewing coffee filled the room, and from the far end conversation hummed among the twenty or thirty people who stood there, waiting for church to begin. Cassie glanced through the crowd, seeking out Katy and Luke.

But when she saw them she stopped.

Nick was with them.

If he was so intent on avoiding her, why had he come on Sunday this week?

Almost, almost, she turned and walked back to her car, but she would have to come to terms sometime with her crazy feelings about him. Why not now?

She stalked across the gymnasium floor and planted herself beside Katy. It seemed fitting, somehow, and even a little mean that he was wearing his cowboy boots today. She lifted her eyes to meet his. He nodded, but out of pity, she thought. With a pasted half smile and an attempt at a cheerful expression, she probably looked like a Chatty Cathy doll.

"Cassie," Katy said. "Great. Let me introduce you to Nick Meyers, Alice's dad."

"We've met. Nice to see you in church."

"I always come, Cassie, but usually Saturday night."

Out of the corner of her eye, Cassie saw Katy's astonished expression.

"You guys know each other?" Katy said.

Brilliant. Cassie hugged her Bible to her chest and waited for Nick to respond. This time he did.

"Cassie and I met in St. Louis," Nick said, "during a blizzard last March. She was coming for her campus visit, and I was on that job interview. Neither of us realized we'd both be at A&M this fall."

So he was there for a job interview. Now she knew.

"But, Cassie," Katy was saying, "didn't you realize last week? I mean, Alice *Meyers*, for goodness' sake."

Cassie watched Nick, curious to see his reaction to Alice's name, but his face remained impassive.

"I didn't know Nick's last name," Cassie said. "And I certainly knew nothing about a daughter. It was . . . how did you describe it, Nick? One of those ships-passing-in-the-night things."

At her tone, Katy and Luke exchanged surprised glances.

Nick shook his head calmly. "Actually, that was the way you described it."

Cassie looked over toward the sanctuary. How much time was left anyway? Could she just walk away? No, she needed some excuse. Coffee?

Katy cleared her throat. "Nick, how's Alice doing? I noticed you had to leave in the middle of Sunday school."

Nick rubbed his forehead and grimaced. "She threw another fit. If things don't improve, I'll have to start going with her—or keep her home."

"Something must be setting her off," Katy said. "She's really not spoiled."

Nick smiled wearily. "You wouldn't be biased, I suppose?"

"Maybe." Katy grinned. "It might just be a phase."

"We can hope." But he shook his head doubtfully.

Luke glanced at the clock on the wall. "It's time."

Katy clasped Nick's arm briefly and then slipped her hand in Luke's. "I wonder what Pastor Escobar has to say about the football game yesterday. He called the last team that beat the Aggies 'uncircumcised Philistines.' Are you coming, Cassie?"

"Go ahead," she said. "I'll be a couple of minutes."

Calling herself a coward, she nevertheless lingered in the bathroom as long as possible, then slipped into the back of the sanctuary to sit alone. If she moved quickly, she could get away at the end of church without talking to them again.

☙ ☙ ☙ ☙

After lunch, at Nick's request, Luke drove Nick to a nearby park. It was overrun with fire ant hills and as a consequence, fairly empty. The two men wove their way carefully toward a picnic table beside the small creek that ran through the park.

"Think they'll ever find a way to get rid of these ants?" Luke asked.

Nick shrugged and let the silence settle.

Luke looked up at the sky in mild frustration. The table was cool beneath his seat, damp from an early morning shower, but the air was warm now, and the silence in the park was punctuated by the buzz of bees and occasional rustling in the undergrowth. Minutes passed, and still Nick didn't speak.

"Come on, Nick," Luke said. "Out with it. What could be this bad?"

"I think ... ." Nick cleared his throat. "I think Wrede falsified some data he sent to the EPA."

"You mean, intentionally?"

"I think so."

"Why? What did he do?"

Nick pushed anxious fingers through his hair. "The EPA asked Wrede to do some GC-mass spec on a new herbicide developed by Cameron Chemicals, over near Houston. The agency has to be sure there won't be any toxic or harmful substances resulting as the herbicide breaks down."

"Right. I understand."

Though it wasn't Luke's field, he knew how a GC-mass spec worked. The two instruments, a gas chromatograph and a mass spectrophotometer, worked together. The GC separated the components of a sample, always in a certain order. Those components went into the mass spec, which produced a spectra, a sheet of paper with vertical lines printed on it called peaks. Though tricky, with practice, a skilled chemist could identify what substances caused the peaks, and in that way know what was in the original sample. For the EPA, the GC-mass spec would show if any toxins or other dangerous substances were left in the soil after the herbicide broke down.

"We started taking soil samples this summer," Nick said, "from a hundred test plots. Wrede asked me to run the GC-mass spec on them—ten per plot. It seemed strange at the time that he would ask me, since this is more Sarah Morgan's field than mine, but I just figured it was another of his ploys to delay my Ph.D. I ran the spectra, did the analysis—with a little help from Sarah. Everything seemed fine—and then about six weeks ago . . ."

Nick rubbed his temples wearily.

"Yes?" Luke said. "Six weeks ago?"

"I noticed a recurring pattern of peaks from one of the test plots. I couldn't identify them, and Wrede was at a conference, so I showed the spectra to Sarah. I thought she might recognize what was causing the atypical peaks. She kept the spectra overnight, then told me I should give them to Wrede. I did, and the next thing I knew a guy was over from Cameron, and Wrede had taken me off the project. Stranger still, I came in the next morning to find all the Cameron data gone from my GC computer—backups and everything."

Luke shook his head. "And now you think Wrede changed the data?"

"I'm not sure. But this last week Wrede announced that the Cameron results checked out, so now the EPA will probably give approval. I asked Wrede about the anomalies, and he told me not to worry about them."

"But you are worried," Luke said. "You think the unexplained peaks might indicate something dangerous."

"The guy from Cameron may have convinced Wrede it was just one batch of herbicide that was flawed, not the actual product. If that's true, the herbicide's actually safe, and there's no real danger."

" 'Convinced Wrede'—you mean with money."

Nick blew out a long breath. "If even one test plot shows anomalies, the EPA could require Cameron to repeat all their testing—which would cost millions of dollars. Or even if it is only one sample that's flawed, the EPA could decide the risk of faulty production was too high and refuse approval on that basis alone."

"So Cameron would probably be willing to pay Wrede off?"

"The thing is," Nick said, "I make my own backups every night. I keep them at the apartment. I have from the very beginning on all my work. I'm really careful that way. So I could easily make copies of the spectra and try to figure out for myself what the strange peaks indicate. Do you think I should?"

Luke rubbed his chin. "Why do you think you need to pursue this?"

"Because I know what the EPA's looking for. The herbicide could produce toxins that would do serious damage to the environment, to groundwater especially, or even to the people living nearby to where the herbicides are used. Isn't that worth worrying about?"

"And you actually think Wrede might take part in a cover-up?"

"I just don't know. And working out the analysis could take a lot of time. It's a lot easier to confirm substances you're expecting than to identify unknowns." Nick thrust himself up from the table. "And you know what's really crazy? For the first time, Wrede actually seems willing to get me out by Christmas—apparently he's decided my time has come. And here I am thinking about messing that up."

"Must be tough," Luke said and waited. Nick was a proud man who seldom asked for help. Through the breakup of his marriage and Sydney's injury and death, through the problems of being a single father, most of the time Nick kept his burdens to himself. Luke thought he probably wanted someone to help him think through the problem with Wrede, not someone to burden him with unwanted advice.

Nick sat back down and silence settled between the two

men. Even the little creek seemed sluggish, and Luke had an impulse to throw something at a nearby fire ant mound just to see them move.

"So," Nick finally said, "what would you do?"

"I don't know. There's Alice to think of. And if you decide to go through with this, you'll come under as much scrutiny as Wrede. The first defense is to attack the person exposing the wrong."

"Not if I can do it anonymously." Nick stared forward, his jaw set.

Luke waited.

"Besides," Nick said, "I could be implicated if any of this came out."

"That's true."

"I can't run that risk, not with Alice." He rubbed his forehead with the palm of his hand and then let his shoulders slump. "But the bottom line is, what's the good of knowing right from wrong if I ignore the distinction?"

"So you'll go ahead?"

"I guess I don't have much choice."

"Then, I know someone who could probably figure out those spectra for you."

Nick's eyes grew cautious. "Who?"

"You won't like this."

"What do you mean?"

"Cassie McCormick. She did environmental work in Illinois. She even mentioned analyzing the effects of herbicides."

"Cassie? No." Nick shook his head. "I don't want her involved with this."

"Still . . ."

"I've even been thinking I should warn her about Wrede. Did you know she came by to talk to him the other day?"

Luke winced. "That was probably my fault."

Nick dropped his elbows to his knees and buried his face in his hands. "What a mess."

"Ask for her help, Nick."

"It's too dangerous."

"It doesn't have to be. You said you'd do it anonymously."

"How can I guarantee that?"

"Look, Nick, whatever you think, we aren't made to go it alone. Maybe this is God's doing, part of His pattern. He brought you together up in St. Louis, led Cassie to A&M. Now she can help you through this. If you're going to do the right thing, you might as well take advantage of the help God's offering."

"Maybe."

They sat a few minutes longer, and then Nick shoved himself off the table. "I've got to get going. In the meantime, thanks." He held his hand out to Luke. "A lot."

ؽؽؽؽ

MONDAY. HIS OFFICE AGAIN.

She plucked the money order from his hand, checked it briefly, and stowed it casually into her leather backpack. "That's all . . . for today."

Today? Good cue. *He pressed his fingers to his forehead.* This was the time. Careful, careful. Don't overdo it. *He leaned down to open a drawer. Not there. Perplexed look. Another one. Pressed fingers again.*

Would she see them? Dice rolling, over, over, everything riding, yes, yes, maybe . . .

"Looking for these?" She leaned across his desk, snagged the pill bottle from beside his blotter, and threw it up out of his reach, laughing at his frustrated attempt to catch it out of the air. "Uh-uh-uh. No relief for you today, not when I'm around."

She pushed the pill bottle into her backpack after the money order.

Careful, careful. Don't let on. Just the right touch of helplessness.

His spirit was singing, humming, buzzing . . . but

no, can't show it. Press lips together, weak eyes. Let her gloat.

She laughed. "I'd better leave, hadn't I? I must be hazardous to your health. Don't cry—at least not till I'm gone. I'm already disgusted enough. Bye-bye, little man."

Hazardous? Hazardous? If she only knew.

He sucked in the air. It rasped down his throat, filled his shoulders, gasping, more air, and all the time wanting to scream, "Die! Die!"—words spewing into his mind in a drumbeat of desire.

Tomorrow or the next day . . . soon, his triumph waited.

When would it happen? Where? Would she see it—death coming? Would she know . . . and fear?

He longed to be there, death crowding her throat, impossible to breathe, impossible to laugh. Utterly vulnerable. Weak. And then gone.

He longed to see, but knowing would be enough.

Five

When Cassie's phone rang the next evening, she thought it might be Katy.

It was Nick.

"Alice and I are going to get some supper. Would you like to come with us?"

"I've already eaten."

"A Coke? Or perhaps a milk shake?"

"What do you want, Nick?"

"Please. I need to talk to you about something, and I should apologize, too, for the other day. So please? I'll come by in about twenty minutes."

Nick arrived in a somewhat battered pickup. Alice was buckled into the front seat next to him, her stuffed kitty on her lap. Cassie smiled down at her as she climbed into the truck, but she got no response from the little girl.

Nick turned south on East 29th Street, and then onto University, heading toward campus. As always, when Cassie approached A&M from the east, she couldn't help thinking of a celestial city. The wide expanse of green on the front campus set off the cluster of sandy-colored buildings behind it, giving it an ethereal aura from the distance. She smiled briefly at the notion. It wasn't that much like heaven up close. Just the normal mixture of human endeavors.

Within minutes, Nick pulled into the McDonald's parking lot across from campus. Somewhat unnerved by the stiff unfriendliness of the little girl beside her, Cassie turned to help Alice, but she had already loosened her own seat belt and was scrambling out Nick's side of the truck and into his arms.

He paused outside the door of the restaurant. "You said you'd met Alice, right?"

"Yes, though I didn't realize, of course, that she was your daughter."

Nick nodded. "Sorry." He pulled open the restaurant door for Cassie.

Was that his apology?

She found a table while Nick and Alice ordered. From across the restaurant, Cassie watched father and daughter in line. Alice was holding Nick's hand, but her neck was twisted backward to watch Cassie, her cheek pressed against Nick's side. At Katy's, Alice had looked almost pretty. Her hair now hung in weak curls around her shoulders, her dress was limp and lifeless, and her tights bunched a little around her ankles. None of that would have mattered if only she were smiling. She watched Cassie suspiciously from under lowered eyelids.

Nick sat down across from Cassie. He took Alice's hand, bowed his head, and prayed, a simple prayer but Cassie's first real sign that Nick belonged to God. When the prayer ended, their eyes met and Nick smiled, a little ruefully, apparently aware of Cassie's thoughts.

He opened Alice's box of chicken nuggets and squeezed some ketchup for her. As Nick worked, Alice stared at Cassie, again twirling her hair and clutching the little kitty to her chest. Cassie couldn't decide if she was merely curious or if she had taken an instant dislike to Cassie.

"There you go, doll," Nick said and dropped a kiss on Alice's head. "And here's your milk shake, see?"

"Don't want ketchup."

"You always have ketchup."

"I want a hamburger." She pushed the package of chicken as far away from her as she could and knelt on her chair to push it even farther, until it was hanging off the opposite edge of the table.

Nick lifted his shoulders. "Suit yourself, Alice. You don't have to eat the chicken, but I'm not buying anything else."

She grabbed her milk shake and started sucking it. She kept her eyes on Cassie.

"Tell Cassie about the movie we went to," Nick suggested. No response.

Nick answered for her. "There was a little girl in the movie just about Alice's age and a frisky little raccoon that kept getting into trouble."

Cassie smiled encouragingly. "I bet that would be fun. Would you like a raccoon, Alice?"

The little girl's glare deepened.

"Alice wants a kitten—a real one," Nick said. "When we move after Christmas, we're going to get one, aren't we, Alice?"

"Move?" Cassie asked, surprised.

"I'll be finished with my doctorate by January."

January? Cassie didn't quite know how to react to this information, so she kept her face impassive. "And Alice can have her kitty." She smiled at the girl.

Not even talk of a kitten could distract Alice from drinking her milk shake and continuing to glare at Cassie.

"Aren't you hungry, Alice?" Cassie asked.

Alice bounced up again and reached for her nuggets—not to eat them but to push them off the table. By instinct Cassie reached out in time to catch them.

"Whoops! That was close. I'll put them over here, okay?"

Watching the little girl react, Cassie felt an absurd desire to laugh. How was she managing to both pout and suck her straw at the same time?

Nick certainly wasn't amused. He finished his hamburger quickly while Alice continued to work on her milk shake. Nobody said anything. When Nick and Alice headed to the rest room, Cassie gathered up her belongings. She stood to meet them as they returned to the table.

"I need to get back," she said.

"Wait." Though the word itself was a command, the appeal in his eyes was evident.

"Why? I mean, this has been—"

"Don't say it. I'm sorry. But please stay. I really do need to talk to you."

This time when he sat, he pulled Alice into his arms and let her lay her head against his shoulder. "Please," he mouthed to Cassie, and she realized the little girl would soon be asleep. For the next few minutes, Nick murmured quiet words to Alice, ruffling his fingers gently through her curls. Her breathing became more regular.

"Thanks," Nick said. He still spoke quietly but seemed confident now that his voice wouldn't wake Alice. "I know this wasn't ideal, but it was all I could come up with. I have something to ask you."

Cassie crossed her arms. "Two birds with one stone? Spend time with Alice . . . sort of . . . and talk with me as well?"

He drew back sharply, and Cassie held up her hands to waylay his response.

"Enough," she said. "I'm sorry. I do sympathize with the constraints you must live with. What did you want to talk about?"

He crumpled a napkin tightly in his fist and glared at it. She wondered if he meant to continue.

"The other day," he finally said. "I put you in a bad spot with Sarah—not the best person to expose secrets to. And I should have looked you up earlier. I saw you almost the first day of the fall semester, walking outside the chemistry building."

"How was it we never ran into each other? Even with as many students as A&M has, the chemistry department isn't that big."

"I don't have classes, just a group meeting every week and a few seminars I have to attend. It's an easy thing to have someone pick up my mail. I just stayed clear of places you might be."

"For six weeks?"

"I know it seems strange, but . . ." He stuffed the wadded paper into Alice's empty cup and then crumpled the whole thing in a tight fist. "That day at the airport, it was great. But I knew here . . ." He looked down at Alice and shook his head. "I'm sorry. I can't seem to get this right."

She grabbed her bag again. "I get the point, don't worry. You didn't have to bring me out here to say all that again."

He reached across the table and gripped her arm. "Wait."

This time when she looked at him, the scattered sounds of the busy restaurant faded away. In that still, intimate moment, something in his darkened eyes spoke to her heart.

"It wasn't you I doubted, but me. And things are really bad in my life right now."

"What do you mean?"

He drew his hand back from her arm and stared at the table.

"Oh, I get it," she said. "There's something else you want, isn't there? You wouldn't have brought me here just for an apology."

He gave another weary shrug. She could see he was finding it hard to continue. "I do need something," he said. "But I want to know—have you chosen a major adviser yet?"

"Why?"

"You did environmental research in Illinois, didn't you? Are you thinking of joining Wrede's group?"

"Why do you want to know?"

Nick tipped his head back. He looked terribly tired—like a man too-long burdened who now found his load even heavier.

"Fair enough," he said. "It's actually your work in Illinois I need to know about. What did you do up there?"

"I worked for a company that did environmental testing."

"Did you ever analyze soil samples—I mean, with GC-mass spec? Have you had much experience interpreting spectra?"

"A little."

Nick nodded. He readjusted Alice slightly. "I need your help. But I need to know first—can I count on your discretion? I mean, if I explain something, will you keep it to yourself?"

She stared at him.

"Please, I need your promise."

"What are you—"

"Please."

"Okay . . . I promise."

"Then, here's the problem." Nick explained about the soil samples, the unknown peaks on the spectra, and the sudden disappearance of data. "If I reprint the spectra from my own backups, can you help me identify the peaks?"

"But if the EPA's already decided to approve the new herbicide—"

"You don't understand," Nick said. "I'm afraid Wrede falsified the data so that Cameron could get its approval."

"No." She stared at him. "Surely not."

"I've gone over this in my mind, again and again, and knowing what I do about Duncan Wrede—yes, I think he would do it. He's tampered with results before. This new grant he's gotten—I know what he based the proposal on, and the data's not nearly as promising as he made it appear. He was pretty selective about what he reported. So, yeah, I can believe he'd destroy data—especially if Cameron paid him to do it."

Cassie stared across the table at him. "I can't believe you're still with him."

"When I started with him, it took a while to figure out what kind of a man he was, and by then I was so far into my research I couldn't face starting over again. Now I'm just trying to finish and get out with some shred of self-respect left." He met her gaze without flinching.

"It's not really my area of expertise," she said. "Someone else in my lab usually ran the GC-mass spec, though I can probably recognize the substances. But how many spectra are we talking about?"

"At least a thousand—a hundred test plots, ten samples each. I'll have to sort through them all to find the suspect ones."

"That'll take some time."

He nodded but didn't speak. It was him against the world again, Cassie thought, the old superior manner that had caught her attention in St. Louis back in force.

Except Cassie's picture of him had changed slightly.

Now he held a little girl in his arms, her blond curls spread over his shoulder and her pink forehead pressed firmly against his neck. In sleep, she looked like an angel, her fingers curled around a fold of Nick's shirt, her cherub mouth slightly open. She stirred briefly in the silence and murmured, "Daddy." Nick put his hand gently on her hair and murmured back to her, calming her instantly.

This was the man who was putting his own future on the line—no independent, self-serving cowboy from the High Lonesome, but a father, a committed one, burdened with responsibilities. In exposing Wrede, there would be little benefit to himself. If he was right, he would earn the censure of many people within his profession who would label him disloyal at best and culpable at worst. But if he was wrong and Wrede ever found out what he was doing, he'd probably never get his Ph.D. He must see the risk.

"Well?"

"I don't know . . ."

"Your name would never come up, I promise. No one would have to know you had helped me."

She bit her lip. "I guess I could look at the spectra—no promises."

"Thanks." He looked too weary to say anything more.

"Or I could give you the name of the guy who analyzed our spectra in Illinois."

"No!"

The force of his voice woke Alice. He took a few minutes to soothe her back to sleep. When he spoke again, he did so more quietly but still forcefully. "Don't show them to anyone. I want to be sure—absolutely sure—before anyone else sees them."

"But you're letting me see them."

He nodded slowly.

"What made you decide to trust me?"

He looked away. She realized she was holding her breath.

"It wasn't just a question of trusting you," he finally said. "I didn't want to put you at risk."

"Even so . . ."

He pushed a hand through his hair. "Luke. He suggested I ask for your help. He seems to think . . ." He shrugged. "I trust his judgment."

Cassie dipped her head forward. She had asked. It was her own fault. "You have a tired little girl there," she said.

"There's just one thing more."

She looked up. His gaze was stern.

"Yes?"

"Sarah Morgan. How'd you meet her?"

"In class. She and Eliot Ross share an apartment downstairs from me. Why?"

"Be careful with her. She's dangerous."

"In what way?"

"She finds people's vulnerabilities and prods them. I know. She likes to see people react to pain. Watch yourself."

What was he talking about?

"Okay, I'll keep that in mind."

"Fair warning." He stood and, still holding Alice, gathered up his trash. "As for the spectra, I'll have to run them when Wrede's not likely to be around."

"I understand. Call me when you're ready."

From her apartment window, Cassie watched Nick's truck drive away and tried to reconcile the man in St. Louis with the man across the table tonight. Several new puzzle pieces had been added to her understanding of him. A father holding his little girl, frustrated at his failure to draw even a smile, coming as close to begging as he ever would for Cassie's help.

How did all the pieces fit together?

❦   ❦   ❦   ❦

TUESDAY MORNING, HIS HOME.

They spoke on the phone early in the morning, before either had gone to work. He took the phone into his kitchen, standing at the counter over an empty coffee carafe.

She began taunting him immediately, and he strained to effect his customary helplessness.

"Yes, yes, I hear you. . . . No. No. That's too much.

*People will suspect. . . . Please, don't. . . . No, please,
I'll do what you say. . . . Yes, yes, I'll add your
name. . . . Yes . . . yes . . . yes."*

*He hung up with the aftertaste of bile in his mouth.
Her name on his latest paper. It would never happen.*

*His own words echoed in his mind—please, yes,
no—each word an agony, each whimper a dagger of
shame.* Please, please, please. *He wouldn't be begging much longer. He picked up the carafe and
smashed it down so hard it shattered over the counter
. . . then delicately, carefully, he swept the remnants—
her remnants—into the trash can.*

It would be so easy, so very easy . . . and yet he
must wait. Don't fold yet . . . don't throw in the cards.
Hold on, hold on . . . you can still win. Day and day and
then soon . . .

So dress. Go. You have to believe it.

Six

*T*uesday, after her first-period class, Cassie stopped by Erin Moran's office. From what Nick had said, an adviser's character mattered almost more than their research. And Cassie had done some computational chemistry in her undergraduate program and enjoyed it. She decided to ask Moran for a place in her group.

Dr. Moran's seriousness impressed Cassie. She wore simple clothes and little or no makeup, her light brown hair pulled into a French braid. It was easy to believe this woman's mind was consumed with eigenvalues and electron densities and other theoretical riddles.

Yet when Cassie announced she would like to join her group in the spring, Erin smiled and a hint of beauty shone through.

"Great. I was hoping very much you would decide in our favor. I know Duncan has a lot to offer a student, especially money, and it'll be a few semesters before I can offer you a research position. You do realize you'll have to continue teaching labs to earn your assistantship? I wouldn't want to mislead you. But we'll try to make you very welcome here anyway."

She personally walked Cassie down to the student office and introduced her to the three students who were there. "You know Luke. And this is Deirdre Butler, who came here from Virginia. David Harper. These three basically do computer research. We have two others in our group, but Renni and Terrence both have their desks in the lab."

Erin showed Cassie the desk they could set aside for her. "Now then." She rubbed her hands together. "When can you get started on research?"

Cassie glanced at Luke, who smiled.

"I think I'd better get through this first semester," Cassie said.

Humor brightened Erin's eyes. "I expected as much. But feel free to use the desk anyway."

Erin stayed with Cassie a few minutes more, listening and smiling as the others warned Cassie to keep a low profile as long as she could. Under the teasing, Cassie could see the respect and even affection that the students had for Moran.

"What do you think?" Luke asked Cassie as they walked down the hall toward the mail room.

Knowing Luke would understand, Cassie said, "Even without money for a research position, she's way better than Wrede."

"You've talked with Nick?"

"Yes. Last night. I said I would help him."

"Thanks. He's okay. Really."

Cassie nodded.

"You still look worried," Luke said.

"It's such a miserable situation, and Nick's not going to come out of it any better off."

Luke nodded. "I know. I can hear people now—the EPA standards are too stringent, the cost prohibitive. More to the point, what business is it of Nick's anyway?"

"It will be Nick no one trusts."

"But remember he's trying to pull this off anonymously. You'll work from your apartment, and he'll do his research late at night. He's pretty tenacious. He'll be all right. But I know what you mean. Science is supposed to be objective, right? Trust granted freely and no betrayal. But sin works its damage everywhere. The science community is certainly not exempt."

Cassie winced.

"It's okay," Luke said. "It will be, you'll see. As complex as things seem, as crazy as the pattern becomes, God still makes everything work out in the end. Nick's pretty certain that God wants him to speak out, and even though in the world's eyes it's a stupid thing to do, this time Nick's doing what God wants."

This time?

As she walked through the corridors to her seminar, the complexity of Nick's life weighed on Cassie. In his place, Cassie wasn't sure she'd be able to catch her breath. She could at least assure Nick of her help.

❧   ❧   ❧   ❧

Nick went home around five-thirty that afternoon and stopped at Katy and Luke's apartment to get Alice. Tuesdays, Katy picked up Alice from her sitter and often kept her through the evening, but tonight she had asked him to come home early. When Katy answered the door, Alice was sitting at the small kitchen table. Flour powdered Alice's chin and nose, and her fingers were gooey with chocolate icing.

"Alice is helping me decorate cookies for a shower at church tonight," Katy said, "for Monica Graves. Her baby's due in a few weeks."

Nick cocked his head toward Alice. "Looks like Alice is decorating herself as much as the cookies."

Katy laughed. "Stay for supper?"

"Thanks."

"Alice promised to eat some, though given the amount of chocolate on her chin, I don't know."

"I will, Katy. I will."

Nick took a seat beside Alice, but she slipped off her chair and retreated into the kitchen to curl herself around Katy's leg.

He sighed. Somehow in the last month or two, Alice had become more and more attached to Katy. In fact, only here, in this apartment, with Katy and Luke, did she seem like a normal little girl. Each time he came to get her, Alice took longer and longer to transfer back to Nick. Though he knew Alice's attitude was a sign of her friendship with Katy—something he wanted and nurtured—it always stung. At least Katy didn't make an issue of it.

He lifted a half-eaten cookie from where Alice had been sitting and held it inches from his mouth. "Yum, chocolate icing. But who took this big bite?"

"Mine, Daddy." Alice came racing back to grab Nick's arm. "My cookie."

He swung her up into his arms and started nuzzling her cheeks. "Well, if I can't have a chocolate-covered cookie, I guess I'll settle for a chocolate-covered girl. Mmm. Lots of chocolate icing here."

Alice dissolved into helpless giggles—and finally Nick was allowed to hug her. Over Alice's shoulder, he smiled at Katy, knowing she sympathized.

Later, after dinner, Luke asked about the spectra.

"I hadn't realized just how much time it would take to sort out my files," Nick said. "I saved them in chronological order, so I'm having to hunt down the suspect results. But I'm going to take what I've managed to find so far over to Cassie's apartment tomorrow evening."

Alice was in the bathroom. Katy came out from the kitchen where she had been washing the dishes. "I'm still a little worried about that sitter of Alice's."

"What was it this time?" Nick said.

"I went right after school to pick her up, a little before four. Everything was spotless, the children all quiet. No toys down at all."

"So? Alice too?"

"She was sitting in the corner. The other kids were eating cookies at the table, quiet—too quiet. But Alice was in the corner."

"I can believe that, these days."

"Regina didn't explain. She just hauled Alice up from her chair—"

"Hauled?"

"She wasn't any too gentle, I can tell you that. She shoved Alice at me and said, 'Good. Now maybe we can have a little peace around here.' " Katy leaned closer toward Nick. "Peace? What's the matter with a little controlled mayhem? Kids need fun."

He smiled and nodded. "Like icing on their chins?"

"Exactly." Katy frowned. "That woman wants kids she can intimidate, Nick, and Alice won't let her. She's too smart, too quick. You have to get her out of there."

"I'm working on it, Katy. I've checked out the day-care centers. Some are crowded and unappealing—they're the ones with space. The good ones are full. I have a note posted at church and have asked around. No response yet." He shrugged. "And given the way Alice has been acting in Sunday school, who would want to take her?"

Katy had tears in her eyes.

"How about Brad Bauer from Tinoco's group?" Luke said. "Wasn't his wife thinking about taking Alice?"

"She hasn't decided yet. And I don't want to move Alice till I have someplace permanent."

The bathroom door opened and there stood Alice, carefully attaching her second overalls strap. She had a smudge of chocolate icing on her T-shirt, and the overalls were a little too short, but when she looked up at Nick her eyes melted his heart. Katy was right: This was a smart little girl who knew she deserved better than Nick was giving her.

"Come here, princess," he said. He wrapped his arms around her and wished with all his heart he could be what she needed.

"I'm sorry, Nick," Katy said. "I know you're trying."

"If I can't find something by the end of the month, I'll keep her with me until I do. I promise."

🦢   🦢   🦢   🦢

The next evening, after cleaning up from the frozen entree she had eaten for supper, Cassie stood in the doorway of her kitchen, looking into the living room. She was trying to see her apartment as Nick would, an exercise sure to dismay. She had rented an upstairs unit in an inexpensive block of apartments. Popular with students, each unit had a compact, utilitarian layout. Outside, railed walkways lined the building, both upstairs and down, with stairs leading to parking in front. Inside looked no less plain, even with Cassie's added touches. She just didn't have enough artistic flair to achieve the cheap chic and homey clutter of Katy's apartment.

Only two items in the room offered any appeal. One was the mission rocker Cassie's grandmother had left to her. It was a genuine Stickley, beautifully finished, with soft leather upholstery on the seat cushion. Cassie loved its simple lines and careful craftsmanship.

More precious even than the rocker were Cassie's dollhouse and accessories, displayed on a table near the couch. The dollhouse was designed in the same craftsman style as Cassie's chair. Her father had made the furniture and wooden people over the years of Cassie's childhood, presenting her with new treasures each birthday. Even now, with his fingers bent and twisted by arthritis, he continued to make her new pieces, love distilled by pain, creating beauty.

So I'm poor and loved, Cassie told herself. A woman could do a lot worse than that.

None of it seemed to matter to Nick anyway. As soon as he entered, he settled Alice on the couch with a coloring book and some crayons and took a seat at Cassie's table.

Alice went to stand in front of the dollhouse. She was biting the thumb of one hand and twirling her hair with the other, her ever-present stuffed kitty tucked under her arm. Her eyes were wide as she gazed into each tiny room.

Cassie smiled. "Do you want to play with it, Alice? You may."

Alice shook her head and turned away, returning to her coloring books on the couch.

"No? Look, Alice. There's a family. A mom and dad and three little kids, just like my own family. One is even a baby. And there's a puppy."

Alice shook her head more vigorously.

"Mmm. Maybe you'll change your mind."

And in fact, by the time Cassie returned from the kitchen with coffee, Alice was standing at the table looking at the figures more closely, and a few minutes after that she began rearranging the pieces.

Nick had already pulled out papers and print-outs from his backpack. From where Cassie stood she could see his profile: firm jaw, strong nose, eyebrows furrowed in concentration. Tonight, as he did most days, he was wearing jeans and an old T-shirt, but there was nothing relaxed about his body or his attitude. From his taut shoulders to his muscular arms, the firm posture of his back and the suppressed power in his legs, Nick Meyers was energy held tightly under control. If anything, his mind was even more intense than his body. She wondered how he released that energy. Perhaps in sports. He would need some way to work off his frustration at the world around him.

He glanced up to find her watching him. For a moment, so brief that Cassie thought afterward she must have imagined it, their eyes caught, and she felt her cheeks warm. Then he shook his head as if to clear it and looked back at his work. "Here's what I have so far," he said. "What do you think?"

For the next two hours, Nick worked with Cassie, marking the patterns they both recognized, separating the anomalous spectra, finding any repetition of unknown peaks. Cassie had been a little nervous that Luke had misrepresented her abilities, but the more she saw, the more confident she became.

"Okay," she said and sat in her chair. "That's enough to go on."

Nick was holding Alice. About an hour into the work, she had begun bothering him, wanting to sit on his lap, asking him to get her a drink, pushing a book into his hands to read to her. He had taken a break, and now she was asleep against his shoulder, her kitty on the floor behind them where it had fallen from her limp hand. The living area behind him was in shadows.

Nick leaned back and stretched, rolling his head in an effort to loosen stiff muscles.

He's tired, Cassie thought, *and maybe a little relieved.*

Perhaps he, too, had been wondering if she could do what he needed.

He turned his face to look at Cassie. "What do you think?"

"It doesn't look good, Nick. I'll check to be certain, but I think this peak right here is dioxin, which is airborne and quite dangerous."

"Agent Orange," Nick said.

"Yes. Bad enough for chemical warfare. But I need to see more spectra, Nick. Sometimes, just burning old pesticide cans can produce dioxin. It might not be from the herbicide at all but from another source altogether."

"That might be what Wrede decided, why he went ahead and recommended approval."

Cassie shook her head regretfully. "Then why didn't he explain it to you? Why hold back and tell you not to worry?"

"I suppose you're right." Nick bowed his head and shook it. "It just gets worse and worse."

Cassie wished she felt comfortable enough to touch him, even just to grip his arm or squeeze his hand. If ever a man needed comforting, Nick did.

"All right," he said. "I'll print some more spectra tonight if Wrede's not hanging around. Alice can sleep at the lab—she's already out. Can I come back here on Friday night, say around seven? I can pick up Alice and get something to eat before that."

Friday night? Two days away? "Okay. But if you want, you can bring Alice and eat supper here."

"You sure?"

Cassie smiled ruefully. "It will be nice to have someone to eat with."

"Thanks. That'll save some trouble."

Cassie had begun to push her chair back when someone knocked on the door. She checked the peephole and looked over at Nick in surprise.

"It's Sarah Morgan," Cassie mouthed. She looked from Nick to the spectra spread out on the table.

Nick didn't dawdle. He pointed to Cassie's bedroom door. "May I?"

Not sure what he meant, Cassie nodded.

He gathered up the papers in a disorganized bundle and took them and Alice into Cassie's bedroom. On his return he pushed Alice's kitty out of sight and lowered himself to Cassie's couch, propped his feet on her coffee table, and thrust his hand through his hair.

It had taken less than a minute for him to remove all trace of their work. He looked as if he had been sitting comfortably on the couch all evening.

Cassie motioned toward the lamp beside the couch. Shouldn't she turn it on?

"Open the door," he mouthed, and Cassie did so.

"Hello, Sarah."

The other woman stepped purposefully past Cassie. She took in Nick on the couch, the shadowed room, and what Cassie knew must be a look of chagrin on her own face.

"What have we here?" Sarah said.

Nick stood up and straightened his T-shirt. Cassie almost choked.

"Well, well, well," Sarah said with much more satisfaction.

"Have you come to borrow some sugar, Sarah?" Nick asked. "Or is it vinegar you want?"

"Maybe not to borrow but possibly to loan. You wouldn't be needing any—shall we say . . . protection, would you? Knowing you, Nick, you're not prepared."

Cassie sputtered, but Nick never lost control.

"What do you want, Sarah?"

"Well, perhaps after Sydney, you actually learned your lesson." Sarah turned to Cassie, who felt like an episode of the *Twilight Zone* had invaded her living room. "Congratulations, Cassie. You seem to be making definite headway with the Iceman. How sweet."

"No," Cassie exclaimed. "Nothing like that. Nick and I—"

Nick abruptly cleared his throat.

"We were just . . . talking," Cassie said. "Did you want something in particular, Sarah?"

"No, no. I saw Nick's car and had to investigate. I'm glad I did." She laughed and swung around to depart. "See you to-morrow, little lovebirds."

Cassie closed the door and turned to face Nick. "How could you? Fixing your hair and straightening your belt. You made it look like we were . . ."

He grinned, his eyes bright with amusement, and she suddenly found herself laughing, too.

"I can't believe you," she said.

He let out a slow breath and shook his head. "Sorry. Desperate measures. I don't want Sarah Morgan getting wind of this stuff with Wrede. Anyway, we're done here, aren't we?"

He brought out his papers first, stashed them in his back-pack, then retrieved Alice. "Next time I come," he said, "I'll park around back. Sarah's less likely to see my car there."

"You want me to help carry some of that down to your car?"

A quick smile lit his face. "With a kiss to send me off? I'm parked right outside Sarah and Eliot's apartment."

She opened the door wider. "Just for that you can manage on your own."

ॐ   ॐ   ॐ   ॐ

THURSDAY MORNING, ON CAMPUS.

He went in to talk to Bob, and she was there. She kept speaking, ignoring his entry, until she finished her tasteless little story.

An Erlenmeyer flask was standing on the bench beside her. In a fantasy so real he felt its cool hardness in his hands, heard the glass shattering as he broke it against the metal sink, saw the terror in her eyes as he lifted the jagged edges to her throat . . .

Bob had to speak his name twice before he realized she had finished and walked out, never acknowledging his presence. The experience was strangely sobering.

Wait, fool. Play out the game.

Seven

*A*fter her seminar on Thursday evening, Cassie made her way through the chemistry department halls to her new desk in Moran's offices.

Seeing her pass the lab where he was working, Terrence Goodman followed her down to the office. Terrence was short, thin, and looked like a teenager, though he was only a year younger than Cassie. He wore baggy shorts and loose flannel shirts, and Cassie kept expecting him to show up at the lab on a skateboard.

"Working late?" he asked her.

"From what I've seen, things barely get going around here before nine. I'm thirty minutes early."

"And med students think they have it rough. They've never had to keep Moran happy."

"She's not that bad, is she?"

On the blackboard above Cassie's desk, Terrence sketched a figure with a whip and added a crouching figure in front of it, hands held up in prayer. Below the cartoon he added the caption, "Please let her get tenure soon."

"There's your answer. Till she gets the big promotion, she's here early morning, all day, through the evening, and sometimes past midnight. Weekdays, weekends. Never a break. She's down in her office now."

"So erase the board, you fool," Deirdre Butler said from behind them. Deirdre was in her mid-thirties, with a somewhat frumpy figure, sharp intellect, and a serious manner—a fitting match for Erin Moran. "Dr. Moran hates it when you complain."

"But it's true, isn't it?"

"And we knew it would be when we signed on. It's like this, Cassie. Moran's young and she's hungry and she gives us a lot of attention, which means we work hard and long but get out faster. Luke will be out of here the end of next summer, a little over four years, which is pretty good. I'll probably finish next winter."

"And what about you, Terrence?"

He groaned.

"He'll be out before any of us if he doesn't wise up," Deirdre answered, reluctantly beginning to smile. "*Way* out."

Terrence didn't look too worried. He winked at Cassie before heading back to the lab.

%% %% %% %%

Nick knew Cassie was joining Moran's group, of course, yet when he stopped by on Thursday evening to see if Luke happened to be around and wanted to get something to eat, he was surprised to see Cassie already at a desk. He recognized her hair first—rich dark brown, falling halfway down her back. And then the set of her shoulders, just a little bit careful, as if wanting to be ready for something. She turned sideways to open a drawer, and he could see her face.

He must have moved. She turned sharply and saw him.

"What are you doing here so late?" he asked.

The question sounded much too abrupt. Her brown eyes widened.

"It's barely past nine," she objected.

"Where are you parked?"

"Remote parking. I've been here since before noon. Why?"

"Stop by my lab when you're ready to go home. I'll walk you out there."

She glanced across the room at Deirdre, who was watching the interchange with interest.

"Where do you park?" Cassie asked her.

"By the English building. My husband has a faculty sticker."

"You're lucky you can park so close."

"But even that close, I call security to walk me over. You can't be too careful, especially late at night."

Cassie turned back to Nick. "I can call security."

"No. Come by. I'll be ready for a break."

He left before he got himself in any deeper. What was he doing anyway? He'd planned to see Luke—now was he hoping for Cassie?

He had to be crazy.

Nick heard his lab door open around ten-thirty. Cassie stood there. She was wearing jeans and a plaid vest hanging carelessly over a loose T-shirt. Her hair was tied back—he had never seen it otherwise—and her hands were at her waist, one nervously rubbing the other.

Afraid of him? Cassie?

"It'll be a few minutes before this run ends," he said. "Can you wait?"

"Sure." She sat on a stool for a few minutes and then wandered around to Izzy's side of the lab. "What's this?" she asked.

Nick saw what she was looking at. "That's an intercom Wrede set up among all his offices—he's an electronics junkie. Izzy's convinced it's really a ruse for Wrede to eavesdrop on us. He's even taken it apart—several times—just to make sure Wrede hasn't rigged it funny. Barring that, Izzy put in a switch under the counter. Now we can hear Wrede, but before he can hear us, we have to turn up our signal."

"A bug? Is he serious?"

Nick laughed. "Who knows? I bet Sarah has some choice words to say about Izzy, but he's okay."

Nick started putting his things away. Seeing his Walkman on the desk she asked, "What were you listening to? Music?"

"No, some tapes Luke loaned me. See for yourself."

He pushed over a plastic case.

"*History of Christian Doctrine*? What kind of tapes are these?"

"Luke got them from the church library and thought I might like them as well. They pass the time in here while I'm waiting for runs to finish. More than that, I'm really interested."

"Which tape did you listen to tonight?"

"One on Pelagius and Augustine. They had a debate around A.D. 400 about what—if anything—we contribute to our salvation."

"Really? Fascinating. And this stuff keeps you awake?"

He leaned back, amused but intent on making her understand. "Most of the time, Cassie, this stuff keeps me sane. I find it comforting to see how God has worked through history. That same church He was protecting back then, through men like Augustine, is the church I belong to today. His interest in everything, even me, is something I like to remember on quiet nights when I wish I could be home with Alice."

"She's with Katy, isn't she?"

"Yes. She'll spend the night there. Katy usually keeps her either Tuesday or Thursday, depending on what works out best for me. The first year Luke was in graduate school, three years ago now, Katy took care of Alice full time. Did you know that? She didn't have a teaching job yet and did day care in their apartment."

Cassie smiled. "When Alice was just a little baby."

"Hard to believe it's passed so quickly."

He popped the tape out of the player and put it back into its case. It would still be a few minutes before the run finished.

"I've been wondering," Cassie said.

"Yes?"

"About her name. It's beautiful, but so old-fashioned."

"Ah, well, there's a story behind that. I like old-fashioned—Mary and Alice and Julia—but my wife wanted something more trendy. We narrowed it down to these—" He wrote three names on the board: Alyssa, Alysia, Elyse. "I agreed to the first one."

"It's pretty."

"But you see, don't you, how all her names had Y in the

middle of them—not just these but all her favorites. It's a popular spelling, but it became too symbolic for me—Y, Y, why—especially given the mess my life was in. When Sydney died I changed her name to Alice." He drew a line through all three names and wrote the old spelling beneath them. "Just plain Alice."

"But—" Cassie bit back a smile.

"What?"

"Now she has an I in the middle of her name."

Nick laughed. "Hey, if it's a choice, I guess I'd rather have old-fashioned egotism over modern-day skepticism anytime. You know what I mean?"

He could see she didn't. He grinned and returned to his work, intent on finishing.

Her next question surprised him. "I was also wondering . . . how did a man like you become a Christian, Nick?"

"Me? What do you mean?"

"You said, in St. Louis, no family. Remember? Half-drunk uncle. I just wondered when God entered the picture."

He leaned back against the counter and crossed his arms, his usual position for thinking. " 'Entered the picture,' " he repeated slowly. "Luke would say He never does that. God *is* the picture, and we're just the background."

He thought for a little longer and shook his head. "No. God is the painter, that's what it is. He's the artist. We're His creation. There wouldn't be a picture without Him."

"Nick . . ."

Seeing her bemused expression, Nick laughed. "Sorry. I guess I get a little philosophical late at night."

"I just wanted to know how you became a Christian."

"Right. Let me get this put away and then maybe we can discuss that over some supper? I haven't eaten yet, and I'll probably be here late."

Cassie bit her lip. He waited, watching the skin between her eyebrows wrinkle, her hands tighten on each other and then release.

"Okay. I haven't eaten either."

"Great." It took her a moment to realize he had loaded everything up and was waiting for her to move away from the door.

"Oh, sorry." She jumped up.

"After you," Nick said.

Cassie rode with Nick to the Denny's restaurant across from campus, where they found a seat and ordered. Outside, traffic on Texas Avenue was still fairly heavy, though at this late hour even a university town slowed down a little. It had been another warm October day, still much like summer, but the night air had grown somewhat cooler.

She'd been told that Texas winters were wet and cold and windy, with barely any snow. She couldn't imagine winter without newly fallen snow. It was God's balance of brightness to the long dark nights and overcast days. The fresh snow, so brilliant and pure, caught the sun's fragile light and reflected it back in shining radiance, igniting hope in even the coldest hearts. It made any inconvenience worth it.

Of course, in central Illinois cities, where snow didn't fall that often, within a day or two car exhaust and sand and dirt along the streets built up to form a grimy pile of black slush. The snow melted, and the depressing, washed-out colors of mud and bare trees and dull lawns appeared again—winter at its worst. But while the fresh whiteness lasted, it made winter worthwhile for Cassie.

Winter rain, on the other hand, had no redeeming qualities. And that was all Texas offered?

"What are you thinking?" Nick asked. He was smiling. "Something serious, it looks like."

"No. Nothing much." Cassie sat back more comfortably. "You were going to tell me how you became a Christian."

"I was, wasn't I? Okay," he said. "How I became a Christian. When I graduated from high school, people tried to get me into college, but there was no way. Absolutely not enough money. And I didn't care. School came easy, but a good time came even easier. I cleared out and moved to Houston."

"Cleared out from where?"

"Remember I said my parents died when I was ten? Until then, I lived with them in East Texas, up in the piney woods area near Tyler. After that, I got shipped over to the Panhandle, south of Amarillo. Small enough town not to have anything much to do, big enough to provide plenty of trouble."

"And you moved from there to Houston? Why not Dallas?"

"The farther the better. It turned out okay. I got work delivering milk—really. People still do that. I drove a truck and dropped off milk at grocery stores and gas stations. It paid the bills. No, it did more than that. My boss was a Christian."

"And he led you to Christ?"

Nick rubbed his neck self-consciously. "Um . . . first I landed up in the county jail. Too much beer and a pretty lady I couldn't have. Woke up with a black eye, a fine I couldn't pay, and a very angry boss. By all rights, he should have fired me." He shook his head. "I still can't figure out why I wanted her so badly. There were plenty of others. Who knows? I was drunk—stewed as prunes."

Cassie realized she was staring. She blinked and took a drink.

"Am I shocking you, Cassie?"

"Sorry. But what's the punch line? I take it your boss didn't fire you."

"He paid my fine, hauled me back to the dairy, and worked my tail off. A couple of days later he took me up to Huntsville for a Bible study in the prison up there. That sobered me up big time. I was just a twenty-year-old kid, but I realized pretty fast I didn't want to end up with those men. After the study he brought me to a place like this for something to eat, and we talked until almost midnight."

"About Christ?"

"And sin. Lots about sin and the consequences thereof. About judgment and grace and what Jesus did on the cross. Within the month I was going to church with him, and three months later I knew I needed a Savior. There you have it."

Cassie had finished her hamburger and fries and was down

to the last leaf of lettuce on her plate. She couldn't remember eating any of it.

"What about you?" Nick asked.

"Me?"

"I don't know much about you. Do you have family in Illinois?"

"Parents. Two much older sisters—fifteen and eighteen years older. I came along late, a little surprise."

Nick smiled. "A happy one, I would think. What does your father do?"

"He farmed. They're retired now. My brother-in-law works the acreage for them."

"So you're a country girl."

"Not really. We live pretty close to Springfield. My mom worked in town, a bookkeeper for the state. What about you? What did your parents do?"

"They were teachers, both of them. My dad taught high school math. My mom taught fifth grade."

"Oh." She brushed her bangs back and frowned, disturbed by the thought of Nick's having lost his parents so young. "I'm sorry."

"It's okay," he said, his eyes gentle. "I'm over it."

"They'd be proud of you now, so close to a doctorate."

"Proud?" He rolled his eyes. "Looking back, remembering some of the other stuff I've done—it always makes me feel a little short in the intelligence department, believe me. I wouldn't have wanted them to see that part of my life."

She smiled. *If they could only see him now*, she thought. He must have seen her approval, for he smiled back, a peaceful exchange.

"Anyway," he said, "ready to go back? I'll drive you to your car now, if you'd like."

"Thank you. Are you still coming over tomorrow night?"

"Sure. We'll both be there."

᱓ᱹ ᱓ᱹ ᱓ᱹ ᱓ᱹ

Friday morning, Cassie found Eliot Ross, Sarah Morgan's boyfriend, in the parking lot. Eliot, a veterinary student, was shorter than Sarah but strong, his shoulders and chest massive, his neck huge. He was lifting the hood on his pickup.

"Trouble?" Cassie asked.

"I need a jump."

"Wasn't that Sarah who just drove off down the street?"

"Yes." Eliot looked away but not before Cassie saw his clenched jaw. "She had to get to class."

"Oh. Well, let me pull my car alongside."

Eliot worked in silence, jamming the jumper clamp against Cassie's engine block and slamming his car door. Cassie fought the urge to cheer. It was about time mild-mannered Eliot lost his temper. Beside Sarah's vibrant personality, Eliot seemed almost timid—they were like pepper and vanilla—yet he made no secret of his desire to marry Sarah. Cassie had a hard time understanding why. Along with the mocking statements Sarah made to Eliot whenever Cassie was with them, Cassie had also seen Sarah volunteer Eliot's help, command Eliot to run errands, mimic his slight speech impediment, and just plain insult him.

How long would Eliot stay angry today? Until the evening? However long, Sarah would probably just laugh at Eliot's show of temper.

His car running again, Eliot came around to Cassie's driver side and said thank you. But his jaw remained clenched.

Poor Eliot.

Nick was sitting on Cassie's desk talking to Luke when she walked into the office.

"Here's Cassie," Luke said to Nick. "Looks like you'll have to park yourself somewhere else after this."

"No fair. I've been sitting here since Tanya dropped out last spring."

Cassie dumped her books next to Nick. He didn't move except to lean over closer to Cassie.

"You heard him, Nick. It's my desk now."

"Can't we work out a compromise?"

Cassie let out a slow breath. Why was he flirting? He didn't have to pretend in front of Luke.

"May I remind you," he whispered—loudly enough for Luke to hear, "that I have some photos you might prefer no one else saw."

"You're blackmailing me?"

"Photos?" Luke said. "What kind of photos?"

Cassie promptly dug into her purse.

"He means these."

She passed over the strip of pictures from the photo booth in the airport.

"You keep them in your purse?" Nick put a hand over his heart. "Cassie, I'm flattered."

"I stuck them into my wallet last spring and haven't cleaned it out. See? I still have receipts from back then, too."

"You're saying it's not because of fond memories? Now I'm hurt."

"You'll live. Can I sit down?"

"Help yourself." But still he sat, not letting her get around the desk to her chair. She stood where she was, less than a foot away from him.

"You never wear your corncob hat," Nick said.

"I gave it to my twelve-year-old nephew." She frowned. "Who was the puzzle ball for anyway?"

"Zoe Calder. A friend from church."

"Zoe?" Luke sounded surprised. "How do you know Zoe Calder?"

"She's usually at Faith on Saturday nights. She helps me keep Alice occupied. Anyway . . ." He lifted himself off the desk, making an elaborate show of relinquishment with his hands. "I'm going home to get some sleep."

After Nick left, Cassie had to ask. "Who's Zoe?"

"A nurse with the county health department," Luke said. "Katy knows her better than I do—they go out to lunch now and then." He chuckled. "Zoe must not have let on to Katy how well she knew Nick. Katy's been trying to get Nick married off for a while now. Seems hopeless to me, but she's determined."

"And Zoe Calder's the right age?"

"She's a prospect, all right."

Cassie saw his eyes grow thoughtful, watching her, and she smiled. "That's good. He could use a wife."

Though if they left him alone he would probably pull one out for himself when least expected. Men did that. Even after sharing a few laughs with someone they worked with.

☙ ☙ ☙ ☙

FRIDAY, LATE AFTERNOON, HIS OFFICE.

The door swung shut behind Bob. Quiet again, but blood pounding, heart beating, rushing, rushing. No going back now. Bob had come in with the news. That wimpy Eliot, her little lapdog, had called.

He took a deep breath and told himself again. . . . Victory. Russian roulette and she pulled the bullet.

He thought about the days ahead. Then of the past . . . the dread of seeing her, the shame, the helpless anger. And now each time, this magic reminder: gone . . . done . . . no more.

Happy Hour at the Crooked Path, and she wouldn't show up.

Group meeting, and never the silent insult of arriving late.

No more money orders, no more demands.

Over. Finished. No going back.

And at a time when everything depended on him keeping his head, he felt as giddy and light-headed as the first time he got drunk.

Careful, man. The game goes on. Even yet she could win.

Eight

*C*assie returned to her apartment around five that afternoon, in time to make some supper for Nick and Alice, who were supposed to arrive around six.

When she began climbing the stairs outside her apartment, though, she found Eliot sitting on the metal steps. He was slumped against the rail, his head bent over and resting on one hand.

"Eliot? What happened?"

"Cassie? Sarah . . . Sarah is dead."

"Dead? Eliot!"

She looked around at the quiet walkway between the apartments, heard the normal sounds coming from the parking lot and the street beyond.

"Did you say 'dead,' Eliot?"

He let his head drop forward again onto his hands. A strangled noise came from deep in his throat.

She sat down and put her arm around his shoulders. "What happened?"

"I came home around two-thirty. I knew she'd be here. We had an argument this morning and I wanted to see her. She was there, in the kitchen, on the floor. Not breathing. There was a broken glass next to her and aspirin capsules on the counter. Apparently she was getting a drink of water when she fell. She didn't even have time to put the glass down."

His voice was beginning to rise.

Cassie hugged her arm more tightly around him. "You called 9–1–1?"

"They came—the paramedics. No chance, but I hoped."

"Do they know how she died?"

"Maybe a stroke. They said something about paralysis—I don't know."

Eliot turned back toward the handrail, his face so pale Cassie thought he might faint.

"How long have you been sitting here, Eliot?"

He didn't seem to hear.

"Eliot, tell me what happened after that."

"I went to the hospital, but what could I do? She was already dead. They sent me home."

And now he can't bring himself to go into their apartment. No wonder.

Cassie hauled him up. She put her arm around his back and began pushing him up the stairs. "You're coming with me. You need some tea. Come on, now, my apartment's right up there, see?"

Half pushing, half dragging the stumbling figure, Cassie drew Eliot into her kitchen, sat him down, and put the teakettle on. Eliot had stopped crying and was staring blindly across the room. "I'm not even her next of kin. They called her parents."

Cassie sat in the chair beside his and clasped his arm. "I'm sorry."

"They're going to do an autopsy. They don't know why she died. They have to make sure—" His voice broke again over the words.

"Sure of what?" Cassie asked.

He looked up at her, his face stricken. "They have to rule out . . . whatever. But they think it was a stroke."

"Oh, Eliot, I'm so sorry. I'm sure it was something normal. Maybe it was a heart attack. The most amazing people can die of heart attacks. Remember that runner—the one who was in such good condition and died while he was jogging? And there was that Russian figure skater. . . . Anyway, it was probably a heart attack. Sarah was so strong, she wouldn't be likely to complain, would she, at the warning signs?"

Eliot's expression grew sharper. "You're right. You're absolutely right. She would have suffered through it. She suffered through enough—I should know." The expression on his face was one of hope mingled with despair. "Oh, man, she won't suffer anymore, will she?"

He thrust his chair back and stood at the kitchen sink, staring down at the garbage disposal as if he might throw up. "I was so angry this morning. I told her if she drove away, I wouldn't be here this afternoon. And now she's dead."

Cassie wanted to hug him but knew he would not give in to comfort. The kettle was whistling. She got up to make the tea, using an herbal mix she often drank under stress. Eliot barely glanced at the mug she set beside him at the sink.

Someone knocked on the open door of the apartment. Cassie motioned Nick in. "Eliot's here," she said quietly.

"Eliot?" Nick seemed surprised, but then he saw Eliot slumped back against the sink. "Eliot. What's going on?"

Eliot turned sharply around to look out the window again.

Cassie answered. "Sarah Morgan died this afternoon, Nick. Eliot found her in their apartment around two-thirty."

Nick stood back, looking from Cassie to Eliot. His face was blank, free of emotion, as if someone had freeze-framed a video. He came forward and put his hand on Eliot's shoulder.

"This must be tough on you, Eliot."

Eliot shrugged away from Nick. "What do you care?" he said. "We all know how you felt about her."

Nick grimaced. "Yeah. You're right. But I know you cared about her, and I'm sorry."

"Sure you are." His lip curled. "I gotta go."

"Wait, Eliot." Cassie followed him to the door. "Are you all right?"

"What do you think? No, I'm not all right. I'm lousy."

Cassie bit her lip. "Stay, please. Drink your tea. You need something for the shock. Talk to me."

"Not with him here. Him and all his kind. They make me want to puke."

And he slammed the door shut behind him.

In the kitchen, Nick was leaning against the counter, his arms crossed. He must have heard Eliot's last words.

"I could have gone," he said.

"He wanted to go anyway. He's feeling edgy, and I wasn't helping." Cassie looked back again at the living room. "Where's Alice?"

"Luke and Katy took her to that playground in the mall."

For the first time, Cassie took in Nick's appearance. He was wearing a sharp plaid shirt with his jeans and cowboy boots. From the smoothness of his jaw she knew he had recently shaved. Good enough to pass Katy's inspection, no doubt, who had probably come up with the playground scheme in response to Nick's attire. It all seemed like a callous joke now.

How incredibly disorienting this was—like stepping on a patch of ice and having the whole world shift beneath you.

"You okay?" Nick asked. He was still standing against the counter, no less tense himself.

Cassie sat down abruptly at the table and let her body slump forward. "She's dead, Nick. It feels like a dream, but Sarah's really . . . gone. It's all over for her."

"How? I mean what caused her death?"

"They're not sure. They mentioned something about paralysis or maybe a stroke. But how could that be? She was so young. So maybe a heart attack."

A muscle tightened in Nick's jaw.

"Nick?"

"You still want to work? Or should I go?"

"Oh. Yes, I guess . . . work. We should eat first, though." She opened the refrigerator, forgot what she had planned, and then remembered. "Is chicken all right? I have some vegetables ready for stir-fry."

He grunted, which she took for a yes. She pulled out the chicken and began cutting it on the counter. "Eliot says they're doing an autopsy. Why would they do that?"

"Probably required when someone healthy suddenly dies like that."

"It must be a little frightening for him. If they were to turn up anything suspicious, he'd be the main suspect."

"Not for long."

"Why?"

"Eliot Ross was the only man in Sarah's world who didn't actively hate her."

She glanced at him in surprise. "Even you? Did you really hate her?"

"What do you think? Sarah Morgan's greatest pleasure was finding people's weaknesses and exploiting them." He pulled open a cabinet door so violently Cassie thought he might break it off. "Plates?" he said. "Dishes, silverware? You want me to set the table?"

"Sure. Here, this one. And this drawer."

She winced as the cabinet door slammed shut again and turned more purposefully to the dish she was preparing. A chair scraped back, and she heard him sit down. She glanced around.

"Oh, don't look so worried," he said. "I'm just upset at myself."

"Why?"

"It puts everything in perspective, doesn't it? She's dead now, without God, without hope."

Cassie sliced another piece of meat into small chunks and pushed them into the frying pan. How could she possibly eat? Her stomach felt awful.

Nick didn't look any better. He was frowning, drumming edgy fingers against the table, his shoulders hunched forward.

"What did she do to you, anyway?" Cassie asked.

He winced and looked away from her.

"Nick?"

"You know about my marriage, don't you?"

"Yes."

"She told you, didn't she? That first afternoon we saw each other at A&M. Soon as you got back to the office, I bet. She wouldn't have been able to resist it."

"I'm sorry."

Nick crossed his arms and let out a slow, labored breath.

"Here's just one example of the kind of thing Sarah did. I often take Alice with me on Saturday to the lab. Yeah, the lab could be dangerous, but she likes it there. She behaves. I have some electronic toys for her to play with, and puzzles and things. She's okay."

"I'm sure she loves being with you."

"Yeah. Well, anyway, most Saturdays we cut out before supper and go to church, but sometimes I work late and Alice falls asleep there. I have a little sleeping bag for her. She doesn't mind, really."

Cassie nodded.

"Sarah came in one night and took Alice's picture. She didn't ask. She just did it. The next thing I knew she was threatening to send the pictures to Sydney's mother, proof that I wasn't caring for Alice properly."

The chicken was crackling in the hot oil. Cassie shoved the pan aside. "I don't understand," she said. "Is Sydney's mother looking for proof?"

"After Sydney died, Walter and Elizabeth sued for custody of Alice."

"And Sarah knew this? Oh, Nick." She pushed aside her bangs with the back of her hand. "No wonder you were upset. What did you do—about Sarah and her pictures, I mean?"

He shrugged. "I told her go ahead. With Sarah, that's the only option. Any sign of weakness, she goes in for the kill."

Cassie winced. Bad choice of words.

She pulled the chicken back onto the burner and added the vegetables. When she turned to set the food on the table, Nick was still staring across the room.

"It's ready," she said. "Will you pray?"

"What? No. You tonight."

Could she pray for Sarah now? Surely not. Had she ever prayed for Sarah? She couldn't remember, but probably she hadn't.

Cassie groped her way through the prayer poorly, the world still shifting underfoot. Hadn't Robert Frost written a poem about fire and ice? Was he right—about the world ending in ice? Cassie trembled.

Oh, Sarah, I'm so sorry.

She opened her eyes to find Nick watching her and lifted her fingers to wipe the tears from her cheeks. "I'm sorry. I can't help it. She's really dead, Nick. Most people I know who've died have been my relatives. I knew they were Christians. We could hold on to that. But Sarah . . . it's . . . it's not very likely, is it?"

"No."

"No hope?"

He thrust his fingers through his hair and scowled across at her. "I know what you're thinking, that I should be filled with regrets, but I can't pretend. If I had moved away, I would never have wanted the misfortune of seeing Sarah Morgan again in my entire life. I would have been glad to be rid of her. Can you understand that?"

She nodded. "Yes."

"Now suddenly eternity comes crashing in, and I'm supposed to revise everything and think of her as some poor lost soul. I can't change my opinion of her so fast."

"I suppose not." Cassie stared down at the golden chicken, the crisp peppers and onions. They might as well have been shards of glass. "I'm sorry. I don't think I can eat this."

He pushed his own plate away. "Neither can I. Should I go, or do you still want to work?"

"Work, I guess."

Eternity breaking in . . . a frightening thought tonight.

Nick stayed until midnight, working with Cassie on the spectra. "Okay," he said. "I'll take this data to the lab and see if I can find similar peak patterns."

"Tonight? This late?"

"I slept all afternoon. Besides, I've got to do this when Wrede's not likely to be around. I don't want him coming in unexpectedly and seeing what I'm doing."

"Would he realize?"

"I have no idea. And I don't want to find out. Based on past experience, though, he'd be pretty ruthless if crossed. There was a student a couple of years ago who complained about him to the administration. I don't know what he was doing, but he must have made her life miserable because she ended up quitting. She's working as a technician out east somewhere."

When he left, Cassie sat on the couch and pulled her knees up to her chest. He must have seen how nervous she felt. "Don't worry," he had said. "I'll watch my back."

But at the lab Nick had a hard time working. The shock of Sarah's death and his own reaction kept intruding on his thoughts. He tried to listen to tapes, but the lectures sounded flat somehow, like a poorly tuned orchestra. He went through the motions of running the GC. At least his research was working, even if his brain wasn't. He decided around three o'clock to get some coffee and a sandwich.

As was his habit, he stashed the new spectra in his backpack. It seemed overkill to carry the pack with him. Instead he stuck it on a lower cabinet shelf and shut the door.

The coffeepot in the computer room was cold. A walk down to the main vending machines would probably do him good. Auxiliary lights lit his way, the dark quiet of the rooms he was passing somewhat eerie, death too close, menace everywhere. At the bank of vending machines in the main building, he pushed in the proper coins, felt the hot cup in his hand, took a drink, and savored the comfort of scalding liquid going down his throat.

Was this the only comfort left him—the sting of hot coffee?

His head sagged forward against the cool glass fronting the vending machine. After all that he'd tried to make of his life, this latest failure weighed particularly heavy. Nothing seemed to change. The sun rose and the sun set, returning again and again to where it had begun, a ceaseless cycle of life and death, over and over, and all of it so wearisome.

He took another scalding gulp and frowned darkly at the bitter liquid. Sensation, the only reality?

He groaned.

It wasn't true. As tempting as it was to believe in such a meaningless existence—individual perception the measure of all things and no demands or decrees from any higher power—the idea ultimately bit back like a scorpion hiding in the toe of his shoe. And yet for all the testimony of the Spirit of truth, life seemed terribly barren.

He should pray, but he knew he wouldn't, not now. He couldn't bear to face God with another failure.

Minutes passed, he didn't know how long, but when he stood straight again, his coffee was lukewarm. He tossed the cup away and bought another one, paid for a sandwich and some chips, and made his way back to Wrede's suite of offices. A light was on in the computer room now.

"Oh, hi," he said to Bob. "I'd have made coffee rather than settling for this vending machine stuff if I'd known you were coming in."

"Not just me," Bob said. "Wrede too. He's wandering around somewhere."

Coffee spilled over Nick's hand. Heedless, he spun around and headed back to his own lab. He should have locked up, should have put everything away.

He half expected Wrede to be there. His heart was pounding, ready to do battle, but the lab was quiet. Everything the same. GC still working. The cabinet with the backpack still closed. And then he saw the print-out of the last spectra he had called up sitting in the tray of the laser printer. He had entered the command to print, gotten the urge for coffee, and walked off before the print-out finished. Would Wrede have recognized it? Of course. It was labeled.

He went again to the door and looked up and down the hall. A light was on under Wrede's door. Perhaps Wrede hadn't noticed the print-out; perhaps he hadn't even come into Nick's lab. He should go, find something to talk about, try to detect a reaction in Wrede. This was the time if he wanted to catch Wrede out. He should go. Now.

But he couldn't move. He stood at his lab door, unwilling and afraid. A coward on top of everything else. He couldn't face

God, and now he was hiding from Wrede as well.

He turned back into the lab and packed up all his materials, retrieving everything that could incriminate him, all the while wondering if it wasn't already too late. What did it matter? He was too tired. He would go home, get some sleep, and start fresh the next day.

Nine

*T*he next morning, standing at the apartment window with a mug of freshly brewed coffee, Katy looked down at the playground equipment in front of their apartment building. Nick was on a bench watching Alice swing.

He had come to get Alice shortly after eight that morning, intending to spend the day at the lab. Alice must have convinced him to stop at the playground.

Katy frowned. Something in the way he was sitting wasn't right.

"Luke, come here. What do you think about Nick?"

"Hmm, tired maybe, but who can blame him? I don't know how he keeps it together."

"This isn't just tiredness. Go talk to him."

"What are you thinking?"

"I don't know. Just don't leave him down there alone. Take him a cup of coffee. And a couple of doughnuts."

Luke kissed her on the forehead. "My Katy. Care for the soul and the stomach both. Could mortal man hope for more?"

She pushed aside the comforting sensation of his old, familiar sweat shirt against her cheek. "I'm worried, Luke."

"Okay, sweetheart. I'm on my way."

Seeing Nick up close, Luke could understand why Katy was concerned. Nick barely shrugged when Luke asked if he could do with a little company. He took the steaming mug of coffee Luke handed to him but shook his head at the doughnuts.

Alice wanted some. She ran over and grabbed two, both chocolate covered.

"Now, go play again," Nick said when she finished.

"But I'm thirsty."

"Then go ask Katy for some milk."

Alice scampered away.

"Think she'll come back anytime soon?" Luke asked.

"Doubt it. She doesn't want to go to the lab. And no, don't even offer. She can't stay with you all day. You've done enough this week." Nick glanced at Luke. "You probably heard about Sarah Morgan."

"There was an article in the paper this morning."

Nick grunted and took another drink from his coffee.

"Weren't you at Cassie's last night?" Luke said.

"Is that why you came down? For a firsthand report?"

Luke struggled not to react to the bitterness in Nick's voice. "No. Actually, I came down to see how you were doing. You okay?"

Nick turned to study Luke warily. After a moment, he shrugged. "Don't mind me. I'm feeling rotten this morning."

"Don't worry about it."

"They don't know why she died, you know."

"They said in the paper they'd know within the next day or two." Luke took a sip of his coffee and eyed his friend over the rim. "This is really upsetting you."

Nick swung his head around to glare at Luke. "What's that? One of those probing statements designed to make me cough up my deepest feelings?"

Luke grinned. "If it is, I can see I was too mild. How about you're feeling distraught, aren't you? Devastated. Really weird?"

Nick held his glare a moment longer, then sighed. "Yeah, I guess. Really weird. There have been times I thought I could have killed her myself, given half a chance and enough of a lapse in reason."

"No," Luke said firmly. "You couldn't have."

"Maybe not, since I didn't get even half a chance and no lapse either. But I sure thought I wouldn't be sorry if someone did."

"Ah. And now you feel like you should be."

Nick stretched back, groaning as tired muscles shifted.

"Isn't that good?" Luke said. "Feeling that way?"

Nick shrugged. "Things were all wrong between us. She threatened me—me and Alice—and I put a barrier up. She was dangerous, someone to avoid. And now all I can think is—another threat gone."

"Pretty grim."

Nick thrust himself up from the bench, took a few steps forward, banged his hand vehemently against his leg, and spun around again to face Luke. "And you know the worst? I've felt all of this before—with Sydney. There. I've said it. I sat by her bed, stayed with her to the end, but my only feeling when I walked away was relief. Do you have any idea how much easier my life is without her?"

"Nick, don't—"

"Come on, Luke. We made a colossal mistake, and we both knew it. Divorce was definitely the next step. And Alice? Would I have gotten custody? Kept custody? Who knows? Sydney would have always been there, like a dark cloud, ominous on the horizon."

"But those last weeks you were so faithful, staying there in Dallas, always there for her."

"I had to try. Even then marriage meant something. If she woke up, saw me, maybe she'd realize that we had something together worth fighting for."

"There you are, then."

"But that doesn't mean I wasn't relieved to get out of that struggle." Nick pushed at the grass with his foot, grinding it into the dirt before looking up again. "I even have her trust fund. Think about that."

"Which you've never touched."

"And what would God do then, do you think?"

"God?"

"He's in everything, isn't that true? Always there, no secrets." Nick sat back down and leaned forward, resting his elbows on his knees. "You know, I became a lot more serious back then about my relationship to Him. But I think now, deep down, I did all that as some kind of payment for letting Sydney die."

"Payment?"

"You're thinking all for the good, aren't you? My life's better. Alice's, too, compared to what it might have been if I'd kept on so carelessly. God used all those problems to turn my life around. But it scares me. I keep waiting for the other shoe to drop."

"Nick—"

"How can it last? He knows the whole story. He knows at the core of what I do is this horrible truth—that I'm grateful Sydney died."

"You're too hard on yourself."

"And now Sarah. What I felt for her came dangerously close to malice. I, who am supposed to—how does it go—act justly, love mercy, and walk humbly with God. I sure didn't love mercy where she was concerned."

"You're being too hard on yourself," Luke said again. "Things may have started that way after Sydney died, but God didn't leave you there."

"You think this is different?" Nick scowled at his mug, then jerked it away from himself, sending the cold dregs of coffee spurting across the grass. "I wish I did," he said. "I sure wish I did."

When Nick arrived at A&M, Bob was there. He followed Nick and Alice into the lab.

"Guess what?" he said. "It wasn't a stroke."

"Sarah, you mean?"

"It was poison."

Nick spun around. "What are you talking about?"

"It's true. Some reporter heard about it. It was on the radio a few minutes ago. The capsules she was taking, that's where the poison was. Pretty powerful stuff. The police have sealed off her apartment, and the crime scene unit is there. Want to go?"

"No!"

Seeing Bob draw back slightly, Nick tipped his head toward Alice. "I can't," he said. "You know."

"Oh, right. Okay. Well, I can. I'll tell you all about it." Bob headed toward the door and stopped. "But that girl—Cassie— she lives right there, doesn't she? You'd even have an excuse for being there."

"No. I'll stay."

"Suit yourself."

Nick could hear Bob whistling all the way down the hallway toward the exit. He shuddered, caught Alice's eyes on him, and tried to smile. He set her up at the bench in his lab and between runs played games or read to her, but her needs did little to drive away thoughts of Sarah's death. Was it really murder?

For lunch, he took Alice to the playground at a nearby park, and in the afternoon, she fell asleep in the corner of his lab. No one would come in today with a camera. Sarah's face would never again appear at the door of his lab. Her dry, slightly husky voice would never mock him again.

She had been one of life's major aggravations and now with her death, a source of guilt. A song they sang in church a lot drifted through his mind, about the weight of sin and being free someday. Nick closed his eyes and sighed. The weight of sin. Why hadn't it felt heavier then, while Sarah was still alive? Would he have treated her differently?

You may cover me, Jesus, but underneath it's still me. How can you bear it? How can I?

As Alice slept, Nick read Lamentations, a book grim enough even for his barren soul, searing with bitterness and gall. And yet in that wilderness there was mercy and compassion that never failed, if he was only willing to wait for God's salvation.

Wait, wait. Knowing what he was, knowing what he should

be . . . wait, believing somehow that God would make the two one.

Around six-fifteen that evening, Alice was awake and sitting at the bench working on her Legos when Katy and Luke appeared at the door of his lab.

"Hi, Nick, Alice," Katy said, "we thought you two might go down to the CowHop with us tonight. Since the Aggies are playing an away game this weekend, we won't have the football crowds. How about it? You could come to church with us tomorrow."

So they could discuss Sarah again? Nick thought not.

Luke pulled the door open wider and Cassie stepped in, moving hesitantly to stand against the cabinet by the door. As usual her dark brown hair was tied in a low ponytail, her bangs pushed off to one side and brushing her eyes. He saw courage in the way she stood, mixed with caution, her chin out, hands in her pockets, her brown eyes dark and intent.

She came closer. "I suppose you heard the latest about Sarah?"

Nick nodded.

Alice scooted off her stool and came running around to greet Katy and Luke. "Katy! We went to the park. And I made a Lego house. Come see it." She pulled Katy along to where she had been working.

Luke repeated Katy's invitation. "We could all do with a little company tonight, Nick."

"What do you think, Alice?" Katy said. "You want to eat cowpies and fries with us?"

Alice's eyes brightened at the mention of her favorite burgers, but Nick shook his head.

"Y'all go without us."

"Sure?" Luke said.

"We're going to church and then home. It's been a long week."

"Are you working tomorrow?" Cassie asked.

"No." Nick picked up Alice, who had come to stand beside him. "Alice and I'll take a day off. She needs a break."

"So do you," Katy informed him.

Nick shrugged.

Cassie propped herself on a stool near Nick. "And what does that mean—a day off with Alice?"

"Sleeping in. Doing the laundry. Shopping. Cleaning house. Alice is my big helper. She picks the best apples, don't you, honey?"

"A day off?" Katy said skeptically.

"It makes a change," he said, "and it all needs doing."

No one said anything for a moment or two. Nick was thinking how normal the next day sounded, the strange sensation of drama played out beside the mundane. In Dallas one day, as Sydney lay dying, he had stood in a grocery store listening to a couple discussing the relative merits of two brands of tomato sauce, their conversation both a comfort and a regret.

Yes, Eliot, laundry and shopping. I'm sorry.

"Were the police at Eliot's apartment today?" Nick asked Cassie.

"Most of the morning. They came by my apartment, too. They're talking to people who knew her."

"No kidding," Katy said. "What did they want to know?"

"They asked how I met Sarah, what I knew about her, my impressions. And about Eliot." She searched Nick's face, her eyes squinting slightly in concentration. "I didn't tell them . . . you know, about what you said."

"What I said?"

Cassie glanced at Katy and Luke.

"Go ahead," Nick said. "Katy and Luke have heard me complain about Sarah often enough."

"About Sarah being dangerous. I didn't tell them."

Nick smiled, her concern endearing. "Thanks, I guess. I'll tell them myself. I never hid my feelings about her before."

"Eliot was with them longer than I was, going over and over who might want to . . ." She glanced at Alice. "You know."

"They probably didn't get much out of him. He's so loyal, he wouldn't speak against her. But they'll find out soon enough what Sarah was like."

"He looks shell-shocked, the poor guy."

"You know," Luke said, "if everyone had your experience with Sarah, I wonder how the police can possibly solve this crime."

They all turned to look at him. He still stood by the door. Glancing out into the hall first, he shut the door and came closer.

"What do you mean?" Nick said.

"Means, motive, and opportunity—aren't those the classic questions? There's no shortage of motive with someone like Sarah. And means all over the place. She was a chemist, after all. Most of the people she knew could figure out how to get poison for a capsule. Even Eliot's a vet student. He said himself that he has access to poison. And opportunity. Anyone could have thrown her that bottle of aspirin. How can they solve this?" Luke turned to Cassie. "Did you hear what kind of poison?"

"No, Eliot didn't say."

Nick had his own ideas about that. Luke didn't work with herbicides. He hadn't heard the warnings about parathion and paralysis as often as Nick and the rest of Wrede's group had. But no sense in bringing that up now. The coroner would know for certain soon enough.

He said, "People may have disliked Sarah, but it's probably a little extreme to say they hated her enough to kill her. That list has to be a little shorter. The police will probably focus on motive."

"Poor Eliot," Cassie said. "They had a big fight yesterday morning. He even threatened to leave her."

Nick scowled. "He says that all the time, but he never would have. Sarah would have been the one to kick him out."

Luke rubbed his chin. "You know, it might be that ex-husband of hers."

"Bradley Stewart?" Cassie said.

Nick turned sharply toward her. "You've met him?"

"Yes, one day at Sarah's apartment."

"I can imagine what happened," Nick said. "Those two can really go at it. And remember, he's a doctor. . . ."

"More poison," Luke said.

Nick nodded. "Exactly. Sarah helped pay his medical school bills, so she gets a healthy alimony check each month. He'd do anything to get out of it, maybe even kill her. One day he came into the office with their wedding picture. He left it on her desk with a knife stuck in it."

Katy and Cassie both winced.

"She laughed. He had just lost an appeal on the alimony. She ordered a bouquet of flowers for him with a note that said, 'My condolences.' "

"Flowers?" Katy said. "Why flowers?"

"With the blooms cut off."

Katy rolled her eyes. "How can people be like that?"

"But maybe showing that animosity was enough to dispel it," Luke said. "Maybe it's someone who's let things build up."

"You mean like Eliot." Nick shook his head. "I keep telling you, not a chance."

"Did you ever hear her mimic the way he lisps?" Cassie said. "Maybe she went too far."

Nick's eyes flared. "She was more than cruel. She was toxic. But still, not Eliot. He was her one redeeming factor. He really loved her."

"And yet, how sad," Katy said. "If the Bible's right at all, we were made for love, not just to receive it but to give it. Did she love anyone, do you think?"

"No. Probably not even herself."

Luke shook his head slowly. "It makes you think, doesn't it? She missed the best, and she'll never have it now."

Silence settled.

"Well, come on," Luke said. "Nick needs to get going if he's going to make it to church."

Cassie hung back after Katy and Luke began walking down the hall. "See you Monday?" she said.

"Wait. There's something . . ." He pursed his lips.

"What?"

"Wrede was hanging around last night."

"You mean, while you were here?"

"He may have seen one of the Cameron spectra. It was almost three in the morning. I'd gone down to the vending machine and when I got back Bob said Wrede was wandering around. I got right back to my lab, I can tell you that. Everything looked the same, except one of the spectra was sitting on the printer."

"And now you're worried." Her eyes tensed.

"It'll be all right," Nick said. "For now you'd better go or Katy and Luke will be wondering."

Cassie didn't even smile. "But I'll see you Monday, right?"

"Sure. Monday."

She glanced back from the door, obviously worried.

After she left, Nick found it hard to concentrate.

It had been a long time since a pretty girl had worried about him. He could see how it could easily become a habit, especially with Cassie McCormick. She had one of the most interesting faces Nick had ever seen, too long for classic beauty, mouth wide and mobile, chin very much there, but altogether full of life and intelligence. Her eyebrows often bunched a little as if she were deep in thought. He liked watching her then, waiting to see if she smiled. When she did, her head usually tipped forward just a little, as if to hide her pleasure, her bright eyes peeking out from under her bangs. And every smile carried the promise of laughter.

But how stupid to be thinking of anything with Cassie. She was just starting graduate school. He would be finished in a few months. And long-distance relationships had about as much chance as a Packers bumper sticker making it through a weekend in Dallas.

No, that wasn't why God had brought Cassie McCormick into his life. What man had a right to ask a woman to give up her future? Especially when he seemed to be mortgaging his own away.

☙ ☙ ☙ ☙

MONDAY MORNING, EARLY, HIS OFFICE.

The door was closed, the desk top cleared—his sanctum. The electric clock on his shelf whirred periodically, and outside, footsteps passed, a door closed, a voice called. He heard each sound, muffled, distant.

In his solitude, only one thought consumed him: another threat, more dangerous.

Murder done and flush of triumph faded, now coldness spread, chilling to the core. He felt drained, the coagulating remains of his anger a white fatty mass, impossible to stomach. How could he have known it would lead to this? Who could ever know what was going to happen?

And yet he must take up the game again, on and on, over and over, never any different except the players. With what result? What did any of it matter, except to him, except for this one small moment, this narrow space, the private reality inside his own head?

And he couldn't find the anger this time. Only fear.

Fear. The need to protect himself, to hedge himself around against a petty, useless passion like Nick Meyers. Full of zeal to no end, a man to be pitied. Self-righteous, deluded, interfering.

But after a fat, satisfying feast of hatred, fear was a thin and watery gruel.

Ten

Two detectives came to the chemistry building around ten o'clock on Monday morning, speaking to each of the students in Wrede's group. Nick was sitting at his desk at the back of the bench when they entered his lab.

"Nick Meyers?"

There were two of them, a medium-height Hispanic who stepped forward with authority, letting his gaze sweep the lab, and a taller, heavier Anglo with blond hair. He stayed by the door, checking something in his notes.

Nick stepped forward. "I'm Nick Meyers."

"Good. And Isaiah O'Donnell?"

Izzy, standing beside his bench, held up his hand.

"Please wait in the other room, Mr. O'Donnell. We'll speak to each of you individually." The man held out his hand to Nick. "I'm Detective Rodrigo Lopez. This is my partner, Jeff Orben. We have some questions about Sarah Morgan."

Nick pulled over some stools and sat down. "Be my guest."

"We'll stand."

This left Nick on the stool looking up at the two men. *Intimidation? Why?* Nick wondered how many murder investigations this man Lopez had taken part in.

"Dr. Wrede has explained about your research groups," Lopez said. "You work under one professor, somewhat in a team but on your own projects, meet weekly for meetings, help each other out."

"Yes."

"Were you close to Sarah Morgan?"

"We knew each other."

"But not close."

Nick stood, feeling the need for some control. What had he said to Cassie? He had nothing to hide. And yet these men, with their analyzing eyes searching him, made the impulse to deceive almost irresistible.

Lopez must have seen his hesitation. "May I remind you, Mr. Meyers, that withholding evidence is a criminal offense."

"Yes, and yet most people probably try, don't they?" Nick clenched his jaw. "The truth is it's unsettling to discover that my strongest reaction to Sarah's death is relief."

"Relief?"

"You must know by now how people felt about her. I tried to avoid her as much as possible."

The other man, Orben, stepped closer. "Why?"

Nick studied the two men, surprised again by the overpowering impulse to put up barriers.

"Okay, let me tell you about my experience with her. It's probably typical." Nick went on to describe the pictures Sarah took.

"What would she hope to gain from this?"

"Not money. Not from me. Merely the pleasure of causing pain." Nick leaned back against the counter and crossed his arms. "But she didn't even gain that. My mother-in-law's no threat—we've worked things out. Sarah apparently went too far with someone else. Find that person and you'll probably have your killer."

Orben opened his notebook. "According to the autopsy, Ms. Morgan was killed by methyl parathion inserted into some pain reliever. We found a bottle with other tampered capsules in her backpack. The poison in these is more concentrated than what is available commercially."

Nick nodded.

"You don't look surprised," Lopez said.

"No. Methyl parathion is used in herbicides. We've got

some on the shelf. When I heard it was poison, coupled with symptoms like a stroke, I figured it might be parathion."

"Anyone could get this stuff?"

"Anyone who knows where to find it on our shelves. Izzy— Isaiah, my lab mate, and Bob and several other students on this floor alone."

"And professors."

"Of course."

"But you don't know who might hate Ms. Morgan enough to kill her."

"Anyone she knew might hate her that much. Like I said, she liked to push people's buttons—and some people are more sensitive than others."

"Eliot Ross?"

"A good man. He seemed to really care about her."

Lopez's eyes sharpened. "Then he would be the one to feel most betrayed if she turned against him."

Nick granted that with a nod. "Though he seemed pretty tolerant."

"What about this Cassie McCormick who lives upstairs from Morgan and Ross?"

Nick tensed. "What about her?"

"She seemed quite friendly with Ross on Saturday."

"No." Nick shook his head. "It couldn't be Cassie. She didn't have any reason to. Sarah was still gaining her confidence."

Orben wrote something down in his notebook. Lopez focused more closely on Nick.

Nick tried to speak more calmly. "I don't have any illusions about Sarah or Cassie. Sarah would have found Cassie's weak point eventually, making her as angry as the rest of us. But not yet."

"Can you add anything else?" Orben asked.

Lopez held up his hand. "What about Duncan Wrede? What was his relationship with Sarah Morgan?"

"Ah. Wrede." Nick leaned back again and took a minute to think. "Not the typical adviser-student relationship, I can tell you that, but Sarah was older than most students and a strong woman. I'm not sure the way she treated Wrede is a sign of anything."

"How did she treat him?"

Nick rubbed his jaw, still thinking. "Well, she wasn't afraid of him."

"And you are? Afraid of Dr. Wrede, I mean?"

"No, but I do have a healthy respect for what he can do for me. Without a good recommendation from my graduate adviser, I'll be in real trouble in the job market. He can slow down my progress here. He can make everything very uncomfortable. I'm not afraid of him, but I'm definitely aware of our respective positions."

"And Ms. Morgan wasn't?"

"She didn't seem to be. But she was flippant with everyone, and she worked hard enough. Nothing wrong there. Maybe it was just something they worked out between them. Their relationship didn't change the way the rest of us dealt with him, that's for sure."

"Give me an example of what you're talking about."

"Every week at group meeting, Sarah sauntered in a couple of minutes late. If any of the rest of us came late, we'd hear about it, but Sarah did it every week, and Wrede just ignored it."

"Okay," Lopez said. "Thank you. We'll be in touch if we have any other questions. Could you send in Mr. O'Donnell, please?"

Nick walked down the hall, thinking about Cassie and what she would say about the conversation. He let out a slow breath, relieved to have it over. He'd see Cassie tonight at supper. He would tell her then.

❦   ❦   ❦   ❦

At six that evening, Cassie put spaghetti noodles into boiling water. Nick and Alice were due any minute. At six-fifteen they still hadn't arrived. At six-thirty, as the noodles cooled in a colander, Cassie wondered if she should throw out that batch and begin again.

At six thirty-five, she heard Alice crying outside her apartment door and opened it before Nick reached the buzzer.

"Sorry," he said. He stepped into the room with Alice in his arms. "She fell at the sitter's and hurt her leg. I can't seem to get her to stop crying." He threw his backpack and Alice's bag on the floor and sat with Alice on the couch. "Sweetheart, show me again where it hurts. Tell me what happened."

With renewed wails, Alice buried her face against Nick's neck and banged her kitty against his chest.

"That's not helping," he told her firmly. "Show me where it hurts. Let's show Cassie."

New, louder wails. Nick gathered her more closely into his arms and began rocking back and forth, crooning into her hair until she became a little calmer.

"Should she maybe go to the emergency room?" Cassie said hesitantly.

He was too anxious to take offense at her suggestion. "Yes, but I took her once before when she'd had an accident and only by some pretty fast talking and my regular doctor's testimonial did I escape getting investigated for child abuse."

"Child abuse!"

"She was eleven months old and just beginning to walk. She fell over, hit her arm on the coffee table, and got a terrible bruise. I was afraid it was broken. They were afraid *I* had broken it. It was fine, but after that experience you can bet I'm not going to the emergency room."

"How about your doctor? He could meet you there."

Nick smoothed Alice's hair away from her face and sighed. "I have another idea. Give me the phone." He dialed. Cassie could hear only his side of the conversation, but she could tell he was talking to his friend Zoe.

"She's coming over," Nick said as he hung up. He explained who Zoe was, apparently forgetting that Cassie had heard his conversation with Luke on Friday.

He shook his head at Cassie's suggestion of a drink or something to eat. As long as he didn't move, Alice didn't cry, though she continued to give little sniffing noises.

Zoe arrived within a few minutes. She smiled briefly at Cassie in response to Nick's introduction and sat beside Nick and Alice on the couch, talking to the little girl first.

Zoe Calder was older than Nick—early thirties, Cassie thought—but very attractive, with long brown hair and a wide, friendly smile. Like Sarah Morgan, Zoe had a vibrant, energetic personality, and her face glowed with intelligence and confidence. But unlike Sarah, Zoe's personality was tempered by an obvious kindness and generosity. No wonder Nick had called her.

Coaxing a brief smile from Alice, Zoe lifted her foot, moving it so gently that the little girl forgot to cry.

"She came home like this?" Zoe said.

"Yes. According to the sitter she fell, around four or four-thirty, I think."

"It's not her ankle. Do you see how the swelling starts higher? And it's not her knee." Zoe very gently touched Alice's leg, mid-calf, and nodded sympathetically when the girl objected with a moan. She laid the foot down again and sat back slightly. "It shouldn't hurt like that, Nick, not anymore. Not if she merely hit her shin. You should definitely have it X-rayed. But . . ." Zoe shook her head.

"What?"

"Given the nature of the break and what we've discussed about Alice's sitter . . ."

Again Zoe stopped, looking with concern at Alice.

"Tell me."

"That kind of break, at that location—I'm afraid it was done intentionally, if you can understand what I'm saying. Let me call Mark Kincaid. He's your doctor, isn't he? If you take Alice to the emergency room, a single father like you, with this kind of injury, they might call Child Protective Services."

"I was afraid of that."

"What would they do?" Cassie said.

"Investigate. Ask questions. Possibly even . . ." Zoe's eyes fell to Alice. "Well, let's not worry about that. I have Mark's home number."

Nick's arms around Alice tightened a little.

While Zoe was on the phone, Cassie went into the kitchen, ladled the steaming, fragrant sauce into a container and the noodles into a Zip-Loc. She doubted Nick would be eating anything soon. But Alice might get hungry. She made a peanut butter and jelly sandwich and put it into a plastic bag, along with a bunch of grapes.

"Cassie?" Nick was standing at the kitchen door, still holding Alice. "Mark Kincaid said he'd see us at his office."

He paused, seeing the sack lunch.

"I thought Alice might get hungry," Cassie said. "This'll take a while, won't it?"

He hesitated, then shook his head. "I'll call you later. Thanks for the lunch."

Left alone, Cassie felt almost bereft. But what right did she have to go along?

As usual, Nick's first thought on seeing Mark Kincaid was that he was too young to be anyone's doctor. The impression was even stronger tonight, with Mark dressed in sweats and tennis shoes, his brown hair slightly messy.

Zoe looked him over and shook her head. "What'd we get you out of, Kincaid?"

Mark grinned a lazy, boyish grin that brought humor to his eyes. "A heart attack probably. I'm getting too old for that crew down at church. Sorry," he said to Nick. "Came straight from basketball."

"No problem."

"Though in return for saving your hide," Zoe announced, "you might at least forego your fee."

Mark's humor lasted a minute longer as he held Zoe's gaze, and then he looked down at Alice and grew serious.

"Well, now, what happened, Alice?"

Always fond of Mark, Alice answered immediately. "I hurt my leg."

"Did you fall?"

At this Alice turned her head back against Nick's shoulder.

"I still haven't gotten a straight answer out of her," Nick said.

The two men exchanged glances, and Mark shook his head sympathetically. Zoe must have described her suspicions to him over the phone.

He led them into an examining room, looked over Alice's leg, and took her in for an X-ray. He came back with the bad news. "It is indeed a fracture of the lower leg. Barely perceptible, but definitely there."

"It couldn't have been an accident?"

"Maybe. But it's an unlikely break. You say she came back from the sitter's like this?"

Nick nodded.

Mark shook his head regretfully. "Has she come home with any other injuries—bruises, burns, anything the sitter might have caused?"

"No! I mean, bruises, but all children get those, don't they?"

"Where?"

"On her legs mostly. Once or twice her arms."

"How's her eating been?"

"She's always been picky."

"But, Nick," Zoe said, "she has been more withdrawn lately. You said that yourself."

"Yes."

"And more nightmares? Didn't you say that?"

Nick winced. "Yes."

"I'm sorry," Mark said again. "I'll have to call Child Protective Services, especially with this kind of injury."

"Why?" Nick demanded, his frustration building.

The eyes that had been so full of humor minutes earlier were now clouded with concern. "We can't ignore this, Nick. There are other children involved."

Nick turned and leaned his head against the wall. Images of Alice's time at Regina's swirled through his mind. He should have taken her out right away. He knew she wasn't happy. No wonder she had been so withdrawn and upset.

"Daddy?" Alice said.

"Oh, honey, I'm sorry." He turned back and picked her up, burying his face in her hair.

Mark put a compassionate hand on Nick's back. "This happens, Nick. Even to parents like you. Kids can take almost anything in stride if they have enough love at home. You'll see. Alice will be fine."

"I should have known," Nick ground out. "I was looking for another sitter—just not fast enough."

"I'm sorry."

Zoe, who worked at the county health department, had perhaps seen more of the injustices of life. "You go forward, Nick," she said, almost sternly, "and Alice will go with you. That's how it works. You have to move on."

Nick held Alice a moment longer, then put her gently back on the table, attempting a funny face for her.

"Why are you crying, Daddy?"

"I'm sorry your leg's broken, honey. I'm sorry Regina was mean."

"Gina got mad."

"Why, honey?"

"She doesn't like me."

"I know, honey. But why did she get mad this time?"

Alice looked from Mark to Zoe and back to Nick.

"It's all right," Nick said. "I won't be mad. Just tell me what happened."

"I spilled my juice, Daddy. I was trying to clean it up, but I couldn't find anything so I got the toilet paper. It got all squashy and drippy so I took it to the potty but it wouldn't go down and Jason wet his pants cuz the potty was all full and Gina got mad and I had to sit in the corner and Jason wouldn't stop crying and Gina got really mad and spanked me and . . . and . . . that's when my leg got hurt." Alice started to cry, not as she usually did, with angry sobs, but silently, the tears streaming down her pale cheeks.

Nick clasped her to him. "Sweetheart, don't be sad. It's okay. You don't have to go back to Gina's. I promise. And the doctor is going to fix your leg, you'll see."

"That's right," Mark said. "I'm going to put a big fat sock around your foot, and we can all color it and put our names on it. I'll go get what I need. Hold on."

"What will Protective Services do?" Nick asked Zoe as soon as Mark had left the room.

"Ask a lot of questions and follow up, I presume, with the sitter."

"They won't—" Nick closed his eyes, collected himself, and faced Zoe again. "They won't take her away, will they?"

"No. They'll have to make sure she's safe, but it'll be the sitter who's in trouble, not you."

"I shouldn't have come," Nick said.

"Of course you should have. And stop taking out your worries on Mark. He's doing us a big favor coming in here late like this, doing nurse's work . . . putting up with you."

Nick scowled. What Zoe said was true. He stood back without saying anything more as Mark and Zoe put on the cast, letting Zoe tease Alice. After Mark finished, Nick slipped an arm under Alice's knees and lifted her up, cradling her against him. "I did check her out, you know," he informed the room.

Zoe put her arm around his back. "Nick, it could happen to anyone."

Nick struggled to keep his face calm. "That's not much comfort, is it? Are we done here?"

"No, first we should pray," Mark said, glancing at Zoe. She nodded. Without further discussion, he bowed his head.

"Now go ahead," Zoe told Nick. "I'll be right behind you."

Outside, Nick strapped Alice into her seat. He put Cassie's bag with the sandwich and grapes into her hand and climbed in beside her.

Zoe came to stand beside the pickup and looked up through the driver-side window at him.

"Thanks," he said. He shook his head as if clearing it. "I guess I got a little crazy there. But it's all so hard to figure."

"He said he'd call CPS in the morning—give you a night's sleep before contacting them."

"I'll be waiting for their call."

Later, with Alice in bed and finally asleep, Nick considered calling Cassie. He even reached for the phone and began dialing her number but hung up. It was too late. She was probably asleep. He would call the next day. Or maybe he'd stop by her office. That would be better.

Alice was okay, anyway. They just needed to get through the next few days, the next few weeks. Time and distance from the pain, a return to normality—that's what they needed.

He'd talk to Cassie tomorrow.

Maybe.

Or maybe he'd just stay in bed.

⁂ ⁂ ⁂ ⁂

Cassie didn't hear from Nick the next morning or afternoon or evening, and as she was preparing for bed she told herself to be grateful. Somehow in the last ten days she had been swept away into Nick's life, and she felt winded now. A breather would be smart.

She did call Katy, however, to find out what had happened.

"I can tell you," Katy said. "Child Protective Services called Nick this morning and raked him over the coals—both sides, well done, he said. They interviewed a few of the other parents but called Nick again tonight and cooked him some more. It's the sitter who's in trouble, though, or they would have already taken Alice away. They've taken Regina's own children and put them into foster care."

"Oh no. How old are they?"

"Two and five. The older started kindergarten this fall."

"That's horrible. How awful."

"Cassie, they can't very well leave those children with a suspected child abuser."

"I suppose not. But how do you know all this—about what's happened, I mean? Have you talked to Nick?"

"Zoe, of course. She's filled me in on everything."

"What's next, then?"

"CPS has turned all their information over to the police, who are doing their own investigation. They'll charge the sitter if that's what they decide, but that'll take a few more days. Zoe says if the child's at risk in the home, things happen real fast, like within twenty-four hours. That's why they moved so quickly with Regina's own children. But since Alice is okay with Nick, charging Regina with her abuse can take a little longer. But they have shut the day care down."

"What's Nick doing with Alice?"

"Why don't you call and ask him?"

Cassie bit her lip. Her silence must have been answer enough. Almost immediately Katy spoke again.

"He's taking the week off but will probably take her into work for a while."

"Wrede won't mind?"

"For a few days, no. For the duration, he might."

Cassie wondered what this would do to Nick's work on the herbicide.

"Okay," she said. "I guess I'll see you Sunday if we don't talk before then."

"He could use a friend, Cassie."

"I know. Maybe I'll call."

Cassie hung up the phone thoughtfully. Easy for Katy to talk about being a friend, but could Cassie really define her relationship with Nick Meyers that way? Colleague, cohort in investigative science, unpaid lackey. Sure, all those.

But friend?

She would let Nick call her—he had said he would, after all—and then she'd have a better idea where she stood with him.

On Wednesday night, with still no word from Nick, Cassie passed Eliot outside the apartment and asked him up for supper. He still looked in shock. As she thawed a pan of frozen lasagna, she asked about the murder investigation.

"They've gone around talking to people. Collected what evidence they could. Even collected things from people's labs, trying to get some traces of methyl parathion. Nothing. So they're left with me."

"Why would you kill her?"

"That's the problem. Sarah had over a quarter of a million dollars in the bank."

"And . . . you get all that?"

"She made a will. Big favor. Now I have 250,000 motives for murder. But, honestly, I didn't even know about it."

"That's a lot of money."

"And yet you saw how we lived. Pizza was an extravagance. She bought her clothes at Goodwill. She drove an old Audi, left over from her marriage. Really, I can't figure it out, but that money's sure getting me into trouble."

"Where did she get it?"

"From her ex-husband, I thought. But even with incredibly profitable investments, his portion would only account for $150,000."

"Imagine, earning money like that and having to turn it over to Sarah. He must be a suspect, too."

"But where'd the rest of it come from?" Eliot sighed. "I'm afraid they'll never figure out who did it, and then they'll arrest me as a last resort—I did have motive, means, and opportunity. Or they'll just leave the case unsolved and people will still think it's me. How could everything be so wrong?"

He was the picture of dejection—slumped shoulders, sagging neck, weary features.

He pushed the food away. "I'm sorry. I don't feel much like eating these days."

Cassie nodded sympathetically. "It might help to talk."

"About what?"

"Tell me how you and Sarah met."

"At a football game, believe it or not. Two years ago. She came with someone else, but it was me who laughed at all her comments about the players and the crowds and everything else. You know how Sarah is—was. Afterward, I asked if she wanted to go out for a drink, and she ditched her date. Just like that. Sarah always did exactly what she wanted."

"I guess."

"No. Don't get the wrong idea about her. Under that hard shell, mostly she was afraid. She couldn't have children, you know, because of an STD—a sexually transmitted disease."

"I know what it means."

"Stewart wanted children, and he made her life miserable because of it. That's why they split up. She picked it up in college, she said, and it wasn't contagious, just painful. She thought sometimes she would die. I think that's what made her so bitter—that pain and being sterile and the whole mess. She took in all that money from Stewart but didn't spend any of it. She did well with Wrede but hated him. She mocked Bob often about his weight and his prospects—he's not very smart, you know. And Nick. She couldn't stand to be around him. But really, she was afraid. All the insults and maliciousness and spite—it was mostly to keep from turning those emotions on herself."

"And you? Did she turn that hate on you, too?"

"She tried, but I thought if I could just love her well enough, convince her she was safe, maybe I could help her. Guess I didn't have that perfect love."

Cassie shook her head. "Perfect love? What do you mean?"

"Didn't you ever go to Sunday school?" Eliot said. "Shame, shame. It's in the Bible somewhere—perfect love does away with fear. Something like that. I thought I could do that with Sarah, but . . . well, she made it hard."

They sat in silence for a few minutes. Finally Cassie said, "You don't go to church now?"

Eliot wrinkled his nose. "It didn't fit in here. Sarah liked to live it up on Saturday night. Sunday was made for sleep, she said."

He shut his eyes, memories still fresh and warm—and all the more painful. His shoulders fell.

"I know people won't believe me, Cassie, but I was lucky to have Sarah. I really was. Given enough time, she would have come around. I really believe it."

Cassie smiled. "Not as lucky as she was to have you, Eliot."

After he left, Eliot's words about God not fitting in haunted Cassie. As if God were old clothes that had gone out of style or a hobby left behind at home.

The thought of God's reaction to that casual rejection made her increasingly uneasy. Church had also been an afterthought for her in college and even since, a familiar prop in her life. Set adrift here where she had to rely on Him more, she was beginning to realize His true importance and the extent of His role in her life. It had been God who had brought Luke and Katy to her—God in Luke and Katy that had drawn her to them.

Poor Eliot. There *was* a perfect love that could have saved Sarah, but it wasn't Eliot's. Perhaps Eliot at least could still find it. She could certainly pray for him.

        ❧   ❧   ❧   ❧

On Thursday Luke convinced Nick to play racquetball while Katy watched Alice. Katy called him back as Luke was heading down the apartment stairs after Nick.

"Get Nick to talk," Katy said. "He has it all bottled up inside of him."

But as Luke waited with Nick for a court at the G. Rollie White Building, he wondered how Katy expected him to succeed. "How's it going?" he asked Nick.

"Fine."

Luke sighed. Like a brick wall.

"How's Alice?"

"Fine too. Really. She's okay."

"What will you do with her now? I mean, for day care."

"I'm working on it. I'll figure something out."

"Katy wanted me to ask."

"Yeah? Well, tell her we're fine. We'll get through this." Nick stood and grabbed his racquet. "Come on, there's a court."

Luke gathered up his racquet and ball with a wry smile. In

the annals of male conversation, not exactly a standout. He knew just how Katy would respond. At least, the way Nick was warming up, it wasn't *all* bottled up anymore. Luke probably shouldn't count on winning any points off him tonight.

"What do you mean—fine?" Katy demanded when Luke arrived home. "That's all he said? Men! You're hopeless."

Luke hadn't even put his racquet down before Katy started grilling him, and now she was throwing on her jacket and heading toward the door.

"Where are you going?"

"Where else? I'm going to talk to Nick."

"He'll be taking his shower."

"Not yet he won't."

She stormed down the stairs and around the building, climbing Nick's flight two at a time, and banged on his door.

"Katy?"

"We have to talk, Nick."

"I'm putting Alice to bed."

Katy stalked into Alice's room. Alice wasn't in her pajamas yet. Katy pulled a few books from the shelf, thrust them at Alice, and patted the bed with her hand. "Sit and look at the books, Alice. Your dad will be here in a few minutes to read to you. I want to talk to him."

Big eyed, Alice did as she was told.

On her way out, Katy pulled the bedroom door shut, assuring Alice again that they'd only be a few minutes. Then she turned around and glared at Nick.

"What's your problem?" he said.

"Fine, fine, everything's fine. That's what you told Luke. Well, I don't believe it."

"Quiet down. She'll hear you."

"And that bothers you? I thought everything was fine?"

He clamped his jaw shut and glared back at her.

"Have you talked to Cassie? Seen anyone from church?

Gone anywhere or done anything besides play racquetball with Luke? You haven't, have you?"

"We're working through this, Katy. That's all I can say."

"You haven't even gone to the lab, have you?"

It was clear he hadn't.

Katy took a deep breath and let it out in a rush. "How can everything be fine?" she said, trying hard to be calm. "This is a horrible nightmare for both of you. If you can't talk to Luke or me, find someone at church. Karen Groves is a wonderful counselor. She can help lead you through this mess."

Nick refused to look at Katy. His gaze shifted first in one direction and then in another.

"Nick, please."

"We're doing fine. In fact, I'm planning to go in to work tomorrow. Now, let me get back to her before she gets worried."

Katy stamped her foot. "You're in denial. Can't you see that? And it's not helping you or Alice."

Nick physically pushed Katy toward the door. "Go home. I know you're trying to help, but go home."

"I give up."

Back at their own apartment, Luke merely shook his head. "If he is in denial, Katy, he probably has to work through it. It takes time."

"But Nick's so smart. And this is Alice."

"I know, but even so . . ."

"Oh, fine. Fine, fine. You're probably right. I'm going to bed."

Eleven

*E*ach day that passed without Nick contacting her, Cassie grew a little more disappointed. She thought frequently about Alice, the abuse taking a strange grip on her imagination. Katy filled Cassie in on the details she knew, but Cassie's emotions continued to churn within her, horror predominant.

She considered calling Nick or stopping by his office but decided against bothering him. If she was so appalled by Alice's experience, what must he be going through?

His silence certainly clarified his feelings for her, however. Something to remember. Nick, after all, wanted to finish up and leave A&M. If he also wanted to leave certain memories behind, who could blame him? What man would want a reminder of such a bad period in his life? And perhaps, really, the man who had stood beside the GC that day—that restrained, cautious man—might be the real Nick. Hadn't she learned yet what happened when she started assuming things about men?

So when Nick stopped by Cassie's desk around eight-thirty the next Monday night, Cassie's response to him was purposely cool.

She had less control over her response to Alice, however, whom he had brought with him. The little girl stood holding her father's hand, looking up at Cassie. Nick had clearly taken pains with her appearance. She was wearing a pink Oshkosh jumper over a white T-shirt. A pink and purple ribbon in her hair matched the purple cast on her leg, which stuck out from under her pants. But it was Alice herself who looked different from the last time Cassie had seen her. Her cheeks were rosy again, her eyes alert and curious.

Cassie found tears unexpectedly close. She wanted to jump up and hug Alice, who looked as though she neither wanted nor needed that form of sympathy.

After Nick lifted Alice up on Luke's desk, she gazed down balefully at Cassie. "This is Luke's office," she announced.

"Mine too now," Cassie said. "I'm working with Luke."

"Oh." Alice looked around the room. Her bearing was as regal as a princess's. "Where is Luke?"

"Not here now." Cassie took a deep breath. "How's your leg, Alice?"

Alice didn't respond—she had yet to answer a single question Cassie asked her. Nick propped himself against Luke's desk, arms crossed in his favorite pose, but he also didn't say anything.

What? Was she on some kind of review here?

Fighting the compulsion to scowl at him, Cassie instead smiled sweetly and pulled a bag of Chee-tos out of her bottom drawer. Turning her chair to face them, she began to munch the snack. After a moment, she held the bag out to Alice.

"Want some?"

Alice bounced off Luke's desk, skipped one-legged across to Cassie, and dug into the bag.

"Cool color on your cast, Alice," Cassie said. "Did you take a bath in grape juice?"

Alice, still munching her Chee-tos, just stared.

"No," Nick answered. "Dr. Mark put it on that way. Zoe liked the pink, but Alice wanted purple."

"It's great, kid."

Another handful of Chee-tos and Alice said, "My leg's broke."

"I know."

"But it's okay, cuz Dr. Mark fixed it. I don't go to Gina's anymore."

"Katy told me."

"I come to work with Daddy."

"Do you like that?"

More Chee-tos and a very thoughtful face. Then Alice nodded. "We go to the park sometimes."

Not quite a direct answer, but close.

Cassie said, "Bet that's fun. Want some more? Here, take the whole bag, Alice. It's yours."

Alice's eyes grew big. She reached for the bag.

"What do you say?" Nick said.

"Thank you." She skipped back to Luke's desk and held up her arms for Nick to lift her. Seeing Nick still waiting, she added, "Thank you, ma'am."

Cassie smiled at Nick. Under all that attitude was a cute little kid.

"I want a drink, Daddy."

"Ah, that's my fault," Cassie said. "I have some juice in the fridge next door. I'll go get it."

Nick followed her into the room and took the juice she retrieved from the small refrigerator the students used. He said, "Stay here. I want to talk. The Chee-tos and juice will keep Alice happy for a few minutes."

Cassie opened her mouth to object, but Nick was already gone, taking the juice to Alice. Instead of following, she walked to the window and took a seat in front of a computer terminal. They hadn't seen each other in a week and he was issuing orders? She should make her stand now. She should leave . . . except she wanted to hear what he had to say.

When he came back, he stood by the door and looked across the room with that same confusing assessment.

"How is she, Nick?"

"Seems okay. No real problems that I can see. Kids bounce back."

"Really?"

"Yes, really."

Father and daughter—the same determined tilt of the jaw, the same stubborn look in the eyes.

Cassie held up her hands to waylay any further claims of normalcy. "Okay. Fine. Go ahead. What did you want?"

"Have you been okay?"

"Busy, but good," she said cautiously. "I've matched your spectra to peaks in the spectral library. Are you still planning to finish that?"

"Sure. Yeah, I am. You still think it's dioxin?"

"Yes. And not incidental."

He nodded and looked down at the floor. "Izzy said he saw you on Saturday."

"A bunch of us went to a football game."

It had been Cassie's first experience of an Aggie football game. With the rest of the students, she stood through the entire game. They were the symbolic "Twelfth Man," all of them ready to go down and play for the team if needed. Another tradition said guys could kiss their dates each time the team scored. She had barely managed to turn her head after the first touchdown to avoid Terrence's kiss.

Terrence. Now, if it'd been Nick . . .

Cassie pushed her chair back and stood up, thrusting her hands into her jeans pockets. "What is it you need, Nick?"

"Right. I'll explain, but . . ." He sighed heavily. "I'm sorry to be putting you on the spot like this. If I could think of any other solution, believe me . . ."

"I understand," she said. "More spectra?"

"No . . ."

"Daddy?" Alice appeared at the door beside him.

"Go back and finish your drink, Alice."

"I'm tired of Chee-tos."

Nick dug into his pocket. "Here. M&M's, but you have to eat them in the other room. Go on. I want to talk to Cassie."

Alice took the bag and left.

Nick caught Cassie's expression and shrugged. "There, you see? A bribe. I seem to be resorting to them more and more. I have to get something else worked out for her while I finish up here at A&M. Hanging around offices and labs isn't that great for her. A woman from church said she would keep Alice every day from eleven to four. I can cover the mornings, and Katy said she'd pick up Alice on Tuesday and Thursday after school.

But . . ." Again the reluctance. "Here's what I need. Would you be willing to pick her up on Monday and Wednesday, take care of her during the evenings?"

"Baby-sit Alice? I . . . I don't know, Nick."

"It's only from now until the end of December, since your schedule will probably change next semester."

"She doesn't exactly like me."

"She'll warm up to you. I'm not worried about that."

"How late at night?"

"Ten, most of the time. Every now and then through the night if possible, though not often. I want to keep her with me as much as I can, but Wednesday's a problem, no matter what, because I have group meeting. Katy has class and most of the people from church are there on Wednesday nights—choir practice and prayer meeting and so forth. But . . . you're free."

"Nick, I don't know. . . ."

"Please."

She swallowed. "Let me think about it. I'll let you know."

He held her gaze a moment longer and then nodded.

She would have returned to her desk in the next room, but he put a hand out and gripped her arm.

"I should have called you last week. I'm sorry."

"It's okay." She kept her face purposely blank. "I called Katy, and she told me what happened."

"Still—"

"Please, you don't have to explain."

His words came out in a rush. "Katy says I'm in denial. She's nothing if not blunt. She says Alice needs counseling, and me too. That we'll get through this easier if we confront it and work through it—the whole sorry mess. I just want to put it behind us. You know?"

Cassie was quiet for a moment.

And you couldn't call me because somehow I was part of the mess? she thought. *Because I was there . . . I saw her when she was hurt? Is that why?*

"I understand," Cassie said. "And about the baby-sitting, I'll let you know."

"In the meantime, I'll keep looking."

After he and Alice left, Cassie went into the bathroom, wet a paper towel, and held it against her forehead. How dreadful this all was—Alice's nightmare and Nick's pain, hurt feelings and crossed purposes. She could so easily help them. Why was she hesitating?

Eliot's verse came to mind: *Perfect love casts out fear.*

How much of her feelings for Nick . . . and Alice . . . were tainted by fear? And Nick—was he also afraid of what was happening between them? His marriage had ended painfully more than three years ago. A second marriage was the obvious solution to Alice's care, yet he was still single. Perhaps there was a reason for that. Perhaps he had planned all along to get away from A&M heart-whole and begin fresh somewhere else.

All the more reason to be careful. *Don't be foolish; avoid hurt.*

And yet she felt certain that God, in His grand intrusion, wanted her to help Nick, even with little hope of anything in return.

From the lips of Eliot Ross, no less—perfect love casts out fear.

Maybe it wasn't romantic love she would have with Nick. Romantic love didn't cast out fear—it caused it. Maybe with God's help, it was His perfect love she could offer Nick instead.

Katy called Cassie later that evening. "Has Nick spoken to you?"

"About baby-sitting? Yes." Cassie drew out the word cautiously.

"Baby-sitting? I meant about *anything* since Alice's leg was broken. I've been so worried about him. He's been holed up in his apartment. Hasn't gone to the lab, to church, to anything, and he hasn't talked with practically anyone. Luke convinced him to play racquetball last Thursday, but even there he didn't say much."

"He was at work this evening."

"Really? How'd he look?"

"Alice was with him. They both looked fine."

Katy squawked, "If I hear that word one more time I'm going to scream—real primal stuff, loud enough to wake the dead. I mean it!"

"Okay. They looked . . . well, you know."

"What did you mean about baby-sitting?"

Cassie explained.

"That's good," Katy said. "That must have cost him, but that's good. Let him figure out that some problems need dealing with and he can't just ignore them. I wonder . . ."

"Katy?"

"Since he was willing to ask you about the baby-sitting, would you do another favor for him—one he would never ask for, just as a friend?"

That word again.

"What?"

"The social worker called this afternoon. The police are arresting Regina Poole this evening, so her bail hearing's first thing in the morning. Nick wants to be there. Do you think you could go, too? Give him a little moral support?"

Cassie bit her lip.

"Please?" Katy said. "Luke's giving a seminar in one of Moran's classes, and I have school, of course. Zoe has work. And you know Nick's pretty much a loner. There's no one else. It would mean a lot if you showed up. The other parents are probably out for his blood."

"Why? They should be thanking him."

"For making them realize they've been putting their children at risk? Even Nick can't deal with it."

Still Cassie hesitated. *Perfect love. Perfect love.*

If her fear was keeping her from being the friend Nick needed, she didn't have the love God wanted. *Lord, am I supposed to trust you in this?* she asked hesitantly. *Is that the idea? But look how things turned out with Richard.*

Cassie nearly jumped as another question entered her mind. *Yes, and isn't that what brought you here?*

She frowned. "Okay. What time?"

"Ten o'clock."

Cassie would miss her eleven o'clock class. She shrugged the thought aside. "Tell me where."

Katy gave directions to the courthouse, then hung up in a hurry. She was probably afraid Cassie would change her mind.

With good cause, Cassie thought, rolling her eyes.

🐦 🐦 🐦 🐦

TUESDAY MORNING, HIS BEDROOM.

He woke up with a headache, the pillowcase beneath his head drenched with sweat. He drew away in distaste and turned the soiled pillow over, trying to ignore the lingering smell.

He couldn't find a comfortable position.

Stupid woman. He almost missed her.

From the kitchen he smelled the coffee brewing, preset the night before. He sighed, sat up, and rolled his head. The small bones in his neck creaked against each other.

An awful night.

He knew why his head hurt, of course. He couldn't shrug away the feeling of impending doom, even in sleep, chance dealing him a disaster, another bullet in there somewhere.

And still no solution.

Stupid woman, all-too-clever man. A far greater danger, if only because this one wanted justice, not money. Justice in a random world. What a joke.

He rubbed his neck, the thought of coffee somehow nauseating. He had to find a way out soon.

If only he weren't so tired.

🐦 🐦 🐦 🐦

Cassie pulled her Skylark alongside Nick's pickup in the courthouse parking lot the next morning, just as he was shutting his truck door behind him. He stood beside the hood and watched her get out. He looked surprised.

"Katy asked me to come," she said.

He frowned.

Cassie gripped her hands together. "Should I stay?"

"What—yes!"

The words exploded out of him. He smiled wryly and his face relaxed. She could see now that his frustration was self-directed. He put his hands on her upper arms. "Until I saw you getting out of the car, I didn't realize how much I was dreading this, walking in there alone, wishing for someone to come with me—thinking about you, in fact. I'm glad you came, Cassie."

He let her arms go and thrust a hand through his hair. "I must be losing it."

"Maybe that's okay," she said.

He froze. "What do you mean?"

She felt tears pooling in her eyes and blinked them hurriedly back. "Maybe you have to realize how bad things are before they can get better."

He stepped back and looked away from her. "Maybe."

A long moment passed. She wished desperately she felt free enough to hug him. What other comfort could she give him? She sighed and motioned toward the courthouse. "Shouldn't we go in?"

"Yes." He took a deep breath. "Yes. Let's get this over with."

Cassie saw Regina Poole for the first time inside the courtroom. Wearing a poorly cut navy blue suit that hung on her thin frame, she walked with rounded shoulders and bowed head toward her seat. At first glance she looked downcast, but on closer scrutiny she had the posture of defense, not defeat, and her eyes darted to and fro throughout the courtroom like a cat on the prowl. Cassie shivered. There was something in the way Regina Poole kept clenching her fists, rubbing her fingers against her palms, that made Cassie afraid. She leaned closer to Nick.

He glanced down at her. "I see some other parents, though they don't look exactly thrilled with me. They're probably here to support Regina."

Cassie shook her head. "That's what Katy said, but I can hardly believe it."

"Denial," a man beside them said. "They don't want to believe they chose such a bad sitter for their children."

"I don't believe I know you," Nick said. "I'm Nick Meyers, and this is a friend of mine, Cassie McCormick."

"Philip Close." The man reached across to shake hands with them both. "We had our two-year-old son with Regina for a few months this summer."

"Oh. You too?"

"Don't be so hard on yourself. In many ways, she was the ideal sitter. She'd take Jeffrey early, keep him late—for a price, but not exorbitant. She was always there, very reliable. Cheap. And children with her were always well behaved."

Nick's jaw hardened.

"Are you saying she was a good sitter?" Cassie said.

"No," the man said. "No. I didn't say that. I said she looked good. She sure did to us. That's why these parents are upset about having her closed down. But I bet the kids aren't." He spoke past Cassie to Nick. "You've done them a favor."

"Why did you take your little boy away from her?" Cassie asked.

"Jeffrey came home the third week with bruises on his legs and stomach. Regina said he had fallen. I could accept that— the first time. When it happened two weeks later, this time with bruises on his back as well, we found a new sitter. Jeffrey wasn't happy anyway. He wasn't sleeping well. He woke up crying. He became extremely clingy—which he hadn't been before. He's generally a happy little kid. He stopped talking, and we had to put him back in diapers."

"And now?" Nick said.

"He's much happier. It was hard at first, but it didn't take long. Kids are resilient."

"Why didn't you do something about her then?" Cassie said.

"We didn't have any proof. Makes you wonder, though, why

a woman like that would be baby-sitting. Wasn't there something else she could be doing?"

Nick was watching Regina Poole as Philip Close said these last words. Cassie squeezed his arm. "Nick," she whispered, "you're a good father."

He turned his head, searched Cassie's face, and reached for her hand. "Pray for me, Cassie. I don't know where to turn except to God, and yet He must be behind this."

"God? How?"

"Just pray, Cassie. This is in His hands."

She bit her lip. How could God be behind something so awful? Couldn't this have just happened—not what He wanted at all—and only now, lately, He was coming to Nick's aid?

As the judge entered and everyone stood, Cassie tried to pray. They sat again, and she gripped Nick's hand in return, wishing she could pass a current of comfort to him.

The judge's decision took only a few minutes. Regina Poole was released on bail, even though the prosecutor mentioned "threats against the parent who had instigated the case." At this, Cassie and Nick exchanged surprised looks, but the judge didn't miss a beat. He stated the amount, banged his gavel, and called the next case.

Regina stood, turned, and settled her gaze on Nick. Cassie shivered and shrank back against Nick. How could he have missed the coldness in this woman's eyes?

She followed him outside into the sunshine on the steps in front of the courthouse. A small crowd of reporters surged up the stairs to meet them, pressing in against them. Questions flew and a barrage of flashes. Seeing Cassie flinch, Nick took her hand and stepped in front of her, shielding her slightly. The prosecutor made a statement, and then Nick pulled Cassie through the crowd and toward the parking lot.

She paused beside her car, wishing they could drive back together. It seemed too abrupt a parting after being together in the courthouse.

Nick must have agreed. "I could do with some coffee. Will you come with me? I could bring you back here to get your car."

She wondered what time it was. Going with him would probably mean missing her twelve o'clock class, too, but if she looked at her watch, he'd retract the offer. "Sure. I'll go with you."

He touched her arm briefly, a mute acknowledgment of gratitude, and came around to open the truck door for her. Neither spoke during the brief ride to a nearby restaurant.

They chose a corner booth, and once they were seated, Cassie said, "Feel better now? It's all over."

"I feel exhausted. I . . ." He smoothed his hand over the menu and looked across the restaurant for a waitress. "Why doesn't she come?"

Cassie gripped his hand briefly, then made a show of opening her menu.

"I'm sorry, but it's been awful," he said, then had to wait as the waitress poured coffee and tried to take their orders. Neither wanted anything to eat. The mere thought of food repulsed Cassie.

After the waitress left, Cassie thought Nick would retreat into silence again, but he continued, as if the choice were no longer his.

"Maybe I have been in denial, like Katy said, but it feels more like anger to me. Malice in plenty, believe me. When I saw her this morning—" He put both palms flat on the table and stared sightlessly down at his cup.

"It's okay, Nick. Anyone would feel the same way."

"No, it's not," he said without looking up. "It's not okay. Look where this got me with Sarah. But I can't seem to stop. Every time I think about what she did—"

"Nick . . ."

He held up his hand to forestall her. "I'm trying. After Sarah—her dying like that—I felt like King David hearing about the poor man's lamb. All she had was this life, and it was taken away from her. I don't want that again, believe me." He held his hand wearily to his neck, turning his head slowly from side to side. "This wanting to exact punishment, to bring about justice—it doesn't belong to us. We have been forgiven much.

We're supposed to forgive in turn, to love mercy. I lost my chance with Sarah. I don't want to do the same with Regina. And really—think about it, Cassie, think about her life—given Regina's circumstances, would I have done any different?"

Cassie made a protesting sound, but he shook his head sadly.

"I know a thing or two about my failures, Cassie. And why aren't my circumstances like Regina's, anyway, if not because of God? If He wants this now, for Alice and me, so be it."

She sat up straighter. "You said something like that in the courthouse, about God being behind this."

"Yes."

"God's responsible?" She leaned closer. "It doesn't make sense."

"Wait," Nick said. "If there's one thing God's been teaching me in the last year, it's this: God has the final say. Remember Job? His children died, he lost everything, even his health, yet he took his complaint straight to God."

"But it was Satan's fault. He made that happen. If Job had known about Satan's role, he might have complained to him instead of God."

"And he would have been wrong. That's the point. Satan had to get permission from God before he could do anything to Job. In fact, everyone and everything was under God: the people who stole Job's cattle, the lightning and tornado that killed his sheep and children, the germs that made him sick. Everything is limited by what God allows." He poked a finger down on the table. "And so is Regina Poole. I have to believe that."

"Oh, Nick." She searched his face for some sign of weakness but saw only conviction. "This is *so* weird."

"I know—you think it wasn't fair to me or to Alice. But I am not innocent, Cassie. I can't claim that His treatment is unjust. I'm a sinner in His hands, very much at His mercy. And so is Alice—don't you doubt that."

"At His mercy!" Her mouth hung open. "What kind of God is that?"

Nick wrapped his hands around his mug and stared down into the opaque liquid. "I don't understand Him either," he admitted. "Like Job did, I want Him to spell out what's happening, the big picture. But the truth is, Cassie, I have no call on God, no right to demand anything from Him—certainly not to call Him to account."

"You're His child."

"By His mercy."

"You did become a Christian. You accepted His salvation."

"By His mercy."

"But He owes you something for that."

"No! Who has ever given to God that God should repay him?" He shook his head sadly. "Face it, Cassie, I'm the one with debts. The Bible's absolutely clear on that. Not by works of righteousness which we have done—remember?"

She huddled farther back into the corner of her booth.

At God's mercy? How could that be?

"Cassie, read Job. Look at what Job says to God. Then see what God says back."

The waitress brought more coffee, but Cassie made no move to lift her mug again. It all seemed so confining. She ran her hand across the molding along the side of their booth. It was defined by a border of green vine, which trailed endlessly along the wall, all around their section of the restaurant, even rising above doors and running under windows. Like a rope around them, surrounding, imprisoning. The table also seemed too close, the booth adding to her claustrophobia. She put her hands in front of her and pushed, to no avail.

"Cassie . . ." Nick said, his voice gentle.

"When I was a little girl," she said and kept her grip on the table, "I had a picture of Jesus in my room—Jesus and a fallen lamb. The lamb is hanging from a cliff. It's caught in a bush. And Jesus is reaching down to it, so sure of himself, His hands safe and gentle." She glared across at him. "That's the God I want. A Savior."

"And you think the shepherd didn't notice when the lamb wandered off? What kind of shepherd would that be, who kept losing sight of us and having to dash off to our rescue?"

"Instead the shepherd *let* the lamb do something dangerous?"

"How dangerous can it be when the shepherd is watching?" She shook her head doubtfully.

He lifted his shoulders. "Like I said, read Job for yourself." Cassie crossed her arms and hugged herself.

Why did it terrify her so much—being at God's mercy? Because it left her nothing to bargain with? Or because she was afraid of how God would treat her?

She raised stricken eyes again to Nick.

"Let me pray," Nick said and began immediately. "God, I know my sin. I know—at least a little—of your holiness. I know what I deserve. And yet you sent your Son to die for me, and every day you meet me with new compassion. You know how I struggle, and yet you say when I stand before you, it will all make sense. Until then, do what you want and help me be strong enough to bear it, even to bear Regina, even to bear what she did, with your grace."

Nick opened his eyes and smiled glumly. Still Cassie stared at him.

"It's a little unnerving, isn't it?" he said. "But the Bible says the fear of the Lord is the beginning of wisdom, not the end of it. Relying on His love—that's where wisdom takes us. I'm not there yet, but it'll come together for all of us, wait and see. In the meantime . . ."

"Yes?"

"You haven't told me what you've decided about Alice. Will you keep her?"

"Where will she sleep? I only have one bed."

"I'll bring a camp cot for her."

"Okay then. I'll take care of her."

"Great. Now come on. We'd better get going. I'll take you back to your car before it gets any later. You've already missed two classes because of me."

As Cassie drove back to campus, she found herself smiling. He knew her schedule? How . . . interesting.

Twelve

*T*hat night after her seminar, Cassie called her sister. Mary had five children. She would know what an almost-four-year-old girl would enjoy. Cassie had her own plans, of course, insights she had gained from baby-sitting her two older sisters' children. But Mary might know of a few fail-safe games and toys Cassie could buy.

It took a while for Mary to understand what Cassie was doing. "Baby-sitting? Cassie, I can't believe you. What's this guy like? You haven't gone off the deep end again, have you?"

Cassie scowled. Mary's husband, Joe, was quiet and easygoing. Good thing, with Mary for a wife.

"I'm helping a friend, Mary. A friend. Yes, he's a Christian. No, this isn't going anywhere. He's going somewhere, after Christmas, when he gets his doctorate. So calm down."

"But I thought you were having trouble with your classes. Isn't this going to make it worse?"

Cassie made a protesting sound deep in her throat.

"You're too willing to help," Mary said.

"I could use some help from you right about now. What about it? Can you give me a few ideas?"

"Well, all right, but I hope you know what you're doing." There was silence for a moment, then Mary spoke again. "Nothing expensive, I suppose? Puzzles, of course. Easy ones that fit into a tray. Get the cardboard ones, not wooden. And I'll send you a list of our favorite books for that age. You can get them from the public library. Other than that—your dollhouse. And some Duplo blocks and Disney videos."

"No TV," Cassie said. "She's had too much of that in her day care."

"Such a personal interest, Cassie."

"Don't get going again, Mother Contrary. Just give me that recipe for play-dough that you like, the one pasted on the wall by your stove. You haven't taken it down yet, have you?"

Mary laughed. "How can I? The wallpaper's faded around it. Here." She read off the ingredients. "I'll send you some of my favorite catalogs as well, when I send that list of books, with some notations of things the kids have liked. But you know, Cassie, it's really *you* that's important. Your attention. That's what'll be best for her."

Cassie thanked her sister and hung up.

Attention . . . like from God? By paying attention to Alice she hoped to show the little girl how important she was, to convince her again that her well-being mattered. Would it be any different with God?

She had always assumed He paid just enough attention to make things work out the way He wanted. But if Nick was right, God's attention went much further than that.

Did she *want* God to pay such close attention?

Cassie shook her head in confusion. If God were that concerned with her life, its every small decision, every idle word, it made everything too important. It frightened her to think of it. How could she know what to do? How could she ever hope to please Him?

How much easier to believe that most things ran on automatic, the little moments slipping away on the periphery of God's attention.

Here, she wished He would say, I'll put you in charge of this little part—your part. Your everyday life. You be a sort of lesser god over that much. A sort of co-creator, co-sovereign. Keep things going, and as long as you don't mess up too much, I'll leave you alone. But if you have trouble give a shout.

That would leave God free to focus on the big things—like

Billy Graham, world politics, Mother Teresa, or the latest earth-quakes.

Didn't that make more sense? And when things became bad, like they were for Nick, God could come in and set things right again.

It *had* made sense, once upon a time. Now it seemed a whirl-wind had swept through her tidy garden and uprooted her dis-ordered notions. She wasn't even sure anymore that she knew which were weeds and which were flowers.

She made the play-dough, then pulled out her books to study. But she couldn't make her mind focus.

The book of Job first, she decided. What had Nick told her to do? Notice what Job said first and then God. She would try.

৯৪   ৯৪   ৯৪   ৯৪

WEDNESDAY MORNING, HIS KITCHEN.

The answer to his dilemma. There it was, plain to see.

He became so excited that he gulped down his cof-fee, only realizing later in the morning when he drank his second cup that he had burned his mouth.

Small price to pay. He gave himself up again to the pleasure of planning Nick Meyers' demise.

That it would also bring Cassie McCormick and even Nick's daughter, Alice, to grief didn't worry him.

Nick Meyers deserved every pain he could inflict. And those unfortunate enough to join him, no less. Bad luck.

Exactly what should he do to pretty little Alice Meyers? The question consumed his thoughts the rest of the morning, but by the time he returned from lunch, he knew exactly what it would be.

Perfect.

৯৪   ৯৪   ৯৪   ৯৪

At three-forty-five Wednesday afternoon, Cassie waited for Nick on the sidewalk in front of the chemistry building. On this first day, he wanted to take Cassie himself to meet Linda Bridges, Alice's new sitter. After today, Cassie would pick Alice up on her own. Only a few minutes late, he pulled up in his pickup. He waited while Cassie fastened her seat belt, then he held out a folded newspaper.

"You'd better look at this."

A large photograph, taken on the steps of the courthouse the day before, appeared on the front page. Nick was clearly the focus. He filled the center of the photo. His jaw was thrust forward, his forehead furrowed in concentration. To one side, slightly behind him, stood Cassie. He had his arm around her shoulder, sheltering her, and she was leaning toward him, almost hiding against him.

When had he put his arm around her? Right at the beginning, when they came outside? She only remembered being so cold. Nick must have seen her shiver and tried to warm her with his arm.

Some friend she had been, needing his strength when she meant to give him hers.

The caption listed her name, describing her as a friend of Nick, and the accompanying article announced to the world that she would be taking care of Alice in the future.

"Sorry," Nick said. "I never meant for you to be photographed. Fortunately, it's just a local story."

Cassie's eyes grew wide. Her parents might have seen this? She hadn't even written them about Nick or the work she was helping him do.

"It'll blow over," Nick said. "Don't look so worried."

"But look what Regina Poole said—these threats."

"Empty words, spoken in anger. Don't worry."

Seeing her frowning still, Nick reached across the seat to grasp her hand. "Please. Don't be afraid, not of Regina Poole. Leave her to me."

"You?"

"Me. And I'll leave her to God."

He took his hand away but gripped the steering wheel so tightly his hands were white.

"Will you?" She ran her index finger across the tense muscles of the hand closer to her. "Can you?"

He grunted, lifted his hands, and shook them out. "Yeah— can I? I'm going to try." He glanced again at her after pulling away from the curb, and something in his expression made her blush. "But what would I do without you, Cassie McCormick? Can you tell me that?"

She made a sound of protest, her thoughts too flurried and confused to respond. Nick let the question ride, asked instead what she planned to do with Alice, and discussed when he would come pick her up that night.

Linda Bridges and her husband lived close to campus in a small rental house. They had two children of their own, who were playing in the backyard with Alice on the swing set when Nick pulled into the driveway. Alice hobbled across the yard to meet Nick and jumped up into his arms. She began chattering about her day.

Nick saw Cassie's reaction and smiled. "Getting back to normal." To Alice, he said, "Slow down. I want to introduce Cassie to Linda. Cassie's going to pick you up from now on, remember?"

Alice looked across at Cassie, her face suddenly still.

Cassie smiled back and held out her hand to Linda. "I'm Cassie McCormick."

"Linda Bridges. Nice to meet you. I've seen you at church."

Linda went on to introduce her own children, then her face grew worried. "In the paper—what was that all about, what she said?"

"It'll pass," Nick said.

"Well, yes, I guess, but she sounded—" Aware of Alice, Linda broke off. "Anyway, we'll pray."

Nick strapped Alice into the front seat of the pickup and took his place behind the wheel. He had told Cassie and then Linda not to worry, but as Cassie watched, a shudder, barely perceptible, passed through him. When he turned to check the traffic, he saw her concern, paused, and let out a weary sigh. She reached along the top of the seat where Alice couldn't see and clasped the side of his shirt, squeezing it briefly.

He nodded again and mouthed the words, "Thank you."

At the lab, after Cassie had taken Alice home, Nick loaded his samples into the GC, pushed the buttons to begin the run, then paused and pressed flat palms against the plastic cover over the instrument. Signs of activity surrounded him. He could hear people walking down the hall, Wrede standing at the door of the NMR room talking to Bob, a car starting outside in the faculty parking lot. Much more going on than at night, but he was having trouble connecting his thoughts to the lab.

Against Katy, he had a few defenses. He could ignore her advice, pretend things would work out, imagine that the past weeks had been nothing more than a bad dream. A hug, some soothing words, a little extra attention, and everything would be okay. *We're back to the real world, kid. Daddy's here. No monsters under your bed.*

But he didn't have those same defenses with Cassie. And although she had not spoken out as Katy had—she was far too gentle for Katy's tirades—he had seen how concerned she was about Alice.

And even more about him.

Why should he continue to pretend anyway? Regina Poole had done more than break Alice's leg. She had broken Alice's relationship with him as well. Even a three-year-old knew who should have protected her. No wonder she felt drawn to Katy. Katy hadn't betrayed her like he had.

He pressed his forehead against the edge of the GC. This was why Katy kept saying he also needed counseling.

Betrayal for Alice; guilt for himself. Not that easy to work through.

It's too hard, Lord, he prayed. *What good can you possibly bring out of this travesty?*

He thought of the days and years ahead in Alice's life, with always this behind her, his role a fault against him. How could she understand the pressures that had contributed to his failure? Would she ever truly forgive him?

Too hard.

He felt his emotions begin to spiral out of control. He wanted to throw his head back and roar, like Beast in Alice's favorite video, waves of sound pouring out of him, louder and louder, until heaven had to listen.

What are you doing, God?

He stumbled to his chair and slumped into it, lowered his head into his hands, and gripped his hair. Why put it off? He reached for the phone.

Karen Groves, the counselor Katy had mentioned, answered on the second ring.

When Nick swept into Cassie's apartment shortly after ten, Alice was on Cassie's couch, curled up under a blanket, clutching her little stuffed cat. "Ah," he said. "She's asleep. It's a wonder she can with this wind."

"No rain yet?" Cassie said.

"No, but it'll come."

"Want some coffee? It's decaf."

"Sure."

While Cassie went into the kitchen, Nick tucked Alice's blanket more closely around her. It wasn't really cold in the room. Storms just brought out his protective impulses.

He glanced around the room. A single lamp beside the computer illuminated Cassie's homework. The only other source of light was the screen itself, flickering dimly. The computer was humming, but otherwise the room was quiet.

He walked to the window. He had never paid much attention to what was behind Cassie's apartment. Her block was the farthest from the street and the most isolated. In front, parking spaces separated her building from the other two buildings closer to the street. In back, across another single row of shadowy parking spaces, a short fence separated the development

from what appeared to be trees and a gully of some sort. Tonight
the branches of the trees were waving wildly, shadows and limbs
and leaves in a melee of motion.

"What's back there, Cassie?" he said when she returned with
the coffee.

She handed him the mug. "Why? What are you thinking?"

"Just . . . wondering. What's on the other side of the
fence?"

"A culvert, bushes, a few trees."

"Where does the culvert lead?"

"Out past the apartment complex to East 29th Street."

So someone could come up behind Cassie's building, jump
over the fence, and no one from the street would ever see.

He turned from the window. Time to tamp down that pro-
tectiveness.

"How'd it go tonight?" he asked.

Cassie brushed her bangs back. "With Alice?" She shook her
head as if to clear it. "Fine."

"Fine. Really?"

"Well, you do have to keep up with her. She has a quick mind
and it's hard sometimes to follow, but she's really cute, too. We
made supper together, sausage and rice porcupines. She made
me write down the ingredients so she can make them for you.
And she had a bath—is that all right? She washed herself. And
we read books, lots of books. She fell asleep in the middle of
Lyle, Lyle, Crocodile."

"There, on the sofa?"

"Yes. If you had called about working late, I would have
moved her onto her cot, but I liked having her close."

"That's fine, Cassie."

She had stepped back from him slightly and was standing
with her arms bent at her waist, one thumb nervously rubbing
against the other hand's palm. That little wrinkle appeared between her eyes again. What was she thinking? It was becoming
so important to him—the tantalizing riddle of that furrow.

"Nick?" Her frown became more pronounced. "Can I fix
you something? Are you hungry? Unless, of course, you think

you need to get Alice home before it starts raining."

"What do you have?"

She smiled. "If you're going to be picky . . ."

"No, no. Anything. How about some leftover porcupines? I'd settle for a couple of quills."

"Funny. Come on. I can tell you what I found out from Job while I fix them."

"Job?"

"You said to read it." She took out a dish of leftovers from the refrigerator and glanced over at him. "Didn't you?"

"Sure, but—already?"

"I was curious."

She set the timer on the microwave. "Pepsi, root beer?"

"Pepsi's fine."

"And I have some salad. I'm right, aren't I—you haven't eaten any supper?"

He put his chin on his hand and looked over at her, busy beside the sink. She turned to put the lettuce back in the refrigerator, saw his expression, and paused.

"Well, did you?"

"No." He smiled slowly. "Sure is nice of you to worry."

"You want to eat this or not? 'Cause if you don't—"

"Yeah. Sure I do. I'm starved."

"Then here."

She filled a small plate with food and sat down opposite him. Steam rose from her mug of herbal tea. Was that why her cheeks were red? He hoped not.

"Thank you," he said.

Nothing.

"Cassie? Thank you. They're good."

She sneaked a look at him from under the fringe of her bangs. "You're welcome, but don't count on supper every night."

Supper with Cassie every night. Now, there was a thought. Maybe she was thinking along the same lines. She *was* still blushing.

Time to let her off the hook. "Tell me about Job."

She lifted her mug, took a tiny sip, then another.

"Okay." This time she smiled more naturally. "Mostly Job complained. At one point he says—wait, let me find it. Here: 'But He'—meaning God—'stands alone, and who can oppose him? He does whatever he pleases. He carries out his decree against me, and many such plans he still has in store.' That's what you were saying yesterday about us being at God's mercy. But doesn't that frighten you? *Many* such plans He has in store?"

"Yes, it does. But not as much as thinking there's no one in charge, that there's no purpose, no reason behind any of it. How devastating to think life just happens."

"I suppose." She held her palm over the steaming mug until a layer of moisture had condensed on her skin. "Maybe."

"And God? What does He say to Job?"

"Mostly He talks about creation. Those chapters where God speaks are beautiful. 'Where were you when I laid the earth's foundation?' Who did this . . . who did that? But He never explains anything, not really."

"He's saying, look at how I made the world. I made it well. I made it wisely. I made it right. If I can do that, I'm wise enough to know what's best for you."

"He doesn't *say* that."

"You can tell from Job's answer. 'Surely I spoke of things I did not understand, things too wonderful for me to know.' "

Cassie wrapped her hands around her mug but seemed to gain little comfort from the remaining warmth.

"But we have more than His wisdom," Nick continued. "Remember? Jesus leaning over the cliff to pull us back, dying in our place, taking our punishment. By His wounds we are healed."

"Job said he despised himself. Is that what God wants us to do?"

Nick leaned closer. "Isaiah felt that way, too, when he came before God. 'Woe is me,' he said, 'I am ruined! For I am a man of unclean lips.' And me too. The closer I get to God, the more unworthy I know I am. That's why I'm glad we have His love.

Wisdom alone might have decreed annihilation—that's what we deserve, after all. But love took Him to the cross."

Nick uncurled Cassie's hand from her mug and with his thumb rubbed a circle in her palm, around and around, until she looked up and nodded. She must know—freedom, safety, comfort, and peace, all tied up in that one act of sacrifice.

"God showed His love by dying for us," Nick said. "And having saved us, He doesn't leave us useless and weak but crowns us with love and compassion. You said it yourself—He calls us His children. That's the love we can rely on, the love we have to rely on."

She looked down into her mug, empty now and cold. "It's so hard sometimes."

"I know. Believe me, I know. Think of Job. Children, riches, respect, and then sitting among the ashes. Hot, cold. Love, shame. Life, death. But always behind it heaven's song goes on, even when we can hardly hear it. God's there, over it all, knowing and loving and working out His purposes."

She nodded. "I guess." She met his gaze and smiled ruefully. "You're a strange man, Nick Meyers."

"Give me your other hand. Brrr. You're cold as ice. Why are you so afraid, Cassie?"

"This being at His mercy—have you forgotten so quickly what it felt like to discover that?"

"No. No, I haven't. But that's the beginning of wisdom, remember? Not the end."

She nodded slowly.

Nick took both her hands in his. She was a special woman, but not yet sure of herself and definitely not sure of God. *Take care of her, please, Lord. Don't leave her afraid. Take her to the end, to respect and awe and faith.*

It was only later, driving home with Alice, that Nick confronted whether he actually accepted what he had told Cassie. It all sounded good, but he himself had talked about the other shoe falling, about payment and punishment. And now this to Cassie. For all his fine words, he had yet to balance a holy fear with confident love.

At his own apartment, Alice asleep beside him, he sat in the pickup, drumming his fingers against the steering wheel. He believed what he told Cassie. He did. But he *felt* what he told Luke about expecting repercussions from God. Belief versus feeling—that was the difference—and God had used Cassie to remind him of the belief.

After all, there was a measure of reality to the other shoe falling. He did deserve punishment. But there was a further reality in God's love; his continued sin a thing of earth, its end—by God's grace—a promise of heaven.

There it was again: the perceived and the real. Time and eternity. The glare of the sun on his face, the reality of heaven even higher.

And where did Cassie fit in?

Cassie McCormick. Leaving the apartment, he had turned at the top of the stairs and seen her standing beside her door. Her head was bent slightly forward, bangs brushing her forehead, her stance now endearingly familiar to him. Seeing him look back she had smiled, her eyes bright and warm, and he had found himself fighting the urge to go back to her, to touch her face, hold her close, and kiss her.

He rested his head against the steering wheel. He couldn't fight it anymore. He was in love with her. A tidal force followed the admission, breaking barriers in its path, letting loose hope and dreams long confined and now set free.

He wouldn't even think about the problems—her graduate school, his career, what was happening between her and Alice. This one fact overshadowed everything: incredibly, after all this time, he loved another woman. This time, he vowed, he would measure love not by how he felt about her, but what he could do for her.

And maybe, with the other mercies God had shown him, He intended to give him Cassie as well—a major mercy, one that might actually take him out of the wilderness, out of waiting, and into peace.

And all on a whim at the St. Louis airport.

Such small moments, quick choices that changed a person's

life forever, the pattern shifting, blooming, nothing incidental, and all of it beautiful in His time.

How did it go with Joseph and his brothers? Nick had meant Cassie for the moment, but God had meant her for good.

He smiled. For good—both a blessing and forever. Not a bad pun when considering God's providence.

Does it make you smile, too?

A sense of God's presence came over Nick, as if in the dark he could reach out and touch Him sitting on the other side of Alice. And more than His presence—His love.

Now all he had to do was win her heart. Nick smiled, knowing God would see his pleasure.

All suggestions gladly welcomed, you know.

༺ ༺ ༺ ༺

The next morning, Thursday, when Cassie returned to her desk after her morning class, Luke said, "Have you seen Nick this morning?"

"No. Why? What happened?"

"Someone slashed his tires during the night."

Cassie drew back in horror. "He's all right? Alice?"

"He's upset, that's for sure. He only has liability insurance on his truck."

"What will he do?"

"I've already called the church. They'll help him out through the benevolence fund—if Nick will take the money."

"Regina? Was it her?"

"What do you think?"

"They should have kept her in jail."

"Don't look like that, Cassie."

"But she already broke Alice's leg. Just a little girl. She could be capable of anything." Cassie thrust her chair back. "I'm going up to talk to him."

"He's not on campus. He borrowed my car to go buy tires. He's changing them now."

Cassie slumped back into her chair, shuddering at the

thought of the woman's vindictiveness. But Nick would say God stood between Regina and Nick, that God had allowed this act.

I don't understand. You rewarded Job in the end. You made his life good again. Can't that happen to Nick, too? Soon?

Luke told Cassie that Nick would bring the keys back during her twelve o'clock class, so dropping her books off, she went upstairs to find Nick.

Duncan Wrede was just returning from lunch as Cassie walked down the hall. He stopped and favored her with a smile that didn't quite reach his eyes. He was looking at some point below her left ear. She had to fight the impulse to duck and swerve slightly in order to make eye contact.

Was he shy? Or was this his way of putting her down?

"Well, Miss McCormick. Quite the celebrity these days."

Celebrity? "Oh. The picture in the newspaper. That was a surprise."

"I understand you've decided to join Erin Moran's group next spring." He favored her with another brief smile and looked away, as if there was something down the hall he felt compelled to watch. "No chance I can change your mind?"

"No, I don't think so. I . . . I want to branch out a little, do something different."

Wrede flicked a finger against his coat lapel. "Did you? And I thought we had the perfect incentive . . . but Nick will be finishing up soon, won't he? Can it be that Erin's group has an equal attraction?"

Did he mean Terrence? He couldn't mean Dave—he was married. So was Luke. Then she saw Wrede's sneer. Cassie bit back her surprise. *He must mean Luke.* She lifted her chin and glared at the man. "Excuse me. I'm sure you're busy."

In Nick's lab, she pulled the door shut behind her, closed her eyes, and tried to banish Wrede's insinuations. Nick's footsteps came closer.

"What is it, Cassie? Wrede? What's he been saying to you?"

She opened her eyes, determined to shake off Wrede's comments. Nick was only a few feet away. "Luke told me about your tires," she said. "How are you doing?"

Nick crossed his arms, the muscles bunching reflexively. In the background, the GC-mass spec was humming, and the faint but unmistakable odor of organics lingered in the air.

"Nick?"

"Not just the tires."

He rubbed the back of his neck and rolled his shoulders with a pained expression.

"What happened, Nick?"

"I left Alice's stuffed kitty in the truck last night when I carried her up. Whoever slashed the tires slashed Kitty as well."

"Oh no. Did Alice see?"

"No, but I had to tell her. She never goes anywhere without Kitty."

"I'm so sorry."

"Well, it is upsetting." A muscle in his cheek tightened, but seeing Cassie's concern, he smiled wearily and shook his head. "Don't look so worried, Cassie. Better the cat than Alice."

"You're pretty sure it was Regina?"

"Who else? She's mad as a red ant. I just hope she works it out of her system." He turned and walked the length of the bench back to his desk. "Now, how's the analysis going?"

They spent the next half hour talking about the herbicide tests, and then Cassie stood to leave. "Lab in fifteen minutes," she announced. "Have to go earn my keep."

Nick nodded. "I . . . uh . . . there's something I wanted to ask you."

"Yes?"

He had stood when she did and was leaning against the counter that held the GC. His arms were crossed, his head down slightly, reminding her of the first time she saw him at the St. Louis airport.

She laughed, suddenly nervous. "What?"

"How about coming over tomorrow night? I'll get some barbecue—have you tried Tom's yet? And I'll get a video, too. What do you think?"

"Not to work on the spectra?"

"A time to weep and a time to laugh. Wouldn't you say it's time for a little laughter?"

"Yes, I suppose so." Was this a date? No, not chaperoned by his daughter. Just as friends, some fun after a horrible week. "Okay. What time?"

"Five-thirty, six o'clock? Come when your Friday afternoon lab is over."

"Okay. Oh dear, I'm going to be late."

Cassie hurried across campus to the building with the freshman labs. Nick would be gone after January. No sense in getting excited. No sense, but the students in her lab probably found her oddly giddy that afternoon.

❧ ❧ ❧ ❧

Friday, on campus.

Walking past Nick's lab, he heard him talking to a man, though he couldn't tell at first who. Nick said something, chuckled, and he heard Cassie McCormick's name. Cassie, Nick's apartment, tonight.

He glanced up and down the hall. No one coming. He stood closer to the wall on Nick's side of the hall, straining to hear.

The other man said something—he couldn't quite hear it. Ah, it was Luke Shepard, Moran's group.

A stool scraped against the floor.

He turned and scurried down the hall to his office, slipped inside, and leaned up against his closed door.

Cassie McCormick would be at Nick's that night.

See? Chance was smiling again.

Would Nick convince her to spend the night? No, probably not. Just as well.

But she would at least stay late. Even better. Dark. Quiet. Tonight. Perfect. Everything working out just as he wanted. So perfect, in fact—maybe they were right and no one else actually existed. Just him, and all of life a running invention of his mind, the rest of them mere props. He the creator, they the creatures in his universe of one.

If so, he wondered, did they know?

Thirteen

Cassie parked her Buick Skylark on the opposite side of Katy and Luke's building Friday night and climbed the narrow stairs to Nick and Alice's second-floor apartment. She knew what to expect. Laid out like Katy and Luke's, but in reverse, the door would open onto a small living room, perhaps ten by twelve feet. At one end an alleylike kitchen stretched to the back of the apartment; beside it a door led into the bathroom. Cassie knew from Luke and Katy's apartment that the two doors on the other wall led into tiny bedrooms, barely big enough for a double bed and dressers.

Nick opened the door for her. He was wearing jeans and a waffle knit gray pullover, and tonight, there were the boots she'd seen in St. Louis. She lifted her eyes to his and saw his grin. "You hardly ever wear them."

"Never in the lab, but they go well with Texas barbecue, don't you think?"

"Mmm." She closed her eyes and breathed in the rich, spicy aroma. "How did I ever live without it?"

He grinned and motioned toward the table with cartons of take-out. "We're all ready, as you can see."

Alice hobbled over to stand beside Nick.

"Kitty's dead," she said, her eyes big.

"I know," Cassie said. "I'm sorry. What will you do now, Alice?"

"Daddy says he'll buy me another one, but . . . I want Kitty."

Cassie knelt down and gave Alice a hug. "You know . . ." Cassie frowned, trying to look as serious as possible. "I was in a store yesterday morning and I heard a little puppy barking. He was so cute, with floppy ears and fluffy brown fur and a funny little black nose. But he was sad. All his brothers and sisters had found homes, and he was left all alone."

Nick made a protesting sound in his throat, but Alice's eyes grew bigger and bigger. Cassie sympathized with Nick, but she wasn't about to break character for his sake.

"Can you give him a home, Alice? His name is Toby."

"Cassie . . ." Nick murmured. His face was a study in conflicting emotions: frustration, determination, sternness.

Cassie took pity on him. Pulling a stuffed dog from her carryall, she held it out to Alice. "Here he is."

Alice pulled back, and Cassie made a whimpering puppy sound. "He's so unhappy, Alice. But if you won't keep him, I will."

One more whimpering sound and Alice reached out for the puppy. She didn't exactly embrace the toy. She ran her fingers over his puffy belly and touched his hard black nose. "Toby," she whispered.

"Will you take care of him?" Cassie asked.

Alice shrugged but carried the dog to the couch and seated him carefully beside where she would be sitting.

Cassie stood up and grinned at Nick. "Gotcha."

"I've been sandpapered," he said, grinning. "Well, come on in."

Cassie stepped forward and looked around. An entertainment unit filled one entire wall in the living area, with television, stereo system, VCR, and speakers.

Nick held up his hands. "I know, I know. The bigger the boys, the bigger the toys. I purchased most of this during my first year of graduate school—or I should say, I acquired them. It took a while longer to pay for them."

"Really."

"Now, wait a minute. Look in here at Alice's room. See? Toys, books. We're really not the video junkies or audiophiles that all this would indicate."

And indeed two large bookshelves bulged with Alice's playthings.

"Elizabeth, Alice's grandmother, keeps us supplied. She also chose the decorations."

Cassie caught Nick's grin and laughed. Frilly and lacy, the room was a charming oasis of femininity, a room any little girl would love, with a canopied bed, a pint-size vanity, and an entire zoo of stuffed animals.

"It's wonderful, Nick. Does her grandmother also keep it clean for her?"

Nick looked offended. "Absolutely not. We handle that all on our own, don't we, Alice?" He laughed. "Actually, Alice and I have been working since four o'clock getting things ready. Just don't expect a tour of my room. We had to have someplace to stash all the clutter."

"I feel honored."

The rest of the apartment was much more casual—comfortable couch, well-worn overstuffed armchair, heavy wooden coffee table, and piled crates filled with books. An eclectic mix, from Cassie's cursory inspection: Christian books, mysteries, some fantasy and science fiction, and a pile of Bible reference books.

"More in my room," Nick said, "which is mostly a study. Just a bed in the corner."

Cassie ran her fingers over the books on one of the shelves. This was the life of a Christian single father, nineties style. Not even a double bed probably. There wasn't room for both a bed and a desk in Nick's bedroom.

He was standing across the coffee table from her, watching her reaction. Again she remembered seeing him in St. Louis. She had thought him handsome back then—mildly dangerous even—a man for fun and diversion.

But roots? Able to sustain growth, produce anything more than momentary magic? Hardly.

And now? Same strong shoulders, same firm jaw, same vital, dramatic, irresistible eyes. But with the background of his life filled in—Alice beside him, one of her crayon drawings tacked up in the kitchen, dishes draining beside the sink, and place mats on the table.

More than that. Faith in the face of trouble. A single bed. Prayer as natural as a telephone conversation. And the knowledge of God watching, noticing, caring.

"Cassie?"

"It's great," she said. "All very nice. Now, what do we have to eat?"

A small table, barely big enough for two, sat beside the opening into the kitchen. Nick had put the cartons of food there. But dishes and silverware waited on the coffee table in front of the couch.

"Hope you don't mind eating in here," he said. "The table would be a little cramped."

"What do we have?"

"I didn't know what you would like, so I got a sample of almost everything Tom sells—brisket, pork, sausage, chicken."

"Is Tom's the place where you only get a knife to eat with?"

"Traditionally, a slab of meat on butcher paper, bread, a pickle, and a big fat knife, good and sharp. Down-home casual—"

"Not to mention dangerous."

"But a lot of fun. You can try it if you want, but you can see I've also set out forks. And we have beans and coleslaw and fries for Alice. What would you like?"

Cassie laughed. "A little of everything, of course. You won't find this Illinois farm girl turning her nose up at meat."

Comfortable now with Cassie, Alice chattered through the meal, easily dominating the conversation. At one point, Nick leaned closer to Cassie and whispered, "Babbling—she does it all the time. But she'll wear down after supper."

Cassie smiled. "And you said you wanted enough kids to surround a big table."

"I still do."

Cassie closed her eyes, imagining the dining room Nick had described. She was surprised by how vividly she saw it, and how much it hurt to see Nick holding another baby. Her eyes opened abruptly. Nick was pouring some more barbecue sauce on Alice's plate, patiently telling her again why the Coke had bubbles.

"But, Daddy, who puts the carbon doxide in? Does God?"

Cassie didn't even hear Nick's answer. She was consumed by Nick's hand reaching out to tuck a stray curl behind Alice's ear. Such a strong hand but so gentle. And his arm, his sleeve rolled up slightly, revealing the muscles of his forearm. And his relaxed grin as he turned to Cassie.

She couldn't know for sure what he saw, but something in her face made him pause, a question flickering in his eyes. She stood abruptly, going to the freezer for more ice.

What was she *thinking*?

For the movie, Cassie deliberately sat next to Alice on the couch, leaving the armchair to Nick. When Alice climbed up onto Nick's lap, Cassie gathered a puffy pillow against her stomach and wrapped her arms around it. She felt herself relax, the threat of shaking gone, but the shock lingered even so.

Nick Meyers. She realized now that outside of her imagination she had hardly known Richard. This man, holding his little girl in his lap, dropping kisses into her golden curls, this man she knew. He looked up to find her watching him, and she turned resolutely toward the television screen.

The movie he had chosen, *The Gods Must Be Crazy*, began oddly, like a documentary, but the story soon developed, and Cassie and Nick were laughing, Alice's eyes sparkling with pleasure at seeing their amusement.

It felt incredibly good to laugh again. At the end, Cassie nestled into her corner of the couch, feeling cleansed and relaxed. Maybe things would be okay, after all. She stretched her arms up and out and let her head tip back against the couch. "That was fun. Thanks. Like having St. Louis again."

Nick smiled, pleased with himself. He glanced down at Alice, asleep in his arms. "Let me put her in bed. Then we'll have"—his voice dropped—"some dessert."

"Can I get it?"

"Ice cream. Blue Bell, homemade vanilla. You'll love it."

But as Cassie reached to open the freezer, she paused and pressed her forehead against the cool white exterior. He wanted her to stay, wanted to talk to her. She bit her lip. How could she talk when she felt so confused? She was falling in love with him, and no wonder—handsome, intelligent, loyal, and loving. But did she really expect him to return her feelings?

He came to help her in the kitchen, squeezing past her in the alley between the counters and the wall. "Not made for two, is it?" he said as he reached above her for bowls.

He was only inches from her. His eyes had flecks of light in the blue. Flecks of humor. He was laughing. Feeling the warmth in her cheeks, she knew why.

"Oh yeah. Let me move," she said. "Sorry."

"Cassie, Cassie. You're welcome anytime—tight squeeze and all."

Cassie grabbed the carton of ice cream and carried it out to the table. She searched frantically for something to say in return, but her mind was blank. Nick didn't seem to mind. He was still grinning when he joined her at the table.

She motioned toward Alice's room. "I take it Sydney's parents aren't still hoping to get custody."

"No. After the suit, we worked it out. Elizabeth comes and gets Alice for a weekend now and then, but she doesn't really want the responsibility. The suit had more to do with grief than anything else."

"Sarah said Sydney's family was rich."

"In tall cotton, that's for sure, most of it originally from oil money."

"Yet you seem . . ."

"Strapped for cash? I won't take any money from them. Sydney had a trust fund, but I've put that aside for Alice's college. I can take care of her myself."

"Umm." That independent streak. "Are they Christians—Sydney's parents?"

"Country-club variety. Pretty clothes on Sunday and big donations for a stained-glass window in the chapel. You know the kind."

Yes, Cassie did. What Nick was describing wasn't that different from the detached relationship her father had accused her of just before she came to Texas—Nick's in-laws designer clothed, her own more down-home, but both the same empty, complacent relationship with Christ.

Not anymore, please, Lord. I do want Your grand intrusion. I do.

She asked, "How did you become so serious about your Christianity?"

"Doesn't quite mesh with the circumstances of my marriage, does it? No—don't apologize. I'd like you to know about that time."

He began by telling her about his experience in college. "A church school in East Texas. Real conservative. Too conservative." Nick planted his hands on the edge of the table and pushed back, as if even now the memory of that time threatened him. "Knowing that I needed a Savior was one thing. Being told I had to wear a tie every day was another altogether. We could barely talk to the female students. No movies. No TV. Everything controlled and censored. I mean, hey, I was twenty years old when I came to Christ, and no virgin, believe me. I went from thinking myself in complete control of my life to having no control at all."

"Why didn't you go to another college?"

"My boss, the one who led me to Christ, got me a scholarship. I couldn't afford to switch. So I worked like crazy to get out of that place—managed it in three years."

"And you came to graduate school."

Nick nodded. He held Cassie's gaze. His eyes were full of regret, but he seemed determined to continue. He did pull back again and turned his chair. So he didn't have to face her? she wondered.

Cassie waited.

He leaned his head back against the wall and took a long, slow breath before continuing. "Sydney was in one of my labs the first semester. Beautiful, funny, and willing, and I went right where all my worst impulses took me. At Christmas she told me she was pregnant."

Nick sighed heavily and leaned forward, shoulders hunched, resting head on hands. "She wasn't going to have Alice at first. It took a little doing, convincing her to keep the baby."

"Why didn't you want to take Sydney's way out?"

"Abortion? You forget, Cassie, what I really wanted. Somewhere I had gotten that picture of a family. The kids, the big table . . . remember?" He stopped and frowned, his expression severe. "Looking back, I see it all a little differently. I believe now that in His great mercy, the Holy Spirit kept us from that sin."

"I'm glad," Cassie said.

"No kidding. Anyway, the pregnancy was hard on Sydney, and murder on our marriage. She threatened to leave after the birth—and did. She went home to her parents, left them pretty quickly, since they kept talking about wanting the baby, and took up with an old friend. You'd think that was when I would become more serious about God—alone with a new baby. But no. Katy was baby-sitting Alice full time. She and Luke tried to get me to church. I wasn't interested—still burned, I suppose, from college. Anyway, six months later Sydney had an accident riding a horse, and things became really bad. Oh, that's right. Sarah probably told you."

Cassie nodded. "And that you missed several months, staying with her in the hospital."

"Five weeks, actually. She was in intensive care most of that time." He frowned. "Have you ever had someone there, someone you know?"

"In intensive care? No."

"It was for head injuries. Three times a day we could visit, twenty minutes each time. All of us relatives and friends gathered outside the ICU, waiting for the appointed time. We would all file in, walking between rows of beds. Patients lying there. Some of them with heads wrapped. A lot looking pretty normal, actually, except sound asleep—always sleeping. For twenty minutes we stood by the beds, talking, some of us singing, brushing their hair, touching faces and hands and arms."

He stopped, the memory so vivid he seemed to have forgotten where he was. A car honked outside. He looked blankly across at Cassie and shook his head, shaking the vision away as he did so.

"Sorry. I got lost there."

"Where was Alice all that time?"

"With Katy and Luke. I found a place near the hospital. People there had quite a business going, renting rooms out." He rubbed his chin thoughtfully. "It was all so strange. My landlady asked me one day, near the end, how Sydney was doing. I hardly knew what to say. Maybe it was the three-times-a-day visits, the numb look on everyone's faces, the helplessness of it all . . . I don't know, but I felt cut off from life during that time, as if I were way off on a cliff somewhere."

He rubbed the back of his neck, his tension obvious.

"I had no idea what lay beyond. Was it oblivion? Is that where Sydney was heading? Or something else? One night near the end, it came to me—Sydney wasn't heading into nothingness, but someplace more real, more important than anything we experience here. Ecclesiastes says God puts eternity in our hearts. I think that's what I sensed that night. Eternity. So close and so real. Two days later, she was gone."

His brow furrowed. "Have you ever sensed that, Cassie? Do you know what I'm talking about? Eternity in your heart?"

"I don't know. Probably not."

"We don't live on the cliff. We live here, under the sun. Soggy cereal, bald tires, videos on Friday night, work, play, church. Down here, heaven's song becomes a little faint. We get so easily distracted. But as I sat in that dark room wondering about Sydney, praying for her, I heard the sound of God's purposes all around me, and I was afraid, Cassie—afraid in a way I had never been before or ever have been since. I understood then what life's really about. At some point I will leave this world to stand naked before a holy God—a God who will call me to give an account of how I've lived, a God who sees everything and lays it all bare. I want to be ready for that moment."

She bit her lip. "But you're a Christian, Nick. You won't have to give an account, will you?"

"Yes, I will, the Bible makes that clear. But by His grace I will come clothed in His righteousness, not in my own sin. I'll stand before His throne, and He'll speak to me face-to-face, as a man speaks with his friend. Think of it, Cassie. God himself."

Nick's eyes were burning with a zeal she had rarely seen in anyone, and yet there seemed to be room in his vision for her. He took her hand and laid it flat between his own.

"There's more going on around us than we can see or know, Cassie, but this much is clear. Either life's a game and it really is all meaningless, utterly meaningless, chasing the wind like Ecclesiastes says, or what we do here, what we choose right now really matters to Him, to us, to all that is or ever will be. I believe it does. On that day when I look into His face, I want to receive His blessing—well done, my good and faithful servant. Nothing else will matter. Nothing else will compare."

"No wonder you're so serious."

He drew back in surprise. "No. Does it seem that way? You've caught me at a bad time. It's joy He saved us for, and joy that He'll reward us for—because joy comes best when we live in His will." A lazy grin spread across his face, and his eyes became warm with humor. "Actually, I take great hope from Ecclesiastes. It says I should enjoy life—food, drink, youth, love—among other things. Let your heart cheer you, it says. Believe me, Cassie McCormick, I intend to."

He was clearly challenging her, and in a way that made her look frantically around for a change of subject. She lifted her thumb toward the freezer. "Want some more ice cream?"

Nick laughed. "You're probably ready to go home, aren't you?"

"Should I be?"

"I wish you lived closer by. Don't you ever worry, alone like that?"

"It's a first for me. I felt better when Eliot and Sarah were downstairs, but Eliot hasn't been there for a week now."

"Oh?"

"He moved out the week after Sarah died. He's been sleeping on a friend's couch. He's even thinking about quitting school."

"Too bad. It must be tough."

And Nick would know, after all. Was it easier for him, with some warning that Sydney might die? Did he still think about her?

He must have seen her frown. "Hey, you okay?" he said.

She stood up. "I really should go home."

"Wait—"

"No, it's late. But I've had a good time tonight."

"Me too. Let me walk you down to your car."

He grabbed a sweat shirt.

"I'm all right," Cassie said from beside the door.

Nick came to stand beside her. "I know you are, Cassie McCormick. You are all right. But I'm walking you down anyway."

The doorknob dug into her back, but she couldn't move. She heard a faint rasp as he breathed out, and then he was leaning forward, the warm bulk of his chest firm under her fingers. He looked down at her hand, and waited, waited. Such mesmerizing blue eyes.

She should open the door, she should. She tried frantically to remember why. Instead her fingers curled into his sweat shirt, and she pulled him closer. Then she was in his arms and he was kissing her.

It was his chuckle, low throated and quick, that brought her back to earth. He knew. He had to know. She had given herself away again. And now he was laughing.

In a panic, she pushed him away and fled down the stairs.

"Wait. Cassie."

He caught up with her beside her car. "Take it easy, Cassie. It was only a kiss."

She spun around. He was confirming it. Just a kiss—casual for him, but so real to her.

The lights of the parking area and from the apartment windows cast a strange yellowish light on one side of his face, the shadows of his neck and eyes making him appear even more unpredictable. She gathered up the remnants of her pride and glared at him. "I don't know what you're thinking, but whatever it is, I hardly know you. This is moving way too fast for me."

He stepped back and held up his hands, palms toward her.

"Okay, okay. We'll slow down. We'll get to know each other. But don't be afraid, Cassie. That's the last thing I would want. This is . . . something special. Let's see what's there for us."

"Us?" She rubbed her hands together. They were so cold. Nick reached for them. His were warm.

"Maybe us. I like you, Cassie. I have ever since St. Louis when you looked up at me through those tantalizing bangs of yours. Let's find out if things will work. Can we do that?"

His hands felt so good. He had turned hers over. His thumbs were rubbing her palms again, his slightly rough, much bigger than hers, very strong, but so gentle.

"Cassie?"

She swallowed and looked up. "You really think we can?"

He laughed, and she winced. How pathetic she must sound.

She held up her hand. "Don't answer that. Okay," she managed. "We'll see what happens. But slower."

"Good." He became much more serious. "You'll call me, won't you, if you're worried about anything?"

What did he mean by that?

She drove home utterly confused, excited by his kiss, about what he had said, and about their relationship, but wondering what he meant about being worried.

She pulled up in front of her apartment and looked at the building. She was reluctant to get out. Why?

Her entire end of the building was dark. At one in the morning that might not be so surprising, but all the parking spaces were also empty. Eliot was gone; she knew that. Her neighbor in the next apartment was an older woman working on a graduate degree who went home to her family south of Houston every weekend. The guys in the apartment downstairs must still be out on the town having a good time.

She should get out. Why was she stalling? Because of what Nick said?

No. She gasped. Something much more real.

The lights at the bottom and top of the stairs—both were out. No wonder it seemed so dark.

She considered heading straight back to Nick's apartment, but that was foolish. The lights were out. Big deal. She would just go upstairs, unlock her apartment door, and everything would be okay.

There was no one on the stairs waiting for her. How foolish. How weak to even imagine it.

Open the car door. Shut it. Oh, that was loud. Loud enough to wake—

Stop it. No one's there. No one except you.

Take one step and another. Up the stairs. Okay, hurry. See? No one on the walkway outside. No sound. No one there.

Key in the lock. There, it's in. Shut the door, quick behind you. Turn on the light.

Nothing.

Cassie jerked back against the door opening, the impulse to run down the stairs overpowering. Instead she closed her eyes. The doorknob was smooth under her hands, the wall beside the light switch warm and slightly rough.

She couldn't run back outside. There, too, was darkness and danger. Someone could be waiting, at this moment advancing toward her.

She locked the door and leaned back against its firmness, gathering her scattered emotions.

The lights were off. Someone, somewhere, had thrown a breaker. The whole end of the building was out. That explained the darkness over the stairway. The lights would come on again eventually.

For now, walk into the kitchen, find the flashlight, get into bed. Tomorrow there would be light enough to solve any problem.

Come on, Cassie, move.

The darkness—dense, liquid, and menacing—was pressing against her, circling, isolating. Near the kitchen, she stumbled roughly against a chair, the hard legs ambushing her, attacking her feet, snagging and pulling her down to the floor. Groping, she felt for the kitchen doorway and dragged herself loose from the chair's grip.

Still crouched, a sudden thought stabbed her psyche.

When had she moved a chair into the kitchen doorway?

A whimper escaped. She hadn't. Not her. Someone else had moved it. *Someone. Else?*

Here? Now? In this darkness? Waiting?

She struggled to take a breath, but a huge scream was lodged in her throat, blocking the air, threatening to erupt.

Torn between fleeing and advancing, darkness in one direction, a flashlight in the other, she crouched in frozen immobility between the overturned chair and kitchen doorway, for how long she couldn't say, but eventually the silent stillness in the apartment settled around her and she was able to catch her breath again.

No one was here. The lights were out. That was all. This was panic—blind, thoughtless, irrational panic.

She was not a child. She was a woman. She had survived a tornado at fourteen, called an ambulance for her mother at sixteen. Just last year she had extinguished a fire in the lab. She was not helpless. She was not stupid.

She was acting as if she were both.

Stand up, Cassie McCormick, and get on with things.

She struggled up from the floor, the remnants of anxiety making her clumsy. Her arm brushed against something, knocking it to the floor.

The lamp. Useless lamp. No light.

She reached out for the doorway, pushing the chair away. She must have left the chair there herself. No one was in the kitchen. No one had been in the apartment. No one on the couch . . .

He might be there, very quiet, breathing, waiting, sickly smiling while she maneuvered around his traps. The panic came rushing back, thrusting her violently forward into the kitchen.

And here, the nightmare grew.

From across the room, near the stove, a voice spoke. A low, inhuman voice. Whispering.

Her name. Over and over.

"Cassie. Cassie. Cassie."

Fourteen

*C*assie turned and fled, diving past the overturned chair, falling, bruising her knee against the hard wood, crashing across the lamp, and finally gaining the door. She fumbled for the lock, her sweaty palm slipping against the latch, pulled the door open, and slammed it tightly behind her, clinging to the doorknob outside, expecting to have it jerked back open from the other side.

With her last dregs of courage, she let go of the door, spun, raced down the stairs, and gained the sanctuary of her car.

Her keys.

Upstairs. In her purse on the floor of the dark living room. She couldn't, no, she couldn't go back in there. The voice—palpable, threatening—the voice had hands . . . hands that would curl around her, choke, smother, strangle her.

No one there yet. The stairway empty, still. She abandoned the car and raced across the parking lot.

The gas station on the corner . . . lights, a man inside, phone.

Don't look back, don't look back. He's there. Don't look. He's gaining. Run. Everything into your feet, pick them up, move, move!

Her feet felt heavy as clay, her knees stiff as a statue's. Her chest burned, her throat constricted. Wind slapped her face, but she couldn't get the air into her lungs. Cut off. Choking.

He must be gaining by now.

Don't look back.

Something rustled behind her—close, inches behind her. Feeling his hand extending, reaching, her spine tingled, her flesh crawled. In an agony of fear she pushed her chest forward, unbalancing herself, and fell to the cold sidewalk. On hands and knees skidding, she scurried forward, spiderlike, hobbling away, out of reach, until she could stand again and run. *Run.*

The last obstacle. The door. Hand on the knob, pull it, quickly, and into the light. Warm, bright—exposed.

She hurried around the far corner of the check-out counter, ducked low, and turned to look. Now surely he would be there, her pursuer, relentless, behind her.

"You all right, lady?"

The check-out clerk. A big face. She raised her head to see him more clearly. Big, burly, two hundred fifty pounds at least. She looked again at the glass doors.

No one.

Where was he?

She shrank back down.

The clerk leaned over the counter. "Is someone out there? Should I call for help? Lady, what's the matter?"

"Uh, no." The words came up hard. Like pulling crumpled chunks of sandpaper up through her throat. She tried to clear it. "I . . . I will phone. You have one?"

"Outside."

"No!" Part word, part wail. Cassie tried again. "Please. Not outside. Please, don't you have one inside? Can't I use yours?"

It took a moment for him to decide . . . a long moment, hope hanging on the rim, slow motion, the phone outside an acre of asphalt away.

The clerk reached under the counter, pulled out a phone, and pushed it toward her. "Sure, why not?"

She lifted the receiver, paused, searched through the turmoil of her mind, and began punching Nick's number.

"Is it your husband? Is he out there? Or your boyfriend?"

Cassie shook her head. No, not that, thank God.

Nick's phone was ringing. She ducked back down where she

wouldn't be seen from the door.

"Hello?"

Nick sounded alert. He couldn't have gone to sleep yet. She could hear a smile in his greeting.

"Hello?" he said more sharply, and she found her voice.

"Nick!" Something caught in her throat. She coughed. "Come get me. Please. Something awful has happened."

Instantly the tenor of his voice changed. "Cassie? Are you okay?"

"I'm at the convenience store. At the corner of the shopping center, down from my apartment complex. Please come."

"On East 29th?"

"Yes."

"Are you in danger?"

"Just come. Hurry."

"Tell me you're all right."

"For now. Please come."

She stayed down, reached across the counter to hang up the phone, and pushed it back toward the clerk, lifting reluctant eyes to meet his.

"Look," he said. "I have a gun. What are you afraid of?"

"Someone was chasing me. I don't see them now." She pointed over her shoulder to the back of the store. "I . . . I . . . I'll just wait back there, okay? There's no back entrance, is there?"

"It's locked. I can call the police."

"No. When he comes—my friend—he'll help me."

"Suit yourself, lady. Get a cup of coffee, why don't you? On the house. You look like you need one."

Across the store, a long walk and visible—standing to reach a cup in full view of the window, a mile from the man at the counter. Cassie shook her head.

She hurried to the far back wall, pushed cans of oil away from the edge of the lowest shelf, and sat down, scrunching up to make herself as small as possible. Her hand rubbed against the shelf, and she flinched. She lifted her hands in surprise and gazed at her palms. Both were scraped and scratched and stinging with pain. She hadn't felt them before. Beneath the thick denim of her jeans, her knees as well were probably lined with scratches. She touched the fabric gingerly. No blood showed through, but her fingers brought forth a sharp pang of protest. She blew lightly on her palms to ease the hurt.

Her eyes were drawn again toward the counter. From where she was sitting, she could see the walkway in front of the door, though not the door itself, and the space near the cash register. Good. She'd have warning.

And she was hidden from the front windows.

Hooks holding gloves ground into her back, and the ridge on the edge of the shelf cut into her thighs, and the muscles in her legs and arms were clamped so tightly against her body she wondered if she would ever be able to loosen them again, and yet she couldn't stop her hands from trembling.

Time seemed to have frozen. She heard the clerk's television, a late-night talk show . . . laughter, questions, booing—a bizarre sound track to her fear. She tore her eyes away from the walkway by the door.

Tiles on the floor in front of her. One had been mislaid. Sideways, when it should have been straight. And dirty. Someone had spilled coffee. No, oil. Dark anyway.

She looked again at the walkway. Too early yet for Nick. *No one else, please. Please.*

Oh . . . God. She hadn't given Him a thought. Only Nick. In all her fear, never a prayer. It seemed too late now. She wished she hadn't thought of Him at all. So much danger and to offend Him as well.

Please, Nick, come.

Praying to Nick?

I'm sorry, I'm sorry. Please don't hold this against me.

The door burst open. Cassie sprang up and was in Nick's arms, crying and clinging so tightly that the threads of his knit shirt were permanently stretched where she gripped them. His arms were warm and strong around her, his voice in her ear husky with concern, his lips against her forehead tender and searching.

"Cassie," he murmured over and over. And then with more authority, "Cassie, look at me. What happened?"

She gulped noisily, pushing the terror back down her throat, and looked up into his face. What must he be thinking? She sniffed and swallowed again, patted his shirt where she had been holding it. Her tears had made it damp. She stepped back slightly.

"Cassie." There was a warning in his voice. "Tell me."

"I—" She bit her lip, the terror coming back.

"Take it easy. We're here now."

Someone behind Nick said, "You're all right."

Cassie shifted slightly to see.

Luke. Like Nick, hurriedly dressed. Nick had pulled a shirt over his T-shirt and sweat pants, Luke a sweat shirt and jeans. Neither wore socks and Luke hadn't tied his shoelaces yet. He saw where she was looking, smiled and shrugged, then propped up his feet to tie them.

"Is Alice with Katy?" Cassie asked.

"Forget about Alice. She's fine. It's you we're worried about."

Luke answered her question. "Yes, with Katy. Otherwise Katy'd be here, too. We're all worried."

"Cassie . . ." Nick said again.

"Someone was in my apartment."

"What—now? When you got home?"

She sniffed again. "Thank you . . . for coming. I'm sorry to be in such a panic."

"Cassie." He gripped her arms. "It's all right. Just tell us what happened."

"When I arrived, the lights in my end of the building were off, which was okay because everyone was gone, obviously, but the lights over the stairs were out, too, and it was so dark. And I kept thinking about how remote that part of the complex is, and when I went upstairs my apartment lights were off, so I went to get a flashlight, and that's when I heard the voice."

"Voice." Nick's grip tightened. "Someone was there?"

"He said my name. Over and over again. I ran. I didn't have

my car keys downstairs. I had dropped them. So I ran. Here."

"On foot?" Luke said. "He didn't follow you?"

"Yes! I . . . I thought so. Now I don't know. I thought I heard something behind me."

"No one's been near here since she came in," the clerk offered. "I've been watching."

Nick and Luke both looked across the counter at Cassie's burly protector, as if aware for the first time that he was listening. He was leaning on the counter, avid eyes watching the entire exchange.

"You want me to call the police?" he asked.

Luke and Nick exchanged glances, but it was Cassie who answered. "Yes. Call them. I don't want to go back there without them."

Nick nodded. "You're right. Stupid to take a chance."

He put his arms around Cassie again, his hand threading through her hair, loosening the rubber band holding it in place. "You've been very brave," he whispered. "We'll go back there with the police, and then you can come home with us."

"You can sleep in our spare room," Luke said. "We have a bed in there."

The hard wall of Nick's chest felt immensely comforting against Cassie's cheek. Yes, Luke and Katy's apartment. She couldn't stay in her own tonight. But then what? Where would she stay tomorrow?

Nick must have realized what she was thinking. He said, "Tomorrow we put in new dead bolts, check the windows, do what we can to secure the place." He leaned back so he could see her face and pushed her bangs aside. With his thumb he smoothed away her frown. "Hey, it'll be all right. Really."

"How about a dog?" Luke said, but two police cars drew up outside the convenience store before she could answer. Cassie looked up at Nick in fresh panic.

"It's okay," he said. "I'll help you."

Nick drove Luke and Cassie back to her apartment. One block to the culvert, another block to the entrance, past the front of the complex, across the central parking area, and then her own building. The distance seemed so short to her now.

"Cassie. . . ?" Nick sounded confused.

"What?" He was looking at her building. She did so, too . . . and froze.

The lights were back on over the stairs. "Oh. Maybe it was just the electricity after all."

She would have scrambled out of the car, but Nick held her back. "You're forgetting the voice. Let the police check it out first."

They were already heading up the stairs, weapons drawn. In a defensive position, they entered the apartment. The lights came on. An officer soon came back out. "All clear," he said, and this time Nick and Luke got out with Cassie.

In the apartment, everything looked normal. No chair blocking the kitchen. The lamp was upright again. No sign of forced entry anywhere. No sign of any danger, period.

And no one in the kitchen.

One of the policemen took Cassie's statement, though she couldn't remember afterward exactly what he'd asked. She did remember his skepticism. Especially after he called the power company—no power shutdown tonight.

She was surprised he didn't check her blood alcohol level.

He took Nick's and Luke's names, too, told her to call if anything else happened, and then both men left.

Cassie collapsed into the chair in front of the computer.

"Hey, don't look like that," Nick said. He crouched beside her.

"Do you think it really happened?"

"Stop that."

Cassie shook her head. "But I was gone such a short time. I ran down to the convenience store. You came so quickly. And now everything looks so normal." She looked at him sharply. "What about the electricity? You heard what the power company said. Why weren't there any lights?"

From where he stood beside the door, Luke answered. "Someone flipped the breaker."

"Someone in the apartment?"

"They could have unscrewed the bulbs over the stairway outside."

"And then . . . put them back in? Why?"

"To make the police leave, perhaps."

"He was here. While I was. He watched me. And if you weren't here . . ."

"You said you heard him," Nick reminded her.

"I did! Don't you believe me?"

"Hey, calm down. I do. But why do you think it's him and not her?"

"Because of his voice."

Luke said, "Tell us again."

"Just a voice. He said, 'Cassie, Cassie.' "

"He knew your name."

"Yes!"

Luke rubbed his chin. "But it was a man's voice? You're sure?"

"Why? Yes, a man's voice. Low. No—actually, strange. Like this." She said her name again, twice, this time keeping the inflection steady, the stress on each syllable the same.

"Like on the telephone?" Nick said. "Maybe it was a computerized voice."

"On a tape," Luke said. "Maybe voice activated so Cassie wouldn't recognize it. Then whoever set all this up waited outside."

Nick was nodding. "She could have used some kind of motion detector, maybe, to start the recorder. That way, even if Cassie somehow found a flashlight, there'd be no one there for her to discover."

Luke frowned. "You said 'she.' Who are you talking about?"

"Regina, of course."

"Regina?" Cassie asked.

"You really think it was Regina?" Luke said. "I would think people who abuse children would stay away from adults."

"But that's the point—she stayed clear of danger." Nick stood abruptly, his face grim. "I agree, slashing tires and stuffed animals is pretty gutless, but this was, too. She probably felt safe."

"But why me?" Cassie said. "Why would she come after me?"

The two men paused, momentarily stumped, then Nick crouched back down and took Cassie's hand. "The picture in the paper, probably. You looked pretty important to our future—mine and Alice's. And the paper did identify you as Alice's future baby-sitter." He held her hand against his face. "This is my fault. I'm sorry."

"Who knows if you're right about Regina?" Cassie said. She bit her lip. "But you do believe me? You think it really happened?"

Nick nodded, still holding her hand. "I believe you, Cassie."

"The police didn't."

"I do," Nick responded. "I do. Look, go get some things. We're taking you back to Katy and Luke's apartment. If you want, I'll spend the night. In case she comes back."

"No! Don't. Leave things."

"If she knows enough to make a tape like that, she could come back and do who knows what. Alice can sleep on Katy and Luke's couch. And tomorrow I'll put in dead bolts. These locks are too flimsy." He saw Cassie still hesitate. "Go on, y'all, get going," he said. He pulled her up from her chair. "I'll be all right."

She nodded. "Okay. Thank you."

❧ ❧ ❧ ❧

He saw them leave. He left his car in the next lot. Until the police left he had stayed hidden in the bushes close to the opposite apartment building. An alert cop should have looked around a little better, but perhaps they had another call.

Better yet, perhaps they didn't actually believe Cassie McCormick. That might be useful. He'd have to think about it.

From his car, he saw Cassie and Luke Shepard come down the stairs and climb into Cassie's car.

Nick was staying. Interesting.

But nothing more tonight, he decided. Stick with the game plan. If he started improvising he would get into trouble. It was his intellect that would be their undoing, his intellect that would drive them away.

He knew just what he would do next. The timing had to be perfect, the circumstances exact. Until then, he would be watching. His chance would come. Wasn't everything going his way?

᪣ ᪣ ᪣ ᪣

As promised, Nick installed double-key dead-bolt locks in Cassie's apartment the next day, as well as sturdy latches on the windows and doors.

"A guard dog would be best," he told her when he was finished. He was standing against the door, while Cassie was on the floor by her coffee table, doing a puzzle with Alice.

She shook her head. "I'd love one, but the landlord requires an enormous deposit for animals."

"I feel responsible for this."

"We don't know it was Regina Poole. It might have been some horrible prank. These things do happen, you know."

"Is that supposed to reassure me?" Nick rubbed his neck. "Look, I think you should stay at Katy and Luke's until this is all over."

"And how long will that be?"

"Daddy—"

"Whoever this is could break in again and steal everything," Cassie said. "What would stop them?"

"Daddy, who would steal everything?"

Cassie and Nick exchanged chagrined glances.

"It's all right, sweetheart," Nick said. "Are you ready for some lunch?"

Cassie stood up. "I have some frozen pizza."

"And I'll call Katy," Nick said. Then more softly, "To make sure they don't mind you staying."

After the call, Nick followed Cassie into the kitchen. "She said of course. I told her we'd be going to church tonight, though. You can come, can't you? Then tomorrow you can sleep in late."

"Okay. But this afternoon I really have to get some work done. Two tests on Wednesday and assignments due on Monday, but supper would be okay . . . and church."

"Great, I'll come by your office around five."

Fifteen

During the fellowship time before church that evening, Zoe Calder came over to commiserate with Nick and Cassie. She brought Erin Moran with her.

"Katy told us what happened last night," Zoe said to Cassie. "How awful for you."

Cassie shuddered. "I don't think the police knew what to make of it, whether to believe me or not."

"What are you talking about?" Erin said. After hearing what happened, she touched Cassie's arm in dismay. "Who could have done this?"

"Nick thinks it's that baby-sitter," Zoe said, "the one who hurt Alice."

"Ah, that's right," Erin said. "She did threaten you, didn't she, Nick? I saw that in the paper. The police didn't pick up on that?"

"I'm not sure they connected me to Cassie. It was all too bizarre, really."

Erin held up a finger. "You know, I think I might have an idea for you. How about calling in a private detective?"

"A detective? Who?" Zoe said. "Oh, I get it. Your friend Sam Devereaux."

Erin explained. "Sam's been in Bryan for maybe three years. He was in the army before that. He has two kids. He's a good guy. You could trust him."

"To do what?" Nick said.

"To catch this woman—tail her. Have someone watch your house, try to catch her in the act."

"It would cost a lot, wouldn't it?" Nick said.

"Oh yes, I'm afraid so. At least five hundred, and that's just the beginning."

Zoe turned to stare at Erin. "You certainly know a lot about this, Erin."

Erin blushed. "He took me to dinner one night. He told me quite a bit about his business. He could really solve this for you."

"Dinner, huh?" Zoe crooned. "You didn't tell me about that."

"Stop, Zoe," Erin protested. "We grew up together. I tutored him in high school—not that he really needed it. He was plenty bright. But as for the dinner, we were just catching up."

Zoe couldn't let it go. "Still . . . a date."

Erin pushed an elbow into Zoe's ribs. "Anyway," she said to Nick, "if you decide you can afford him, call him—he's in the phone book. He'll straighten this out for you."

Nick and Cassie took their seats.

"Would you?" Cassie said. "Ever call him, I mean?"

"Too rich for my blood."

"Too bad. Dr. Moran seemed to like him."

Yes, she did, Nick thought. Hard to reconcile his image of Dr. Erin Moran, assistant professor, soon to be tenured, with the woman he'd just been talking to—blushing and stumbling over words and poking Zoe.

Nick wasn't sure he would have spoken so openly to Erin Moran. There was a definite divide between graduate students and professors. Zoe, independent of the university, saw Erin in a completely different light than Nick did.

Pastor Escobar made the announcements, and Nick bowed his head for the opening prayer, but he didn't really hear it. He was thinking perhaps Cassie was right, that he should have approached Moran sooner.

He had never actually discussed anything relating to God with her. Clearly he hadn't credited her with being a sister in

Christ, someone who would support him because of their shared faith. He had seen her only as a professor, one who would close ranks with Duncan Wrede. Yet he had seen her here, week after week, worshiping. He should have thought of her differently.

He was twenty-nine and still a student. Would he be able to dispense with these barriers once he got his own job?

᪻   ᪻   ᪻   ᪻

Katy and Luke had already gone to church the next morning when Cassie woke up. She found a note waiting: "Coffee's set—push ON. OJ in fridge. Bread and cereal in cabinet. Help yourself. We'll be back in time for lunch."

Cassie had her breakfast and headed to campus. She went first to Nick's office and found both Nick and Alice there. Alice was playing computer games on Nick and Izzy's PC.

"Hi," she said. Nick turned to smile, but Alice climbed off her stool and came over to grab Cassie's hand.

"Come see," she said. "I'm drawing a picture."

"Yum, nice colors, Alice. What fun to have a computer to play on."

"Do you want to try, Miss Cassie?" She hopped up into Cassie's arms. "You can. I don't mind."

"You don't call Katy 'Miss Katy,' " Cassie said. "Can't you just call me Cassie?"

Alice looked at Nick and waited.

"Katy refused," Nick explained. "It's the custom around here, what I grew up with."

"Oh." Cassie lifted pleading eyes to him. "Can't I have a dispensation as well? Every time she calls me that, I feel like I should be wearing a hoop skirt and magnolias in my hair."

Nick laughed. "Okay, but you and Katy make it hard on a poor man just trying to raise a civil daughter."

Cassie winked at Alice. "I thank you, sir," she said and dipped a bow to Nick.

He laughed again. "Southern you may not be, Miss Cassie,

but you sure have a southern woman's knack for getting her own way."

"Thank you. I'll take that as a compliment." She sat down in front of the computer and settled Alice onto her lap. "Now, shall I draw something from my home? How about a snowman?"

Alice pulled back and looked at Cassie. "I made a snowman. Last year. But it melted."

"I bet—probably by lunchtime around here. Well, here's one that won't melt so fast. Print a copy, put it by your bed, and you'll have it as long as you want. We can even make it purple."

"No, white. It has to be white."

"Then here, we'll make the shadow purple. How's that?"

Alice leaned forward, eagerly adding suggestions for the perfect winter picture.

But Cassie was having trouble concentrating. Nick had come across the room and was leaning over the central workbench, watching Cassie from behind the computer monitor. The air between them seemed to be dancing, music swirling, all on the strength of Nick's smile.

"Hey, Alice," he said, leaning closer when the picture was finished. "You try a snowman now and let Cassie come here . . . if she will."

Cassie's eyelashes fell to her cheeks, her blush deepening. She ducked a kiss to Alice's head. "Nice job, Alice."

Nick couldn't wait any longer. He came over, took Cassie's hand in his, and pulled her gently to the other side of the bench, the open shelves providing some measure of privacy. "Coward," he whispered.

"Bully," she shot back.

He ran his hands up and down her upper arms. "I'm glad you're okay. Have you been to your apartment today?"

"No."

"I'll take you later if you need to go. I don't want you going by yourself."

"Bossy too," she said.

"Protective." He pulled her into his arms. "Guarding, defending . . . it's a guy thing. You have to play along with it."

"I do, huh?"

"It's either that or the caveman routine."

"Club and all?"

"No, this—" and he pulled her into his arms and kissed her.

"Daddy?"

Alice had come around the end of the bench and was watching from a mere two feet away. "Why are you kissing Cassie?"

"Because it's so much fun. Kissing Cassie. Kissing Cassie. See? Sounds like a poem."

"Stop it," Cassie said. "Sounds like a snake, you mean."

He laughed. "No snake has ever felt this good." But he let her push him away easily enough. He picked up Alice and set her on the bench beside him. To Cassie he said, "You probably have more work today. Those tests again?"

"Yes. I should go down and study."

"You couldn't do it here?"

"Well, I guess so." She bit her lip. "You don't think—I mean, it's safe here, don't you think? At A&M?"

"Maybe we just want you to stay," he said. "Alice and I."

Cassie rubbed her foot across a scuff mark on the floor. It reminded her of the convenience store the night before. "Okay," she said.

"Great. And I have an alternative to Katy and Luke's tonight. How about my place?"

She stared. "Me? Overnight?"

He laughed again. "Ah-ha. Got you that time. That's to get even for Toby. Actually, I was hoping to work through the night. You could sleep in my apartment."

"And look after Alice?"

"Yeah, but only if you wouldn't mind."

"How's the herbicide research going? Are we almost finished?"

Nick pushed his fingers through his hair. "I think so. I've been thinking I'd pass it on to Moran."

"Why not just go to her now and get it over with? I know you're worried about Wrede finding out."

"I'd rather have everything organized first. I'll write a report tonight—before I start accusing my professor. It's too easy to think I'm getting even with Wrede for something. Too much chance for repercussions if she doesn't believe me."

"But she would."

"I don't know that. I'd rather wait. Anyway, tonight, my apartment? I'd sure appreciate it."

She didn't answer, just looked at him and grinned.

"What?" he said.

"This hardly qualifies as taking it slower, does it?"

"You mean kissing you just now?"

"I mean me spending the night at your apartment. What *would* my father say?"

"To lock the door after I leave, if he's like most fathers."

That and more, such as, "Nice guy, Cassie, and smart to be worried about you. You might want to keep your eye on this one."

Oh, Dad, if you only knew.

ஜ   ஜ   ஜ   ஜ

Cassie went out with Nick and Alice for a supper of tacos. Afterward, they drove to Cassie's apartment.

"Wait here," Nick said. "It looks safe enough—"

"The lights over the stairs are on," Cassie said.

"But I still want to be sure. Give me your key."

Cassie bit back a smile. "You're pretty bossy, aren't you?"

"Okay," Nick said, "*please* give me your key."

With exaggerated motions, Cassie reached into her purse, withdrew her key, and held it up to him, declaring with her eyes that she was doing so under duress.

It must have worried him. "I'm just trying—"

She reached across Alice and put her fingers on his lips. His concern gave her courage. "I know, and I'm glad. I think I could get used to these guy things—you know, guarding, defending . . . as long as the guy in question is you."

She sat back and watched the play of emotions on his face.

He let out a pent-up breath. "Expect a response to that later. For now, I'll check upstairs."

He disappeared into the apartment. Lights came on throughout. Then he came out on the landing and waved down to them. Cassie unbuckled Alice and helped her climb out.

"All okay?" she said at her doorway.

"Far as I can see."

Cassie walked through the apartment, wondering what she had expected. Nothing seemed disturbed, nothing out of place.

As always Alice went straight to the dollhouse.

"Daddy . . ." she said. "Look at the mommy. And the daddy, too, and the little girl. Why did Cassie do that?"

"What did she do, sweetie?"

Nick knelt beside Alice so he could see better. He rocked back abruptly onto his heels.

"Daddy?"

"Cassie, take a look."

She crouched down to see, then slumped to the floor. Someone had looped fine cord into nooses and tightened them around the necks of the mother, father, and little girl. They hung now from the rafters of the dollhouse.

"Nick . . ." She groped for his hand.

It had to be Regina—angry because Cassie had taken her place with Alice.

Nick was explaining to Alice that maybe whoever had played with Cassie's dollhouse had wanted the family to fly. "Like Peter Pan."

"Oh, Daddy. The mommy and daddy didn't fly in Peter Pan."

"Well, I don't know, then."

"Who was playing with it?"

"Someone. Let's get them down. They don't look too happy."

Cassie stumbled to the kitchen and hid her face briefly in a wet washcloth. What else had Regina done? She didn't seem bent on theft, only harm.

"You all right?" Nick said when Cassie came back into the living room.

She sat down at the computer and turned it on. The familiar start-up routine filled the screen, the Windows 95 graphics shimmering interminably while she waited for the blue screen to display her program icons.

Nothing.

She moved the cursor to find the Programs file. Still nothing.

"Nick, I can't find anything on my computer. Everthing's gone."

Nick was standing behind her. "Everything?"

"Look." She felt panic rising. "Nick, all my work, everthing I've entered . . ."

"Easy, now. Whoever did this might just have entered a delete command, in which case all we need is a good utilities disk to get everything back."

"*Might* have just entered a delete command? What's the alternative?"

"If they crashed the entire hard drive, your operating system wouldn't be working." He rubbed her shoulders. "Let's try retrieving your files before getting too worried. Do you have a utilities disk?"

"No."

"I do at home. For now, I suggest we pack up your computer and the dollhouse and anything else you wouldn't want to lose and get out of here."

She sat limp, as if in a dream. From behind her, Nick ran his hands up and down her arms, trying to rouse her.

"Now, Cassie, get some boxes. I'll call Zoe and ask if we can store some things at her house. And Luke will come help. Let's get going."

Two hours later everything of value in the apartment had been packed into boxes and carried down to the pickup. The furniture would stay.

"If you'll drive her to Zoe's and help her unload," Nick said to Luke, "I'll drive Alice on home. She's ready for bed."

"I'll bring Cassie back to your place. Ready, Cassie?"

On the way to Zoe's, Luke glanced over at Cassie. "You okay?"

"It's just so repressive, this feeling of having someone after us."

"I know. I keep checking to be sure no one's following us."

Cassie swung around in alarm.

"There isn't," Luke said quickly. "But it's hard to keep perspective, I know."

Cassie scrunched back against the seat. The image of the hanging dolls came back to her. She felt sick, her throat tight, as if she were the one with a rope around her neck. What protection did any of them have, really, against someone like this?

🐦　🐦　🐦　🐦

Sitting on Alice's bed, Nick said, "Cassie's going to stay with you tonight. What do you think about that?"

"Jeremy has new black shoes, Daddy. I saw them at church yesterday. They have a red light that flashes. Can I have some?"

Nick smiled. Perhaps a more oblique approach. "Those porcupines you made at Cassie's house sounded good."

Alice sat up straight. "Can we make some tonight? When Cassie comes over? She said we'd make chocolate chip cookies next time. Is this next time?"

"I think she meant the next time you go to her house, honey. You might be sound asleep by the time Cassie comes tonight."

"No." Alice shook her head. "I'll stay awake."

"So you can say good night to Cassie?"

"And tell her about Jeremy's shoes."

Nick kissed Alice's forehead. "Lie down now anyway, Alice. I'll bring Cassie in when she comes."

He switched off her light as he left her room.

"I'll stay awake," she called after him.

But when Cassie came, Alice was asleep. In the glimmer of the night-light, she looked like an angel. Cassie smiled up at Nick but waited to speak until they were back in the living room.

"She's happier now, isn't she?"

"We're getting some counseling, did you know that? I caved in to Katy's badgering. We met Tuesday with someone at church—Karen Groves."

"How'd it go?"

He shrugged. "Alice was distracted the whole time. Ignored most of Karen's questions. But just before we left, she looked up at Karen and said, 'My daddy won't let me go back to Gina's. She hurt me. Daddy made the police come get her.' "

"Was that good that she said that?"

"According to Karen. I put Alice in a position to be abused—that was a betrayal—but I made things a little better by taking her away from Regina. Redeemed things, maybe."

"A betrayal?" Cassie's eyes were dark with concern. "Is that what you would call it?"

He rubbed the back of his neck wearily and shrugged again. "One thing about being a single parent. You learn pretty quick that you can't be everything your children need. With two parents, maybe there's an illusion of being sufficient. But not when we're alone. Every day is a lesson in guilt. This is just the worst."

"I'm sorry." Cassie took his hand and pulled him gently back toward Alice's room. "Look," she whispered.

Alice's golden curls were spread over her pink pillowcase. In one arm she clasped Toby, the stuffed puppy Cassie had given her. The other arm she had bent up under her face, one small hand under her rosy cheek. Her breath was easy and regular— the picture of peace.

"She's beautiful," Cassie said. "Healthy, energetic, bright. Isn't there a lesson in that, too?"

"Yes, of grace," Nick responded. "That's what it all comes down to. His grace is sufficient—"

"For His power is made perfect in weakness," Cassie finished. "Even I know that verse."

Nick smiled at Alice, shifted his gaze to Cassie, and tugged gently on her hand. "I have to go," he whispered. In the living room, he said, "Thanks, Cassie. I'll be back around eight in the morning."

"You won't sleep at all?"

"At the lab, if I need to. I'll be okay."

Nick picked up a sack from the kitchen table. "Food," he explained to Cassie and opened the door to leave. He paused and looked back at her. The room seemed suddenly very quiet, the dimmed light from the living room lamp casting a warm glow over Cassie's face. She brushed her bangs back nervously, and Nick laughed.

"No, I won't kiss you," he said. "But I'd like to. Think about that tonight as you're going to sleep."

He slipped out and down the stairs to his truck, still smiling.

At the lab, he set right to work. A couple more days on the project, and he'd have the data in shape to show someone. He still resisted going to Moran until then. Everything would be much easier if he waited.

And Duncan Wrede seemed oblivious to what Nick was doing. After the one night when Nick thought he might have seen the Cameron spectra, Wrede hadn't reacted at all. Nick now carried all the data with him wherever he went. And he scrupulously purged the GC's backup files after every use. As for Cassie, no one would ever suspect she was working with him on the project, when there were so many more interesting reasons for them to spend time together.

He was smiling as this thought occurred to him. In the past years Katy hadn't been the only one to think Nick should remarry. The prospect had also occurred to him because of Alice. But having been married once before, Nick knew better than to think marriage would solve every problem.

Attraction was easy. If that were all it took, Nick could have married three or four times since Sydney died.

But marriage required more. Real love and sacrifice, a dogged determination to make things work and to meet each other's needs in submission and generosity—that had to be there, and even then, making it work took courage and stamina. Probably the reason why things hadn't worked out with Sydney.

With Cassie the attraction was there. She was warm, generous, fun loving, and gentle, with a heart that reached out to people—even Sarah Morgan. And although her commitment to

Christ was only now beginning to take root and flourish, Nick could see God affecting her life. Even there he could find hope. For her the work would be worth it—whatever it took.

So, yes, Cassie McCormick. If you want it, I do, too. I do.

Nick opened his eyes. He was leaning against the counter in his lab, his hands holding on to the edge. He grinned. This would be a good time to pray. He bent his head forward again. *Father—*

The door swung shut behind him.

Nick spun around. Who had been there?

He opened the door and looked up and down the hall. A door clicked shut. Nick's head turned. Duncan Wrede's.

Wrede? How long had he stood at Nick's office door? Nick held his breath. What had he seen?

Nick turned and shut his lab door again, leaning weakly back against it, trying to see the room as Wrede had. His earlier assurances had obviously been wishful thinking. He had felt completely safe—how foolish. That wouldn't happen until his work had been turned in, the problem someone else's.

He looked again at what Wrede might have seen.

Nothing, he told himself. *Stop worrying.* He would only have seen him working on the GC . . . his notebook on his desk against the far wall—much too far for Wrede to see. He would assume Nick was doing the final work for his dissertation. Of course he would.

Unless he had seen that spectra all those weeks ago.

It was suddenly hard to breathe again.

❧ ❧ ❧ ❧

SUNDAY NIGHT, LATE. OUTSIDE NICK'S APARTMENT.

Yes, there was her car, parked outside Meyers' apartment. She was spending the night.

He glanced around the lot. At the far end, where he was parked, the last streetlight had burned out. Perfect cover. A short ten feet to the shrubs by the build-

ing, enough space behind them to walk comfortably.

But already? Could he take the next step so soon?

He had everything ready. The ether, the tape with the computerized voice.

How ridiculously easy it had been last night. Just one more good hand and surely he'd win.

As long as the little girl didn't wake up too soon.

❧   ❧   ❧   ❧

Cassie checked the apartment door after Nick left. It had a massive dead bolt in addition to the sturdy regular lock. Nick must have felt they'd be safe.

Cassie chased this thought away. She tried to sleep on the couch first, but as Nick had warned, it was about a foot too short for her. She picked up the quilt Nick had supplied and headed into his room, feeling awkward and intrusive, but most of all tired.

The room was smaller than Alice's. Along one wall, Nick had placed his desk and a file cabinet. The adjoining wall had a closet and small bookshelf. A single bed sat in the opposite corner, with a dresser beside it.

But no computer. *He must rely on the one at work.*

She lifted Nick's pillow off, put it on the chair in front of his desk, and put her own in its place. Still exhausted from the previous night, she was soon asleep.

She woke to hear the phone ringing. She pulled herself up to conscious thought, groggily remembered where she was, and stumbled across the room to where the phone sat on Nick's desk. The clock on his dresser said two-thirty. What could Nick be wanting?

She picked up the phone, said hello, and waited.

She heard breathing.

"Hello," she said more forcefully.

"Cassie. Cassie."

She almost dropped the phone. The Voice. She couldn't feel anything in her hands, and her palms were sweaty.

"Who is this?"

"Cassie. Cassie."

She forced herself to listen. Luke was right. The inflection was all wrong. This was a computerized message, each syllable disjointed and random.

"I'm hanging up! Do you hear me? I'm—"

The Voice was speaking again. She missed the first word but caught the rest: "—is Alice?"

"What?"

"Where is Alice? Where is Alice?"

The Voice droned on and on, but Cassie wasn't listening anymore. She dropped the phone and ran into Alice's room.

An empty bed, sheet pulled back, pillow and blanket missing.

Where *was* Alice?

Sixteen

Cassie gripped the edge of the empty bed. She couldn't focus. Her pulse was throbbing, surging, and she felt dizzy. Where was Alice? The question crowded her brain, pounded around, pushing up and out and against her skull. She couldn't stand it. She was going to faint. The darkness rose around her and in her—

No! She shook her head. She couldn't. She had to find Alice.

The bathroom? Could Alice be in the bathroom? The kitchen, then.

The apartment was too small for Alice to be hiding anywhere, but Cassie looked anyway. Under the couch, behind Nick's bedroom door, under both beds.

Crouched beside Alice's bed again, Cassie curled herself into a little ball and hugged her knees desperately against her chest, one hand pushing the top of her skull down.

The Voice. The Voice had taken Alice. Had come into the apartment while she was sleeping and carried Alice away. How had this person kept Alice quiet? Why hadn't Cassie woken up?

That voice. *Cassie, Cassie.* Inhuman, vile, horrible voice.

"Where are you, Alice?" she cried aloud. The shock waves from the sound reverberated through the small apartment.

She would have to call Nick. Nick—

Oh, God, I can't bear this. What would Nick think of her now? *Help me.*

She picked up the phone reluctantly, began to dial, and

heard the Voice still droning on.

"Where is she?" Cassie screamed into the receiver. "Bring her back, you worm, you beast, you wretched, sick person."

Inhuman, unhearing, the Voice droned on.

Cassie tried hanging up, but she couldn't break the connection from her end. She considered driving to the lab, then remembered Katy and Luke.

But—outside? She would have to walk around the building. There were shadows and bushes and who knows what, waiting. . . .

She covered her cheeks with her hands, then tried the phone again. Still talking, taunting.

Well, fine then. Outside.

Like Esther, if she perished she perished, but she would not let him win without a fight.

She had never undressed for bed, not wanting Nick to come in and find her, so all she needed was to thrust her bare feet into tennis shoes. The door made her pause. Would it lock, leaving her trapped alone, outside in the dark? What if by some disaster Luke and Katy weren't home?

She left the door open, rushed down the stairs inside the building, then shrank back at the door leading outside. Lights flooded the parking lot and extended to the walkway that circled the building. Lights that would reveal her, expose her to watching eyes . . . somewhere.

She almost ran back upstairs, but there the Voice waited.

So into the chilly November air. A gust of wind struck her as she stepped outside. She shivered and began to run, and even inside and up the stairs outside Katy and Luke's door she couldn't stop shaking. She stood pounding and calling until Luke opened the door; then she almost fell into the apartment. Luke was in pajama bottoms and a T-shirt and was pulling on a robe.

"She's gone!" Cassie cried. "She's gone." And before his astonished eyes, she slammed the door shut and crumpled down into a huddled ball against the door.

He knelt beside her. "What is it, Cassie? What's the matter?"

Katy was standing at the bedroom door. She came quickly across the room to put her arm around Cassie.

"You look awful. What's happened, Cassie? Where's Alice?"

"Alice," Cassie gasped. She grabbed Luke's arm and hung on. "Someone took Alice. I picked up the phone, the Voice again—'Cassie, Cassie'—and Alice wasn't there. Her bed. I have to call Nick."

She stumbled to the kitchen, and Katy followed her to the phone.

"What do mean she's gone? Who took her?"

But Nick had already answered. Somehow she managed to tell what happened in straight sequence, but when she told about the empty bed, he stopped her.

"She's really not there—anywhere? The bathroom?"

"I looked everywhere."

"I'm coming home," he said. "Call the police. They'll have to help this time."

Cassie held the phone out weakly to Luke. "He said call the police. I don't think I can."

"Katy will. I'm going to look around outside."

Katy took the phone and began dialing. Cassie collapsed onto the kitchen floor and pressed her cheek against the lower cabinet door. It felt cool against her hot skin. She hadn't ever noticed before that the cabinets were metal. How tacky. Were they the same in Nick's apartment?

"Cassie?"

She forced her eyelids open. Katy looked so worried.

"Come on. We'll go back to Nick's apartment. The person who's doing this might call again."

"What?"

"Cassie, we should go back to Nick's apartment."

She let Katy pull her up and followed along behind. Down the stairs, outside again, through the light, the shadows, her feet making scrunching noises across the concrete walk.

The Voice might call again? No. Nick was coming back. What would he say?

As Cassie climbed the stairs behind Katy, the open door

waited, waited, offering a mixture of dread and hope, but the apartment was quiet, like a tomb—empty, but no joy.

Katy pushed her toward Nick's couch and wrapped a quilt around her. "You're frozen. I'm making you some coffee. Cassie?"

"What?"

"Sit down, Cassie."

"Oh. Okay."

She felt Katy hug her. "It will be okay, Cassie. You'll see. The police will come."

"But her kitty. Nick said a knife—oh, Katy, where is she?"

"No, no, no." Katy put a cool palm against each of Cassie's flushed cheeks. "Not like the kitty. Alice is in God's hands. You'll see."

Outside, a car screeched into the parking lot. Footsteps pounded up the apartment stairs and Nick burst into the room. He looked first at Cassie and Katy and then forged across to Alice's room. He didn't go in. His hands gripped the molding around the door for a long, agonizing moment and then he swung around again and looked at Cassie.

"You sure she's not here?"

"Nick," Katy said.

He lifted his hand in a brief apology and went into his own room.

Luke came in the front door. "I looked outside—couldn't see anything."

Cassie stumbled up from the couch and stood at Nick's bedroom door. He was holding the telephone receiver in his hand. She could hear the dial tone from there.

"They hung up," she said.

Nick nodded. His eyes had a tight look to them, as if his perspective on life had suddenly become small and private. He lifted the receiver, put it carefully back in place, then turned his gaze on Cassie.

"I'm sorry," she cried. "I'm so sorry."

"No, no, don't. Don't, Cassie." He lifted his hand, made a small beckoning sound, and she stumbled into his arms. "Don't blame yourself. We'll get through this."

Again footsteps on the stairs.

"It's the police," Katy said from the doorway.

Nick let his arms drop, squared his shoulders, and stepped around Cassie and into the living room.

But it was Cassie they wanted to talk to. They took her story down and called in for backup. More police came, this time detectives. They introduced themselves as Michael Buchinsky and Eddie Gardner. Cassie told her story again, and then again, and with each telling the police became more assertive. She knew they were beginning to suspect her.

Nick was standing behind Cassie at the kitchen table. His hands massaged her shoulders. "Are you sure it's not Regina Poole?" he said to the police. "She's the one who set up that stunt last night. And my tires. I reported that."

The two detectives exchanged glances.

"Regina Poole left town yesterday," Eddie Gardner said.

"She broke her bail?"

"Exactly."

"But she might still be in Bryan. You didn't actually see her leave town."

Gardner shook his head. "She's not likely to stay. We believe she's headed east, to the Louisiana border."

"But you don't know," Nick said again.

"You want your daughter back, Mr. Meyers? Then let us do our job."

"But why are you interrogating Cassie like this? She hasn't done anything wrong."

"It's all right," Cassie told Nick. She reached up to clasp his hand. "If it'll help to go through it all again, it'll be worth it."

But neither man seemed interested in asking her anything more. Eddie Gardner crossed his arms, leaned back, and stared absently across the room. And Michael Buchinsky began tapping his pencil against the table. He flipped it over and tapped it again, over and over. Cassie watched it, growing mesmerized . . . over, tap, flip, tap, over and over. It saved thinking about—

She banished the thought and concentrated on the pencil,

letting her mind get foggier and foggier.

Michael Buchinsky's voice broke into her reverie. "You know," he said, "whoever's doing this has quite a proficiency with locks. Broke into Ms. McCormick's apartment yesterday. Broke in here tonight. I wonder if Regina Poole has a locksmith somewhere in her background."

Gardner nodded. "Maybe an illegal locksmith."

"Which would mean a record. Let's get Jamahl working on that. He knows how to tweak all those computer records."

Nick took his hands from Cassie's shoulders and leaned sideways against the wall. "I've been wondering . . ."

Michael Buchinsky looked up from his notes. "Yeah. What?"

"Why did Regina call tonight? If she was so intent—" He swallowed and grew very still, gathered his strength, and spoke again. "If she was intent on keeping Alice . . . hurting her . . . why didn't she give herself more time to get away?"

No one said anything. Cassie could hear Nick breathing. Shallow breaths, cautious, careful.

"Go on," Buchinsky said.

Nick cleared his throat before he spoke. "Friday night, whoever did that at Cassie's apartment stayed in the shadows. You know? Nearby. Out of danger. No one was actually in her apartment when she came home."

"You know this?"

"We think so. And whoever did this tonight—I still think Regina or maybe someone connected to her—this person wanted to make trouble, but nothing too serious, nothing that would put her in danger."

"Taking your little girl's pretty serious," Buchinsky broke in.

"And Regina Poole is basically a coward," Nick said. "She abuses children, after all. She doesn't want to be caught. Take Alice, sure. Scare us, absolutely. Become the object of a statewide manhunt? Not a chance."

Eddie Gardner grunted. Michael Buchinsky rubbed his chin. To Cassie, neither seemed convinced.

"I'm right, aren't I?" Nick said. "This is more serious?"

"Of course," Gardner said, "but I'm not sure I get your point."

"That's why she called. So we would find Alice pretty quickly. I think she's nearby, close. I'm sure of it."

"Alice, you mean?" Gardner said.

"Yes. Alice."

"Like tied up, you mean," Buchinsky said, "mouth taped, stashed into a hiding place somewhere?"

Cassie felt Nick's hand on her shoulder again, this time gripping it. She glanced up over her shoulder. His face had grown noticeably pale. "You are at least searching outside?" he said.

Gardner nodded. "Yes. We've got men out there."

Nick pushed off from the wall. "I'll go help."

"Me too," said Luke.

Buchinsky shook his head. "Stay put. You'll only get in the way."

Nick leaned his head back against the wall and closed his eyes.

Cassie thought he must be praying. On the wall above him, the flashing lights from the police cars were giving everything a surrealistic effect, like a strobe light in some weird drama. She shuddered at the thought of Alice in a small dark place.

Well, this time she would pray as well. What was it Job said? *I know that my Redeemer lives . . . I know that my Redeemer lives.*

She let the words sweep through her mind like fresh air on a house too long closed and dormant. *Please, God . . . Redeemer . . . save us.*

One of the uniformed police came in with a message for the detectives. Even with the prayer, Cassie couldn't bear to stay still. She walked across the room toward the window. Below them, police were moving around the edges of the parking lot, bending down to look under cars, checking with flashlights behind bushes. Residents from other apartments stood in their doorways, clutching their coverings in the chilly night air. It all seemed so hopeless. If Alice were out there, wouldn't they have found her already? How many places could there be?

She blinked. Her gaze again swept over the figures searching between the cars. Perhaps . . .

"Nick," she said, "I have an idea."

Nick's head came up. "What, Cassie?"

She went back to the table and faced the detectives. "About the locks . . . well, there really aren't that many places to hide Alice. The bushes, I suppose. Everything else is pretty exposed. But if I knew how to pick a lock . . ."

Nick gripped her arm. "A car," he said.

"Yeah," Gardner echoed. "In the trunk. Ah, shoot, you got those picks on you, Chintzy?"

"What about my car?" Cassie said. "I mean, to taunt us."

"Not his?" Gardner said. "Wouldn't that be more likely?"

Nick was already at the door. "I have a pickup. Come on. What are we waiting for?"

Alice was there, curled up in the trunk of Cassie's Skylark, her pink pillow under her head, her blanket around her, as if the trunk of the car were the coziest place in the world to sleep. Cassie shivered in the night air. This time Alice's stuffed puppy was spared. It lay next to her body, but she wasn't holding it.

In fact . . . her hands were slack, her neck oddly tilted.

A strangled sound came from Nick's throat. "Is she—?"

Buchinsky was taking a pulse at Alice's neck. "Asleep. Just asleep. Probably drugged." He leaned closer and sniffed. "Ether. You can smell it. Call for an ambulance, Eddie. She should see a doctor."

Nick stepped forward to pick her up, but Gardner held him back. "She's okay where she is for a minute or two more. Step back, everyone. Let the crime-scene guys have a go at this."

"You think she's hurt?" Nick asked Buchinsky. "You said a hospital."

"To check her out, don't you think? Just to be safe?"

Cassie touched Nick's arm and he pulled her against him. "She's okay, Nick. She's asleep. Look. She doesn't know any of this is going on."

Nick's breathing was labored. Calm during the crisis, but now that Alice had been found, he seemed ready to panic.

It was less than five minutes before the ambulance came, another five minutes after that when they moved Alice onto a stretcher and into the ambulance. It must have felt like a lifetime to Nick. When the ambulance left, he went with it.

Detective Buchinsky was over near Cassie's car, talking to one of the other policemen, but as Cassie stepped back after the ambulance drove out of the parking lot, she found Eddie Gardner watching her. Luke stepped closer to Cassie and put his arm across her shoulders, and Katy took Cassie's other side, her arm around Cassie's waist.

A united front. Cassie smiled, tears close. Their support was comforting, especially given what Gardner was probably thinking.

"I suppose finding her in the trunk of my car makes me look even more of a suspect," she said.

"No." Gardner rubbed his forehead, and for the first time since arriving at Nick's apartment, he laughed. "Truth is, Ms. McCormick, I can't figure out a motive for you to do this. We pulled up the file on your complaint Friday night. We figured maybe you were trying to get Meyers' attention—you know, make a play for him. Women have done worse to catch a man's eye. But from what I see, the guy's already plenty interested. More than interested, I'd say. So why would you pull something like this?"

Cassie couldn't think of anything to say. She knew what the police had thought. Exactly what the Voice had wanted. His efforts had succeeded with the police, but not—*thank you, God*—with Nick.

Then Gardner's words sank in. If even a police detective could see how Nick felt, surely Cassie herself could begin to believe she wasn't dreaming.

She looked up at Luke and Katy, who were both grinning. Katy squeezed Cassie's waist.

"Can we go now?" Luke asked.

"We have a little more work to do in Meyers' apartment,

looking for evidence, but your apartment's nearby, right? We'll catch you there if we need you."

"I'll go wait at Nick's," Luke said, "just to make sure everything's okay. You two try to get some sleep."

Cassie followed Katy to their apartment. She thought she'd never be able to relax, but she was asleep within minutes.

Seventeen

Monday morning, Cassie opened her eyes to a silent, empty apartment. This time Katy had left a longer note for her: "When you're done, Nick wants to talk to you. Alice woke up in the ambulance. They kept her awhile and let Nick bring her home. She looks okay! Unless it's after lunch—in which case you must have really been tired!—he's still home with Alice. Go see him."

Cassie stumbled to the bathroom, took a quick shower, and hurried to Nick's apartment. But when Nick opened the door, he still looked worried and weary. "What's happened?" she asked.

"Problems," Nick said. "I came home from the lab in such a hurry last night that I left my notebook and the copies of spectra where they were. I remembered them on the way home from the hospital and stopped by to pick them up. They were gone."

"On the Cameron study? *Those* spectra?"

He glanced at Alice. She was watching them, alerted perhaps by the tone of their voices. "Go make some coffee," Nick said to Cassie. "I'll get her settled with a video."

"*Beauty and the Beast*!" Alice said.

"Sure, sure," Nick agreed, "but you might not get to watch it all. No complaints if I have to turn it off."

Alice was already settling herself into Nick's big armchair. With the video running, Nick came to Cassie in the kitchen. The coffee was dripping.

"The spectra?" Cassie reminded him. "Are they all gone?"

"Not all of them. Only the copies I reduced for my notebook."

Cassie leaned heavily back against the counter. "Well, that's okay. You can collect the data again—I think I could recognize dioxin on a spectra in my sleep."

"I'm not worried about reproducing the work. But I've been thinking." He frowned at the floor. "What if we're all wrong about who's behind this? What if it's Wrede, not Regina? And it's because of the falsified data?"

Cassie poured two mugs of coffee. "Here," she said. "I think we could both use some of this. Now, tell me what you're thinking."

He leaned back against the wall. "First, there's the tape in your apartment. It must have had a motion detector attached to it. When you came into the kitchen, it switched on. That would be easy for an electronics buff like Wrede. And the ether. We've got that all over the chemistry building. And the expertise with locks? And messing up your computer? I didn't know Regina Poole well, but I doubt she could come up with such sophisticated schemes and actually pull them off."

"But what would Wrede hope to gain?"

"He must have seen the Cameron spectra that first weekend in my lab. He didn't want to do anything drastic—he's the kind of guy who'd have stayed in the shadow of his mama's apron if he could have. He just wanted the problem to go away—which meant getting rid of me."

Cassie shook her head. "You think he was at my apartment and took Alice?"

"Regina may have been the one, actually, to slash my tires. That gave him the idea. If things got bad enough, finishing my degree would be the logical way to get away from her. She'd never follow me—her resentment wouldn't reach that far. He probably counted on me blowing off the herbicide problem completely and concentrating on my dissertation. He's been making it easy for me to finish ever since the dioxin problem surfaced this summer."

Cassie held her palms to her cheeks. "Okay. He finds out about the herbicide research. He wants to chase you out of town, so he makes it look like Regina's harassment is getting worse. But why me? Did he know about my part in the research?"

His eyes softened. "Because he could see I was beginning to care for you. He knew he could scare me most by harassing you and Alice."

He held out his hand to her. She hesitated for only a moment and then she was tucked up beside him, her cheek pressed against the rough knit of his shirt.

"And it helped make it look more like Regina was behind it," he said, "since you were the one who took over that part of Alice's baby-sitting. Remember? It was in the paper."

She shuddered. "Maybe showing your data to Moran will make him stop."

"I hope so." He reached over for the phone and punched in Erin's number. After a brief conversation, he hung up. "She agreed to see us in half an hour."

"You didn't explain why?"

"I thought that could wait until we saw her. I just wish she were already tenured. If this could cause me trouble in my career, it could do the same for her."

"She'll know how to handle it, you'll see."

He tilted his head toward Cassie, his eyes warm again. "Thank you. I can't tell you how much it means to have you here."

She smiled and ducked her head.

"Hey," he said. "Looks like things got speeded up for us, anyway. Are you okay?"

She crunched a fistful of shirt into her hand. His body beneath the shirt was firm, his cheek against her forehead scratchy. Such small assurances that this wasn't a dream, but so necessary. She rubbed her forehead against his chin, reveling in the roughness and felt his kiss burrowing in between her bangs.

"Cassie?"

She slipped her face down into the hollow of his neck. "I

was afraid. It seemed impossible to believe that you would ever care. That you ever could. And when Alice disappeared, I thought you'd blame me."

"No."

"But instead you were worried about me, even with Alice gone. You stood up for me."

"What would I gain if I got Alice back and lost you in the process?"

She drew back to look at him. "Greedy man. Luke said one time that you were tenacious."

"He did?"

"Yeah, way back when I still thought you were a cowboy."

"Well, if I'm a cowboy, it's time to choose up sides for the OK Corral. Come on, Alice. Time to go."

Erin Moran was in her office. She motioned for them to take seats. Her hair was pulled back into a loose braid. An oatmeal-colored sweater topped brown slacks and leather shoes. Eminently practical, yet still graceful and feminine.

After Nick explained, Erin looked worried.

She pulled her chair closer to her desk, crossed her arms, and rested them on the surface. "No small thing you're claiming here, Nick."

"Can you help us?"

"I'll certainly try." She frowned. "You really think he was in Cassie's apartment Friday night? Isn't that reaching a little?"

Nick explained how they had come to that conclusion. "And last night, the ether, the same voice on the telephone, and my notebook with the analysis of the Cameron spectra. It was missing when I got back to the lab. Who besides Wrede would have taken it?"

"You have a backup on the spectra?"

"In my backpack. And he didn't get all of the suspect spectra anyway—only copies, reduced to fit in my notebook."

"And I have some of the missing analysis," Cassie added.

Erin's gaze shifted to Cassie. "Ah, I see. You were helping Nick with the analysis."

Cassie nodded.

"And you didn't think I'd want to know about this, Nick?"

Alice had been sitting on Nick's lap. She was beginning to squirm, perhaps because of the gathering tension in the room. He pulled a puzzle out of her bag and laid it on the floor for her to do. Only then did he respond to Erin. "Yes, of course, but I wanted to be sure. This wasn't the kind of thing to throw around on a whim."

"No kidding. The federal government hands out stiff penalties for falsifying environmental reports—I just saw something on TV about an apple juice bottler somewhere on the East Coast. He was facing a possible twenty years in prison, I think, and according to the newscaster it sounded like he hadn't done anything intentional or even harmful. Who knows what Duncan would get? He's in big trouble if you're right." She held out a hand. "Let me see what you have."

Cassie passed over copies of her analysis to date.

Erin lapsed into thought, the fingers of one hand drumming softly on the desk top. No one said anything.

She finally looked up. "You're sure of these results?"

Cassie nodded.

"And Cameron's expecting approval?"

"Though in fairness," Nick said, "Cassie seems pretty certain it was just the one batch of herbicide that was bad."

"Most likely a problem in production," Cassie explained.

Erin again took a few minutes to think. She let out a long, slow breath and stopped drumming. "Okay," she said. "What you say makes sense. The question is, now what?"

"We thought—" Nick lifted his shoulders. "You would know."

"Oh." Erin leaned back and crossed her arms. "Sure. Carry on secretly, all on the sly, using one of my students, no less, and now you want me to bail you out." But she was smiling. "This must be the price of authority, though I think I'll pass the buck. In the meantime, I mentioned Sam Devereaux last night, Nick.

Why don't I call him and see what he says?"

"You mean about the data?"

"No, no. I know what to do with that. Or at least that's not where Sam can help us. It's the other. This person who's harassing you. Sam can find out about that."

"You don't think it's Wrede?"

Erin tapped her thumbs together. "Let's say I can believe he falsified data—and hope he did it unintentionally. You say you have evidence for that. But this other stuff—taking Alice and breaking into your apartments—you're just guessing on that. Sam could help find out who's really behind it."

"But you said it would cost money to hire him."

She smiled. "If I ask him, he might give us a . . . well, let's call it a free consultation. Sam owes me for those tutoring sessions in high school anyway, even if they didn't do him any good."

She made the phone call and sat back again. "He'll be over in about twenty minutes. So. You had quite a night."

"What will you do about the herbicides?" Nick asked.

"I'll call the department chair," Erin said. "We've worked together on committees, and he's a good man. Fair and honest. I'll do just as you have with me. Pass the information on, and let him decide what to do with it. Wherever this buck stops, it's not on my desk."

"Will this hold you back on tenure?" Cassie asked.

Erin shrugged. "These things have a way of sorting themselves out, some people would say by chance. I prefer to believe it's God, working out His justice. Slow sometimes, but certain. We can be sure of one thing anyway—we can't let possibly dangerous herbicides out on the market. Not when there are relatively safe alternatives."

Erin paused and cocked her head toward Nick. "You know, you could use Wrede's eagerness to get you out of here to your advantage. Ask to move up your dissertation defense. Make a great show of working on your writing. Push hard to finish quickly. Wrede will probably support you in that. He'll think his plan has worked. He won't know that I have the data. I could wait to move forward on that until after you defend your research."

"You would do that?"

"It's this other thing that worries me—the harassment. Ah, this is probably Sam."

Sam Devereaux was a little over average height—perhaps five eleven—and he had a receding hairline and scruffy hair, as if the only comb he'd used that morning were his fingers. His face was thin and sharp, and his jaw stubby with beard. He must have looked a little frightening to Alice, who climbed up again into Nick's lap, but when Sam reached across to shake Cassie's hand, his eyes shone with a depth of humor and charm that made Cassie instantly feel at ease. Even his cheeks had smile lines.

"Sam Devereaux," he said to Nick. "I guess you've had a hard night here. I heard about your daughter on the police band."

"Oh?"

Sam laughed. "No, I don't usually make a habit of staying up to listen to police radio. I was on a stakeout. I tune in when I'm doing that, just to know what's happening. I had no idea the little girl was connected to Erin."

He propped himself against the wall. Nick got up to offer his chair, though he looked equally weary, but Sam shook his head. "After being up all night, believe me, I'll be more alert if I stand. Okay, what can I do for you?"

"We need some advice," Erin said. "Nick, tell him what you told me."

"About the data, or about Cassie and Friday night?"

"Everything," Erin said.

Once again, Nick related the story. When he had finished, Sam scratched his chin, caught the others watching him, and grinned, his face transformed by humor. "Didn't have time to shave. Stuff sure gets scratchy." He held up his hands. "Okay. Here's what I suggest, though you're not going to like it. Call the police. Tell them what you told me. Gardner and Buchinsky, they're good guys. Family men. Hardworking. They'll sort it out for you."

The others stared back at him. Even Erin seemed surprised.

"What?" Sam said. "You think that's a bad idea? Well, consider this—and I get the idea graduate students are a little hard up—these guys you've already paid for. Me? I'd bring in a fresh bill for you."

"The police think Cassie did it," Nick said.

"Nah. They may have considered it, but I sincerely doubt they're holding on to that theory. Look, I know this probably isn't what you were hoping for, but it's your best bet. Call them, tell them the whole story, and if you still think they won't come through for you, I'll come back. But try them first." He pushed off from the wall, looked around the office, and nodded. "This is nice, Erin. I like the Monet prints. Don't forget, I'm always up for dinner again, anytime."

Erin stumbled as she stood up. "I'll . . . I'll just see him out, okay?"

After they left, Nick stood and reached across Erin's desk for the phone. "Might as well call Gardner. I'll see if Luke can watch Alice while we go over to the police station."

꙲   ꙲   ꙲   ꙲

The two detectives took Nick and Cassie into a conference room at the police station and indicated chairs for them, but only Gardner sat down. Nick wondered if police instinctively positioned themselves to give a height advantage or whether this was something they learned in their training.

It took them a while to fully understand Nick's story, but when they did, Buchinsky and Gardner exchanged glances.

Buchinsky rolled his eyes. "You didn't think you should mention this to anyone?"

"I might as well call in Lopez and Orben," Gardner said. "Hold on to your hats."

"Lopez and Orben?" Nick said. "Why them?"

"Come on, think, man. Sarah Morgan, of course. If you're right and this guy Wrede is willing to cook up this kind of stunt to chase you out of town, why not pull something a little more serious on the other woman? Maybe she knew, too."

"And there's the money," Cassie said.

Buchinsky gave her a sharp look. "You know about that?"

"What money?" Nick said.

"Quarter of a million, give or take." Cassie heard Nick's startled murmur and nodded. "Eliot Ross told me. Sarah's bank balance was much larger than anyone expected, by at least a hundred thousand dollars. Maybe she was blackmailing Wrede."

"See?" Buchinsky said. "It makes sense he might have murdered her."

"Where would Wrede get that kind of money?" Nick protested.

"From the chemical company, I suppose. You thought they might be paying him off."

Nick considered this for a moment. Now it made even more sense to him that Wrede had trod lightly when he found out Nick was reproducing the spectra. Something more drastic would have exposed his motive for murdering Sarah.

"How about your little girl?" Buchinsky asked. "She okay now?"

"Yes. She slept, but not too long. You know, the timing was so tight, finding her like that just before she woke up. I've been wondering if Wrede would have called again if we hadn't found her in time."

"You're pretty sure he did it?"

"Yes, now."

"How would he have known we hadn't found her?"

Nick scowled. "Maybe a listening device?"

"Huh . . . a bug. Maybe."

"Too farfetched? He is into electronics, big time. A real gadget man."

"Well . . ." Buchinsky shrugged. "I suppose we could check."

"Look," Nick said, "he wanted to scare me, not her, and he did call to let us know she was gone."

"For her sake? You're giving him a lot of credit."

"I have my little girl back, Detective." Nick rubbed his forehead, the memory of the night apparently coming back in force. "I don't like what he did to her—or to Cassie, if he was the one—but both could have been so much worse."

Cassie held up her hand. "But how did he get her away in the first place? Surely I would have heard her cry."

"He probably used a mask with a portable flask for the ether," Buchinsky said. "Can she remember anything?"

"No."

"Might have nightmares, though." He must have seen Nick flinch. His face softened. "I have two daughters myself. They're pretty tough."

"I hope so," Nick said. "She's had a hard couple of months."

Gardner came back with Orben and Lopez.

"Go ahead," Gardner said, wincing a little. "Tell them what you told us."

As Nick finished, Orben scraped his chair violently back from the table, almost knocking it to the floor. What he had to say to Nick was even more expressive than his actions.

"You should have told us earlier," Lopez agreed, more mildly than his partner.

"What're you being so nice for?" Orben nearly shouted. "We should have *these* two arrested for obstructing justice."

Buchinsky and Gardner were noticeably silent.

Orben thrust his hand through his hair and groaned. "Do you know how much time we've wasted because you didn't have enough sense to tell us about this earlier? Not to mention saving you a little agony, as well. Huh? Did you think about that?"

Nick struggled to keep his voice even. "I . . . I'm sorry. I just didn't connect the two. Falsifying data—it's an academic thing, white collar. Not like murder."

Orben slapped his hand against the table. "Well, start thinking now! Like how much money this company would have saved. And how much money Wrede might have gotten. I'd have asked for a couple hundred thousand dollars, at least. And what about his tenure? He'd have wanted to protect that. None of this occurred to you? Let me tell you, Bubba, for a supposedly smart man, Ph.D. and all that, you sure were dumb."

Nick shrugged. "The timing was bad."

Cassie explained. "The Monday after Sarah was killed, his daughter came home from her day care with a broken leg."

"Yeah." Lopez nodded. "We heard about that. If you're right, it all played into Wrede's hands."

"*You* played into his hands," Orben grumbled.

"Mmm. I'm just wondering . . ." Nick paused.

"What?"

"Are you going to be able to trace any of this to him? Actually prove that he did this, either taking Alice last night or killing Sarah Morgan? How long is this going to go on?"

Orben scowled. "Let me tell you, if you'd only—"

"Maybe," Lopez broke in. "This gives us some more leads."

Orben stormed up from his chair. "Come on, Drigo. Let's get out of here before I break something."

Buchinsky and Gardner, sitting almost primly on their chairs, waited until the other two men left.

Gardner breathed out slowly. "Orben in a temper is something to see."

"Better Lopez than me," Buchinsky agreed. He saw the expressions on Cassie's and Nick's faces and grinned. "Don't worry. This kind of stuff happens all the time, witnesses holding the key to the entire investigation and not putting two and two together. He'll get over it."

Nick shrugged. "But what I said . . . about proving anything. What can we do? I'm afraid Alice isn't safe, or Cassie, and I don't feel invulnerable myself."

"What's happening with the data thing?" Gardner asked.

"I've already turned over the results I have to a professor," Nick said. "She's going to deal with it."

Cassie leaned forward. "We're hoping to convince Wrede he's won. Nick will abandon the herbicide research and concentrate on his dissertation. Move up his defense, try to get out of here by Christmas."

"You can do that?"

"If Wrede cooperates—and since it was his idea to rush me out of here, we figured he would."

Buchinsky stood up. "Well, that's a start. We might get a break. You never know."

Eighteen

Katy was home from her Monday night class by the time Nick and Cassie came to pick up Alice, who was ready for bed. Instead of eating out, Nick put Alice down on Katy and Luke's bed, and they finished a chicken casserole that Katy had pulled out of the freezer.

"They think Wrede killed Sarah?" Katy said.

"Think about it," Nick explained. "Means, motive, opportunity. And if he's behind the harassment, he's got the personality for it, too. Have you noticed how whoever's behind this doesn't want any kind of face-to-face confrontation? Poison. Taped messages. A frightening abduction but quickly concluded. Wrede has always ducked confrontation—he leaves notes with instructions, for example, and never quite looks you in the eye when he is delivering criticism firsthand."

Katy shuddered. "I wonder what he'll do now."

Luke nodded. "I only hope the police can move fast on getting evidence against him."

"Until then, Cassie can stay with us," Katy said.

"Thank you."

Nick stood up. "That can be my exit cue. We could all use some sleep."

"Wait," Luke said. "Let's pray before you go."

After Luke finished, Nick got Alice from the spare bedroom and motioned with a smile for Cassie to follow him out onto the landing. He pulled the door shut behind him, winking at Katy's grin. Holding Alice against his shoulder with one arm, he pulled Cassie closer with the other. She felt the warmth of his breath against her hair and heard the peace in his sigh. Alice stirred between them but didn't wake.

"I'd better let you go," he said.

She stood where she was, unwilling to leave the comfort of his embrace.

"Go," he said. "I have lots to say, but this isn't the time. Get some sleep. I'll see you tomorrow. Come over for breakfast, if you want. I usually try to get Alice to stay in bed until seven, so . . . seven-thirty?"

But the next morning, when Cassie went over to Nick's apartment, he didn't look as if he had slept much. Though he had already shaved, his hair was still somewhat rumpled, and he didn't have his shoes on yet. "Come on in," he said. He looked around the apartment distractedly. "We're getting a late start this morning."

Cassie grinned. "How do you know? With your schedule, I wonder sometimes how you keep track of when you're supposed to eat."

"Uh, yeah, well, don't worry. I remember."

Alice pulled on his shirttail. "I'm hungry now, Daddy."

He looked vaguely toward the kitchen.

"I see your method," Cassie said. "You have Alice to remind you."

"Daddy . . ."

Nick didn't respond.

What was he thinking about? Cassie wondered.

"Come on, Alice, I'll get you some cereal," she said. "Show me where."

When she turned back toward the table, he was still standing by his bedroom door. "Nick, are you all right?"

He thrust his fingers through his hair. "Tired, I guess. I didn't get much sleep. I got to thinking about how much he knew. . . ." His voice trailed off again.

"Pretty frightening," Cassie agreed.

"I wonder . . ."

She emptied corn flakes into Alice's bowl, sprinkled sugar over them, and reached for the milk.

"Thing is," he was saying and then his words broke off.

The next thing she knew he was jerking the milk jug from her hand. Liquid slopped onto the table beside Alice.

"Nick," she protested.

As if in slow motion, Cassie saw Alice dip her finger into the spill . . . raise it to her lips—

"Don't!" Nick yelled. He yanked Alice up and pulled her into the bathroom. She began crying in fear.

"What, Daddy? I'm sorry, Daddy."

Cassie could hear the water running. Nick emerged, hugging Alice to him. Alice's hand was dripping.

"I'm sorry, sweetheart. I'm sorry. I just don't want you to be hurt."

"But, Daddy!" she wailed.

He shook her gently. "Come on, sweetheart. See? I'm not mad. I'll tell you what. Why don't we eat out this morning? Pancakes at IHOP? What do you say?"

Alice sniffed. Her lower lip was trembling.

Nick pulled her close again. "Sweetheart, I'm sorry. Did I hurt your feelings? I love you."

Cassie hadn't moved from where she was standing over the table. She stepped slowly away, still confused.

Nick saw it but didn't explain. "Let Cassie put on your shoes, Alice. I'll find mine and we'll go."

But before disappearing into his bedroom, he turned again. "Dump that milk down the drain."

"Okay, Nick. Anything you say."

"And don't drink anything—orange juice, coffee. Or eat anything."

Stranger and stranger . . .

❧ ❧ ❧ ❧

"Now," she said, once they were settled in the restaurant, "tell me what you were thinking."

Alice had insisted on sitting next to Cassie, though she had perked up slightly when Nick let her order chocolate chip pancakes. She was still pressed up against Cassie's side but was apparently absorbed in coloring her place mat.

He nodded. "Here's the thing. Wrede doesn't know about Erin, right? So we're still the threat. The way I see it, he has two options. Either he'll run, which I sure wish he'd do. Or he'll come after us, which I'm afraid is more likely."

"And the milk this morning?"

His eyes grew more intense. "Think about it, Cassie. He knows how to get into my apartment. And yours."

"Nick!"

Alice looked up, startled by Cassie's tone.

"Don't worry, sweetheart," Nick said. "Look, here's your milk."

"Milk, Nick." This time Cassie spoke more calmly.

"Well, you know what happened to Sarah."

"You think"—Cassie swallowed—"it was the milk?"

"Or something else. How can we know?"

She shook her head. "Nick. Are you . . . do you think . . . Katy and Luke, too?" She remembered Alice and bit her lip. "Nick, what can we possibly do?"

He sucked his breath in. "I have some ideas, but we can talk about them later, okay?"

She followed his gaze around the restaurant, at the servers moving among the tables, the people at the booths—drinking coffee, talking, some of them laughing.

He smiled and nodded. "See? No problem here. No one listening. We can relax."

He reached across the table and gripped her hand. "Everything's happened so fast. Maybe for a little while, here, we can relax."

"I'll try," she said.

And for the rest of the meal, they did—almost—forget the threat hanging over them.

In the apartment parking lot, Nick zipped up Alice's coat and they all walked around to the playground. It was a chilly day, slightly overcast but with little wind. Alice took off to join the other children playing there. She seemed so different from the first time Cassie had seen her, now laughing and playful and looking over as much for Cassie's attention and approval as for Nick's.

Cassie sat on a bench and scooted closer to Nick. "You sure we're okay here?"

He winced. "Maybe. I'm sorry to worry you."

"Let's not think about Wrede. Not now."

He shook his head. "We can't forget him. I'm serious, Cassie."

"What are you thinking? Tell me what we should do."

"First, I'm calling Elizabeth."

"Alice's grandmother? Why?"

"To see if Alice can visit. I want her away from here, somewhere safe. And—don't be upset—" His eyes were dark with concern, intent and severe. "I wish you'd think about doing the same."

"Me? Go away? Where?"

"Home. Back to Illinois. Anything could happen if you stay here."

"Now you *are* scaring me, Nick."

He took her hands in his, the muscles on his forearms tightening as he held hers. Seeing the anxiety in her eyes, he leaned closer, touched his forehead briefly to hers, and drew back again.

"I'm sorry, Cassie. But will you go home? For me?"

She looked down. Careful, capable hands, neatly trimmed nails, slightly rough skin, yet strong and so gentle. He held her own smaller hands in his, touching her heart in ways no other man had. She lifted her eyes to his, felt courage and spirit build in equal measure, and shook her head.

"No. I can't go, Nick." She gripped his hands in return, seeking to communicate more than words. "Whatever Wrede's planning, *this* is my home now. I can't leave you."

Nick's face became very still and thoughtful.

The sounds of the playground grew dim around Cassie. The air began to move slightly, the clouds parted, and a brief ray of sun fell upon them. Another cloud shifted, and shadows fell over them again. She shivered.

"I'm still afraid," she said. "What if this is just the beginning? What if this goes on and on until he finally does do something to Alice, or to you?"

"No, Cassie." He drew her hands to his chest. "Don't be afraid. I'm sorry. That's not what God wants."

"How can I not be?" She gazed up at him in confusion. "Here you are, more than I ever hoped for. And Alice—look at her. And somewhere this man who waits in the dark. What's going to happen, Nick?"

"Ah, Cassie. I'm ashamed." He lifted her hands to his lips and held them there for a long moment, his gaze holding hers. Then he took a deep breath and sat back on the bench. "I shouldn't have scared you, Cassie. It isn't true that anything could happen, not to us. It's God who brought us together and God who we should depend on. Job knew that."

"But Job—that's what I mean, Nick."

"What? Tell me."

"Are we at the beginning of Job's story—his children dead, his cattle gone, him weak and sick, all that horror—or are we at the end? I know God gives and God takes away. Which is it for us, Nick?"

He shook his head. "How can we know?"

Her shoulders sagged in defeat.

"No, listen, Cassie." He squeezed the hand he was holding. "We have a sense of His higher purpose. We can hear His song, especially when we pray and read the Word. But most of the time, here, under the sun, it's hard to fathom what He's doing. The dissonant chords get so loud, blaring, drowning out the melody, so that just the barest hint of what He's doing comes through to us. But we have to believe He's there."

"I wish I had your faith."

"My faith? Is that what it looks like to you—that my faith is strong?"

He closed his eyes, took a deep breath, and let it out slowly.

"The truth is, Cassie, most of the time there doesn't seem to be much sense to what's going on. The fastest runner doesn't win the race, the brilliant don't get wealthy, the wise go hungry. Life seems like one long accident—here, under the sun."

He turned to face her, his eyes so fierce that he almost frightened her.

"But life isn't a game of chance, beginning or end, full of random events with no pattern or design. There's a reality beyond what we see, the reality of what's happening under heaven, where everything has a purpose, where we matter to Him—tremendously. We have to believe that. In the meantime—" He closed his eyes, shuddered, and opened them, resolute again. "We see Jesus, who loves us and suffered death to bring us to glory. We can rely on that even if the worst comes."

"The worst? Oh, Nick." She shivered again. "It seems impossible—"

He made a noise low in his throat, though whether in protest or comfort she couldn't tell.

She shook her head hurriedly. "No. Wait. I know it's true, what you said—about something greater out there, about that being the place we're heading, where our true home is. But this is plenty real, too—"

"Yes," he said slowly.

He didn't understand. Cassie could see that. She pressed on. "The love, the fear, the pain, it's all so close. I know I should trust Him, but it's hard. Surely God understands how desperate I feel sometimes. Even Jesus—who knew better than anyone how quickly it would all pass away—even Jesus wept."

He sighed. "It's our burden, I think. To know eternity but live in time."

"And we're supposed to go on as if Wrede couldn't hurt us? That sounds so reckless. You're the one who thought he might poison the milk."

"No. If God didn't love us, maybe. If He couldn't help us, certainly. But He does care and can help us, so we should be confident, not afraid. It's true, Cassie. We have to be, or we bring Him shame."

She touched her lips and frowned, thinking perhaps she did understand. It was what Eliot wanted for Sarah but couldn't quite give her. And what she wanted for Nick and Alice. Yet only God had the love that inspired that kind of confidence. She took a slow, deep breath, opening herself to His presence, welcoming His care and protection. Maybe it made Him happy—this need to be confident of things not seen. Or maybe it was preparation for heaven, so that once there, she could know the joy of a heart set free. Either way she would have to accept the burden as a necessary sacrifice and somehow trust Him.

"What is it, Cassie? Are you okay?"

She smiled. "It's His perfect love, isn't it—the love that casts out fear? That's where the joy comes from."

"Yes, I suppose so," he said slowly. He studied her thoughtfully. "Yes, even when it's someone we care about who's at risk."

Something in his expression confused her. She waited, suddenly breathless.

He touched her face, his finger brushing her jaw. "I'm afraid, too, but you must know why I feel so protective." His voice was warm and fervent. "I want to marry you, Cassie. I want to live with you and make our life together. I know it's all happened fast—Wrede and danger and falling in love. And you're just starting graduate school, and I'm finishing. Who knows where I'll get work? For us to stay together, you'll probably have to leave A&M. And I'm not sure what will happen with your plans for graduate school then. I know all that. But I do love you."

He paused, his features tense. "Can you give this up and marry me?"

She clasped his hand to her heart.

"Can you?" he said, his voice still tight.

"Yes." She laughed a little shakily, charmed by his doubt. "Yes, of course I can. I love you, too, Nick. I can't imagine staying at A&M without you."

Joy shone from his eyes. He gave her a quick, fierce kiss,

lifted his face to the sky and murmured thanks, then stood up. "Hey, Alice, come here." He swung her up into his arms. "Cassie said she'd marry me, honey."

Alice smiled, unsure what Nick meant but happy to see him smiling.

"Time to go in," Nick said, filled with purpose. "I'll call Elizabeth. Want to go see Grandma and Grandpa, Alice? And after calling, I'll drive you over to school, Cassie. I think you'll be safe enough there."

He hurried up the stairs and sent Alice in to go to the bathroom, then waited at the top for Cassie.

She stopped a few stairs down. "Where will you be?" she said.

"Over the river and through the woods—going to Dallas, of course. If Elizabeth agrees, I'll take Alice this afternoon."

"Oh."

He grinned at her reaction and pulled her up the remaining stairs into his arms. "I'll be back tonight. Don't worry. Or better yet, you come with us. You'll have to meet them sometime."

"No. Those tests, remember?"

"Too bad." He shuffled her into the apartment and shut the door behind him, keeping her in his arms. "Now, kiss me properly—I've waited long enough."

What began with laughter, drew strength from love, and ended in wonder and joy and freedom. She nestled her face against his neck and breathed in a deep sigh of contentment.

"Ah, Cassie," he said. "So much to thank God for. You know, for the past few weeks, I've been looking at schools that need a sabbatical substitute. My first thought is always the same: 'Would Cassie like Alabama? Or Detroit? Or Grand Forks, North Dakota?' "

"Texas to North Dakota?" She drew back enough to put her arms around his neck. She was laughing. "Cowboy, you don't know what snow is and you're thinking North Dakota?"

"Anywhere with you, Cassie."

"Daddy!"

His gaze lingered on Cassie and then, keeping his arms

around her, he shifted his smile to Alice. "What, sweetheart?"

"Are you and Cassie married now?"

"What did you say?" Nick said.

"Is Cassie my mommy now?"

Cassie drew in a quick breath and struggled to keep a straight face.

"Would you like that, Alice?" Nick said. "If I married Cassie?"

Cassie made little headshaking motions to Nick, but he didn't seem to notice.

Alice gave a big lower-lip frown. "You mean you're not?"

"Alice," he said sternly, "you didn't answer me. Would you like it if I married Cassie?"

Cassie held her breath.

Alice slowly nodded her head, picking up speed as she did so. "Yes, Daddy. I want a mommy. Who stays all night and makes cookies and fixes my hair. Just like Cassie!" She put her arms around Cassie's knees and hugged.

Nick grinned.

Cassie loosed her hand from Nick's and hugged Alice right back. "Thank you, sweetheart. I love you, too."

Nick grinned down at Alice, who was tugging on his arm. "Okay, honey, up you go. There's room in this hug for you."

Later, when Alice had squirmed down to play in her room, Cassie rolled her eyes at Nick.

"You should be ashamed, asking her something like that. What if she said no?"

He laughed. "I knew she wouldn't. Like father, like daughter. We're both going to love you—you might as well get used to it."

And what could Cassie say to that? She blinked back sudden tears.

Nick leaned closer. "Someone who stays all night sounds pretty good."

She smiled. "Not to mention someone to fix your hair on mornings like this."

"All kinds of reasons we need you." He lifted her hand for a gallant kiss.

"Isn't there something in Ecclesiastes, Nick, about two being better than one?"

"Yes, definitely, two are better than one, and three even better. You and me and Alice—with God, of course, at the center."

"And Luke and Katy and Zoe and Erin helping us, too." Cassie shook her head. "Poor Wrede. How can he ever hope to win?"

"That's the spirit. All the same, I'd better call Elizabeth."

But even as he was reaching for the phone, it began to ring. Apprehensively, he lifted it to his ear. In quick succession his face went from concern to calm to amazement.

"No kidding. Really? You're sure?"

He covered the receiver. "It's Detective Gardner. They took a search warrant to Wrede's house this morning. When they got there, he was gone."

"Gone?"

"What do you mean—gone?" Nick said into the phone. "No kidding. . . . No. Not a chance. That would be all I need to make my nightmares complete. Thanks, but no thanks. . . . Okay. Sure."

"What?" Cassie said after he had hung up.

"He cleared out, Cassie. Vacated. Sometime during the night. They're trying to trace him now. It seems he hasn't withdrawn any money from the bank, and he's left everything behind, even his netsuke and porcelain, which I find hard to believe. He must have left in a tremendous hurry. The minute he tries to access his bank accounts, they'll have a trace, but chances are he set this up ages ago, transferring other funds out of the country and getting things ready. At any rate, he's definitely gone."

"This is what you wanted. Remember? Either run or come after us. He decided to run."

"But get this—talk about creepy. They found electronic surveillance equipment in his house—pretty sophisticated stuff, too. And locks for practicing on. And the motion-sensitive tape recorder he used in your apartment. Gardner asked if we wanted to come see it. I hope you don't mind—I said no."

"I heard." She shuddered. "Thanks."

"But from what the police said, they found a tape of us talking yesterday morning. Remember? When we decided to turn it all over to Erin? I think that was the first time he realized you were helping me. No wonder he panicked. On my own, this would have taken much longer. When he heard we had all the evidence we needed, he must have decided to clear out."

She covered her mouth.

"What is it?" he said.

"Are they listening in now, do you think?" she asked, glancing around.

He grinned. "Hope they're romantics."

"Wow. But it was those bugs that probably drove him to run. Who knows how long this thing might have gone on otherwise."

"I don't know that they'll ever find him."

"Oh, Nick. You don't suppose—"

"Stop." He grasped her shoulders. His eyes burned with purpose.

"But he could come at us anytime, Nick. A glass of milk, a cup of coffee, a pain pill, for goodness' sake."

"No, Cassie. Don't." She had never heard him speak so sternly, not even to Alice. "You must remember—God between him and us. I refuse to be afraid of Wrede. Not after this morning. Let's lay that burden at His feet and get on with life. I mean it, Cassie. We'll fear God, if anyone. *Not* Duncan Wrede."

"Then pray," she said. "Say it to Him, out loud, so I can hear and remember. And I'll pray as well."

And with the prayers the joy came again, hard won, but very real.

On opening his eyes, Nick said, "I hope Moran's right about switching advisers. She said the school would work something out if necessary, since I've had all but my introduction to the dissertation approved."

"I'm sure it will be okay. That's why you have a dissertation committee, isn't it?" Cassie took a short breath. "Anyway, now I can move back into my own apartment—can't I?"

He winced. "Maybe one more night, to be sure he's really gone."

"And Alice?"

"I think I'll still call Elizabeth, just to be prudent. It's past time for Alice to have a visit anyway."

"You'll be back late?"

He glanced at his watch. "Not really. We could still celebrate tonight. Want to look at rings before dinner?"

She laughed. "Tonight? Oh no—it's Tuesday, isn't it? Nick, look at the time. I have a class in twenty minutes. I really should go."

"Wait."

She already had her hand on the doorknob.

"When will I see you again?" he said.

Standing against the door, she glanced back at him. He looked so much like that first time. The strong jaw and intelligent eyes, the same slow grin, but now his hand was reaching for her, and his expression was eager, gentle, concerned. Now would he always want to know when he would see her next? Would it matter this much? Filled with wonder, she touched his face. She could definitely get used to seeing him like this.

"I'm pretty busy all day," she said, laughing as she pulled back from his kiss. "Seminar on Tuesday nights."

He drew her close again. "We'll make it a late dinner, just the two of us."

"I can't. Remember? Two tests tomorrow."

He sighed dramatically. "Real life with a vengeance. Okay. Tomorrow night. But I still want to choose a ring."

It was only later, sitting in class, that she realized it would be their first real date. Shopping for a ring on the first real dinner date. . . . Did that qualify as a whirlwind courtship?

Nineteen

SOMEWHERE OFF PADRE ISLAND

He had stolen the boat from a pier on Padre Island, loaded tanks of gasoline on board during the night, and moved away from the shore in darkness. At dawn he cut the engine. As the sun rose, he ran binoculars along the horizon. No one. He had outdistanced the shrimp boats and fishing boats on the Gulf. He was alone.

He stood and faced the sun. It rose before him . . . huge, close . . . as though he could touch it, could steer the boat toward it and disappear into its flames.

And in a way, he would.

He smiled to himself. A nice thought, but like everything else insignificant now. The sun would rise again the next day, as it had day after day after day, setting and rising in its endless cycle, but he would be gone.

To the horror of the shade? He shuddered. He wouldn't believe that, couldn't believe that. No. Nothing beyond. No scroll, no punishments, no gate—strait or otherwise. Only, all, ever, bludgeonings of chance. He should know. All of it over now—as if that mattered.

He looked around at the small boat, knowing what lay beneath the deck.

This was his only hope of lingering in their minds— to vanish completely and leave them wondering, wondering, would he come again? His only chance of continued oppression.

But he knew. No more games, no more pretending. Even that would end. In time, days and weeks, they would forget. Nothing really lasted. Not him, not his work, none of the sorry accumulation of possessions and degrees and honors. And he was too weary to begin again.

What did it matter anyway?

But still he stood on the small deck and faced the sun, watching it rise slowly from the horizon. He stretched his hands out to his side, finding some small pleasure in the warmth on his face, the brightness of the light. It rose higher and higher and still he lingered, wondering.

Perhaps he should have played it safer, played by the rules, been more careful. But what then? He would have ended up at the same place anyway. Perhaps not here with the sun rising higher above him. Not here and not now, but someplace, sometime. Sarah had gone first, sent on her way to the same darkness she came from. Now it was his turn. Nick Meyers' would come eventually. The same sun, the same weariness, the same final darkness. He had to believe that, had to hold on to that. They were all the same, no better than animals, even his poor kind, cursed with the burdens of hope and desire, envy and ambition. Pity the poor pretender.

Enough.

He went below and began pouring gasoline throughout the cabin. This would work. He could smell the fumes. So volatile, the gasoline. It loathed the liquid, its vapors rising into the air, seeking escape from *its sorry existence. And in the air, oxygen—his ticket out.*

Earth to earth, ashes to ashes. Time and then time and it would all happen again, none of it new, even gasoline following an endless cycle. Earth to earth, ashes to ashes.

And when the fumes exploded, it would be over quickly, taking the boat, the furnishings, the tanks, and his poor collection of molecules with it, severing all the electrical connections, all the little chemical reactions that governed who he was, all ended, and him back to dust.

So be it. Ashes to ashes. Molecule to molecule. Energy to energy. And what did it matter?

He would have to hurry. He wanted enough oxygen left for the boat to burn even after the explosion.

He took out the match, knowing his annihilation would be fastest if he stayed where he was below the deck. Yet he longed to feel the sun one more time, longed to feel its warmth.

Sensation, useless passion.

And he'd be warm enough in a moment.

వ్ వ్ వ్ వ్

Chunks of wood and metal flew through the air, some charred, some still burning. The fire licked at whatever remained, consuming, never satisfied, the flames rising and falling with the movement of the waves, until the sea overwhelmed the bulk of the wreck.

The wind, passing by, caught the few sparks and ashes still rising, caught and blew them, chasing them around in eddies and puffs, and carried them away, until finally at some distant place the small specks of dust settled onto the water and vanished below.

Twenty

Somewhere between St. Louis and Springfield, the snow began. They had left Texas the day before, driving Nick's pickup loaded with his belongings and towing Cassie's Skylark fully packed with hers.

Nick glanced over at Cassie, who was driving. The snow didn't seem to worry her. It was a light fall, hardly sticking to the ground. But Alice, curled up against Nick, was frightened by the snowflakes rushing toward the windshield.

"Look farther away from the car, Alice," he told her. "See how gently the snowflakes are falling out there? It's only close to you that they look so scary."

"There'll be snow on the ground tomorrow morning," Cassie said. "You can build another snowman, and if the weatherman's right, it won't disappear by lunchtime. And sledding and snowball fights and cocoa by the fire. My family loves a good snowfall."

Nick reached across to rub Cassie's shoulder. "And what will they think of you bringing home a Texas orphan with a tag-along girl?"

"Nick, you're not really worried, are you?"

"Why are you surprised, Cassie?" He smoothed the back of two fingers down the side of her face and around the curve of her jaw. "You're a beautiful woman. Intelligent, funny, with a rare kindness and generosity. I know they love you. They must. Look how much I love you after only four months. They're bound to be a little apprehensive about this new man in your life.''

"But I told you about Richard. They're expecting glasses and a pocket protector, and look what I'm bringing home instead. A cowboy.''

"My point exactly.''

"A *handsome* cowboy.''

"Worse and worse, I would think.''

"No. My mother will love you for Alice. And my father. Whatever you said in your letter sure impressed him, and the fact that you're insisting we wait to marry until April. Take him off somewhere and talk theology—your Pelagius and Arius and all of that. He'll love it. You've already done a lot by writing to him. Anyway, there it is, across the fields.''

In the late afternoon light, Cassie's home looked to Nick like an island of green in a world of winter white. Only as they turned into the driveway did he see the house hidden inside the pine trees. Closer in, clear Christmas lights drenched the smaller trees, already sparkling in the twilight. A safe place, Nick thought, bright and glowing.

"What do you think, Alice?" Cassie said, stopping the car. "Lots of room to play.''

As stiff as he was, Nick still hesitated to get out. "Big trees,'' he said.

"They break the winter winds coming down off the Canadian prairie. You can tell how long we've lived here from their size.''

Alice unbuckled herself and bounced up on the seat. "I want out, Daddy.''

"In a minute, Alice.'' He took Cassie's hand. "Your father must be a forward-thinking man.''

"My great-grandfather, actually. You're marrying into some pretty extensive relations, you know. Aunts, uncles, sisters, cousins. They go on and on.'' Cassie grinned. "Look, there's Mom and Dad at the door, wondering why we're still sitting out here. Come on, Nick. Show time.''

He pushed open his door and lifted Alice to the ground. She

hung back to wait for him. "In you go, Alice. Now you're stuck to the car?"

"She's as reluctant as you are," Cassie said, laughing. "Come on—I'll hold your hand."

Inside the living room, after a flurry of introductions, Cassie's father looked Nick over. "So this is the one."

"George, be nice," Fern McCormick said. Nick could see Cassie in her eyes and in the gentle way she smiled at her husband.

"I intend to be, Fern, believe me. An old maid like Cassie, we can't take any chances."

"Daddy . . ."

"In our neck of the woods, young man, twenty-four's over the hill."

"Daddy, I'm twenty five."

"See what I mean? Even worse."

Nick was holding Alice in one arm. Cassie turned and pressed her face against the front of his other shoulder. She was laughing. "And you were worried. I told you."

Nick pressed his cheek against her forehead. "Glad to know you'll let me have her," he said to George. "Now, about the dowry . . ."

Cassie giggled.

"Which you'll no doubt need," George said. "I know how much a college professor makes."

"Hush," Fern said. "Come and sit down, all of you, and tell us your plans."

Cassie leaned over. "Alice, do you need to use the bathroom?"

George grinned. "She's already sounding like a mother, Fern. What do you think of that?"

"I like it, George."

Not as much as he did, Nick thought as he squeezed Cassie's hand and smiled at her, feeling his burdens being lifted daily.

Alice shook her head in answer to Cassie's question, and everyone sat down, Cassie beside Nick, Alice still on his lap.

"What I want to hear about now is this idea of quitting graduate school," George said. "How'd that happen, young lady?"

"It's all right, Daddy. I quit school to be near Nick, what else? I want to stay home with Alice until she goes to school, and by then . . ." She glanced at Nick, who smiled. "By then we might have more children."

"But in case she changes her mind," Nick said, "I'll be looking for a job near a university where Cassie can continue her graduate work. We should be able to manage that."

He had given the same assurance to Erin Moran, who had been aghast at Cassie's willingness to throw away her career. Nick had braced himself for whatever Cassie decided, but he found himself deeply grateful that she was willing to invest her many gifts into their family. He gripped her hand more tightly, and she smiled up at him.

"For the next six months, Nick's filling in for someone on sabbatical at Donnally College in western Indiana. About three hours away. And I'll stay here until we get married in April."

"Cassie says you won't mind some company on weekends," Nick said.

"Of course not," Fern agreed. "And Cassie and I will stay busy getting ready for the wedding."

George came to shake Nick's hand. "Welcome to the family, son. We're happy to have you."

A few minutes later, other family members started arriving, bearing food and greetings and a lot more jokes. In all, two sisters, their spouses, and nine children, as well as assorted aunts and uncles and cousins. Cassie had warned Nick on the drive up, so that he knew most of the adults' names, but the children were a different matter. As for Alice, she spent most of the evening on Nick's lap, even during dinner. It would take some getting used to, being part of such a big clan.

Much later that night, after the relatives had left and Cassie's parents and Alice had gone to bed, Nick joined Cassie in front of the big picture window. She snuggled back into his arms, savoring the warmth of his embrace.

"Your family's wonderful," Nick whispered. "All of them."

"I know. And it was like your dining room, wasn't it, the

one you described in St. Louis?"

"Yeah. Someday ours will be just as crowded."

Outside the snow continued to fall, blanketing the world in white. The lights on the trees twinkled like diamonds through the snow. *How silently, how silently, the wondrous gift is given,* she thought. *And of all the blessings of heaven, Jesus, you are the very best.*

"You know, Nick," she said, "I've been thinking, we'll probably never know what happened to Wrede, will we?"

"Maybe not."

"But that's it, isn't it? That's what you said—we can't always fathom what's happening from beginning to end."

"True."

She tipped her head back against his shoulder. "It's weird how everything with Wrede ended, so frightening and then the danger gone. But I've decided not to be afraid, even if he could come rising up out of nowhere someday like a monster in a horror movie."

"Horrible thought."

"Because Wrede doesn't mark the beginning or the end—not for us. Jesus does. That's what the Bible says, doesn't it? He is the beginning and the end."

"The Alpha and the Omega, the First and the Last."

She turned and put her hands in his. "He is heaven's song, Nick, both the music and the reason. He sang the first note, and He'll sing the last, so wherever we are, whatever's happening around us, we can know He's there, bringing His will to pass."

Nick placed a kiss against her forehead. "I'm just glad that part of His plan was for us to be together."

Acknowledgments

Many, many thanks to R.C. Sproul of Ligonier Fellowship—anyone who has listened to his lectures on Ecclesiastes will see his influence throughout this book. Thanks also to Clarence Josefson, a colleague of my husband's at Millikin University, who knows about so many things, including herbicides and poisons; and to Lydia Ecks of Wichita Falls, who explained Texas's social services to me.

I also want to ackowledge the excellent chemistry department at Texas A&M. I chose this setting because of its unique and colorful traditions and because it's the institution I know best—not because it's a likely place for a murder. We owe a great deal to the faculty there and are proud to call ourselves Aggies. Please keep that in mind as you think back over this book.